In the Band

In the Band

Jean Haus

SKYSCAPE

SKYSCAPE

Text copyright © 2013 Jean Haus
Cover design by Silas Warren

Printed in the United States of America.

Published by Skyscape, New York

www.apub.com

Library of Congress Cataloging-in-Publication Data available upon request.

ISBN-13: 9781477847077
ISBN-10: 1477847073

Printed in the Unites States of America
First edition

TO AWESOME READERS EVERYWHERE

Chapter 1

My finger hovers over the mouse button that will change my life forever. I take a deep breath and will myself to move, but I hover. Come on. One click and the end will be official. I close my eyes and lower my finger. Somehow, I press the button. Whoosh. My future down the toilet with one e-mail. I lay my forehead on the computer desk and resist the urge to bang my head against the wood.

The smack of my bedroom door opening brings me back up against the chair.

"Hey, Riley," Jamie, my little sister, says. She's wearing a baseball cap backward, a yellow polka-dot bathing suit, and boots. Seeing her eight-year-old sense of fashion helps lessen the sting of the e-mail. Just a little. She bounces into my room. "Chloe's coming over, right?"

Keeping my face neutral, I nod.

There's an open box between us, and she flips its lid back and forth. Packed boxes that never went anywhere. "So can I invite Mandy over to swim?"

Still unable to speak I nod again. I'm rewarded with a bright smile. "Cool."

As she bounces away, a human pogo stick, I will myself not to cry, not to remember hours and hours of drum practice. Not to think of the glorious freedom I just gave up. But I'm giving it up for a good cause. Two good causes actually. And I'll still go to college. Still have a future. Just not the one I'd planned on.

With a sigh, I log into the local university and pay for classes— awful choices left in August—with the bank card connected to my college fund. I didn't want to pay for my eleven credits of Philosophy 101, Ancient Roman History, or Calculus III until it was official.

And now it's undeniably official.

The twist in my future completed, I sit staring at the screen saver of my one and only boyfriend who I'd lost to college in another state two weeks ago. Dressed in our band uniforms we stand with heads together, sunglasses on, and drums in front of us. We look happy together. Last year. Though I knew the breakup was coming, I'm still hurt and wishing I could call him. It doesn't seem like anyone stays together anymore. I really need to change my screen saver, but my hands stay in my lap.

"Hey, girl, you coming down?" Chloe yells from the bottom of the stairs.

Melancholy interrupted, I shut the lid to my computer and yell back, "Just a second!"

I find Chloe already on the deck overlooking the above-ground pool. Wearing a halter top, a wide-brimmed hat, and catlike sunglasses, she looks like she belongs in a forties movie. Instead, she sits in the shade of our table umbrella with its dangling Mickey Mouse lights. Her platinum-blonde hair and curves only add to the movie star look. With my long dark hair, big brown eyes, and stick body, I look like I belong with the lights. Physically, I can't seem to get past the age of thirteen. Emotionally, I feel like a thirty-year-old lately.

Splashes and giggles sound from beyond the deck, and the smell of chlorine hangs in the air. Mandy must have run over from across the street as soon as Jamie called.

Chloe nods toward the pool. "I told them I'd watch until you came down." She offers a plastic cup with a straw. "Mocha Frappuccino? Slushy caffeine and chocolate got to help a little."

"I'm all right," I say, grabbing the cup and sitting under the umbrella with her, in the chair closest to the pool. Though I haven't come to terms with what went down today, I don't want to worry my friends. It's just something I have to let slowly settle inside. It's been settling for a while though. However, I'm not one to dwell. Rather move on and do what has to be done.

"Yeah, right. Redonkulous." Chloe takes a drink of her coffee. How she can drink hot liquid on a hot August afternoon is beyond me. "Every drummer is okay when they give up a percussion scholarship."

I glance at my sister and her friend bouncing in the water. "Keep it down. I don't want Jamie thinking I'm upset."

"Like they can hear us." She waves a hand toward the giggling and shouting. "And to think you probably would have made their drumline. How many times have you watched that lame movie?"

Recalling the hours Marcus and I sat playing *to* the movie, I snap, "Are you trying to make me feel like shit?"

She rears back in her chair. It's almost a head snap. I sense more than see her blinking behind the dark glasses. "No. I'm trying to get the mourning over with."

I lean back and take a long drag of caffeinated slush while the giggles in the pool turn into squeals. I roll the cup in my hands like I usually do with my sticks. "No need. I've been thinking about this since May."

She jerks her glasses off and smacks them on the table. Green eyes, heavy with mascara, narrow on me. "Riley Jones Middleton, you've been keeping secrets from me."

"I wanted to figure it out on my own," I say with a shrug.

Her fingers drum on the glass. Each ping indicates her annoyance. "Same reasons?"

I glance at my sister twirling in a floatie ring while waves of water encircle her. Jamie with a sitter almost every day until nine o'clock at night was the biggest reason. There were others though. My mother already on the brink of financial ruin. My father not being able to help as much with dorm fees. My mother's growing depression. All of these stem from one thing. "Yeah, the divorce."

"Divorce sucks." Chloe takes a long drink of coffee and slides her glasses back on. "What are you going do if that university band lady e-mails back?"

"Tell her I'm sorry. What else can I do?"

"Suppose that's true. But it was kind of rude to e-mail her two days before you were supposed to show up."

I shrug again. "It was. I just couldn't force myself to do it until today."

The creak of the gate behind me sounds and then a bam as it hits the wooden fence. Chloe's lip curl confirms my suspicion. I don't have to look over my shoulder. "Thought you weren't going to talk to me?"

"That would be too awesome," Chloe says under her breath.

"So you did it?" Marcus, my other best friend, asks from the bottom of the deck steps.

"Yeah, but you could have just texted."

Instead of replying, he races up the stairs and envelops me in a hug. "Aw. Riley, I'm pissed you had to do it, but I understand."

With the Frappuccino cup wedged between us, I say, "You didn't have to skip practice to offer your condolences."

"Sure I did." He pulls away and flops down on the nearest chair. "But we were near perfect this morning. Got the afternoon off." He sweeps his unruly blond mop of curls from his eyes.

My brows rise. "Really, what kind of bandleader do you have?"

"College band is different than high school. People actually practice." He glances at Chloe but only offers her a nod. "And I wanted to talk to you about something."

Chloe lifts her coffee as if toasting him. "You got named tool of the month?"

I give her a look. I'm not in the mood to listen to her and Marcus trade barbs.

"Tool of the year actually," he says snidely, and digs in his pocket. "I noticed this on the message board in my dorm the other day." He unfolds the paper and flattens it on the glass table.

I frown at him. "I'm not moving into the dorm."

"Yeah," Chloe says. "What kind of dork lives in a dorm thirty minutes from their house?"

"What kind of bimbos go to cosmetology school?" he says with a sneer, then adds, "Oh, ones named Chloe."

Her eyes narrow. "I'll remember that next time you want a haircut."

"Like you can remember that long."

That actually causes me to chuckle. Not because Chloe's an airhead but because of Marcus's overly long hair. Feeling a glare from across the table, I gesture to the paper. "What's so important you came all the way from the dorm?"

"Well . . . there's this band and they need a drummer."

My drink almost slips from my hand. "You're going to join a band? Like a rock band?"

"From this"—he points to the paper—"they play a variety of stuff, not just rock. But no, I don't have time for a band. I wish." He leans forward, his eyes intense. "But you could."

The splashing and shouting from the pool grows louder in the sudden silence. Stunned at the idea, I simply stare at Marcus.

Chloe breaks the silence with a snort. "That's a wicked idea."

I don't break my stare. "You've got to be kidding me."

He shakes his head. "Why would I be kidding? You're the best drummer I know."

My face twists into an incredulous expression. "In a marching band."

"I'm not kidding," Chloe says excitedly. She slaps Marcus's shoulder. "I've got to give it to you, tool of the year. Your idea is the cat's ass."

Marcus gives her a grin then looks back to me. "Come on, Riley. You've been playing my drum set as long as me."

The frightening mental image of me onstage in front of rowdy fans has me snapping. "Goofing around."

"Your goofing around is ten times better than my totally serious," he says with a grunt. "And you don't goof around. Shit. After about two rounds of a song, you play it better than me after four hours of practicing it. You'd be perfect for this."

They both stare at me with anticipation lined on their faces. I slowly set my drink on the glass table. "If I don't have time to be in the university band, what makes you think I have time to be in a stage band?" Marcus had begged me to let him talk to his bandleader when he found out I wasn't going to Virginia, but my watching Jamie almost every day wouldn't allow me the time.

"That's the beauty of it." Marcus taps the paper. "They only practice twice a week and do about two gigs a month. They're all in school just like us."

"He's right. It's perfect," Chloe says. "You'll still get to play, not much time away from your mommy duties, and it actually might be cool. Hot guys could even be involved."

Marcus scowls at her before they both return their gazes to me.

I push my chair away from the table and wrap my arms around my knees. "You two have fallen off the deep end. I do not belong in a band. I don't even look like I'm out of high school."

"Four hours." Chloe's red nails shine as she spreads four fingers out. "Okay, maybe five hours"—she adds her thumb—"some dye, some makeup, and some clothes, and I'll have you looking like a rock star."

Chloe, me, and all of those things together in a room for five hours has me shaking my head. And me in a band? Um, no—just thinking about it freaks me out.

Marcus leans forward, scrunching his *got milk?* T-shirt and rests his elbows on his knees. "Listen, they're playing tonight. We could check them out. If you like their style, tryouts are next week. You can think it over and have some time to practice."

A light shines out of their tunnel of craziness. "Can't tonight. My mom has a late night at work. Inventory."

"Weak try," Chloe says. "I can watch Jamie. I could watch her during your practice sessions too."

My teeth grind as I resist throwing the rest of my slushy all over her perfectly primped form. She's trying to help. Wants to help, after I was there for her during her breakup with Neil—the boy who was supposedly *the one*—but this is going beyond help.

"Come on," Marcus says in a pleading tone. "You need to get out. You're like a cat lady without cats lately. This will be fun."

I look between them as they both nod their heads yes. I'd like to smack those heads together. Tightening my arms around my knees, I watch the girls kick a raft across the length of the pool before returning to the waiting stares of my friends. Peer pressure is a bitch. "If I go and I don't like the band, you'll both let this go?"

"Scouts honor," Chloe says, and salutes me with a hand across her chest.

Irritation wrinkles Marcus's brow. "Scouts don't salute like that."

She rolls her eyes. "Whatever."

"Marcus?" I press.

"Yeah, sure." He shrugs. "If you don't like the band, then I'll drop it. But I can't see you happy unless you're playing."

Relieved they've both given me their word, because regardless of my true feelings, I won't be liking the band. "Okay, I'll go."

Marcus grins. "They don't go on until ten, but I thought we could hit the skate park since we're going downtown."

"Oh, reliving our youth are we?" Chloe says. "Maybe you should ask the babysitter?"

"Marcus," I say in a groan, "I haven't been on a board in almost two years, and Chloe's right. It would be beyond rude to leave her here with Jamie while we went out."

He puts his hands up but Chloe waves a hand. "I'm just being a bitch. He's right. You need to get out of this house. Let me play mommy for a bit. Hell knows motherhood ain't happening for me until after thirty-five anyway. If then."

Marcus's stoked expression has me internally groaning. I'm not even sure where my board is. "Fine, we'll go to the skate park, but you're buying dinner." Maybe I'll break an arm falling off my board and this ridiculousness will be null.

He grins. "Hot dog stand here we come."

"I'll put the lasagna in the oven and set the timer," I say to Chloe.

She smiles wolfishly. "That's why I'm here. Your cooking is the one good thing about your new mommy status."

Ignoring her, I stand and tell Marcus, "Just let me find my board and I'll walk over to your house."

"You're not changing?" Chloe asks.

I glance down at my yellow tank top and loose khaki shorts. "Yeah, I should probably at least put on capris. I'll wipe out at least once."

"Riley," Chloe whines, "you're going to a concert. Guys will be there. Hot older guys."

I give her a look. "I'm taking a break from guys. And hot older guys sound out of my league."

Her look is icier than mine. "Aaron is so not worth this."

Marcus clears his throat.

"Go home. I'll be there in five," I say to him, and move toward the sliding glass doors while Chloe mutters in the background. It might be more like fifteen minutes by the time I find the bottom of my closet. If my board is in there. Sliding the glass door open, I'm actually excited to go skateboarding and even to a concert.

But I am so not trying out as their drummer.

Chapter 2

I haven't eaten like that in months. I pick at food lately. After two chili dogs and splitting a cheese fry with Marcus my stomach feels like it's going to burst while my legs and arms feel like rubber from two hours of boarding. Yet I didn't do too bad after two years off the thing. Not great, but not too shabby either. From about fourth grade to tenth, besides drumming, skateboarding was my life. Though boys had been on my radar since eighth grade, one boy in particular caught my eye the end of sophomore year. Aaron. It took a year for me to come out of my tomboy stage—Chloe thinks I'm still partially in it—and three weeks into our senior year for him to finally ask me out, but he did.

Now we're no more.

And now I'm back on a skateboard.

Maybe Chloe's partially right. I'm just regressing back to a tomboy. In fact, I don't think I've touched my makeup bag since Aaron and I broke up. I haven't given two shits about what I've looked like for most of the summer. Now standing against the balcony banister waiting for the band to start and surrounded by girls dressed like hoochies, I'm wishing I'd listened to Chloe just a bit. I feel *extremely* unattractive in an ancient pair of jean capris and a tank top. A bit of hoochieness would help my self-esteem at the moment.

The old movie theater we're in is packed wall to wall. Both the main level and the balcony. A murmer of conversation surrounds us and floats up to us while music plays from speakers above. The packed crowd has me realizing the band is more popular than Marcus led me to believe. He'd been trying to sell me on the fact that they're just a college band. This crowd implies more than just a college band.

"So tell me something, Riley," Marcus says, pulling his gaze from the cleavage of the girl next to him. "Did your mom even try to talk you out of letting the scholarship go?"

My eyes narrow on him before I look at the crowd below us. "Are you implying my mother's selfish? You know she's going through a rough time right now."

"I love Mags," he says, and I can hear the grin in his voice. Though my mother's name is Maggie, he's called her Mags since sixth grade. At least behind her back. He bumps me with his shoulder. "You know that. I'm just curious."

I grip the scarred wooden banister of the balcony. "She asked several times if I was sure I wanted to stay home." I'm not about to share the relieved look she wore each time I said yes.

"And your dad?"

I shrug. "He's busy with his new girlfriend."

"Why did your parents have to go and get divorced? You know Chloe and me were going to tolerate each other and take a road trip to see you perform in the drumline?"

My stomach starts to hurt. I wish everyone would quit bringing up the damn drumline. "We'll come watch you."

"The Hawks don't have a drumline. Shit, Riley, we're barely a Division Two university."

"Well, that sucks."

"And you had a free ride to a Division One in a warm state."

Cheese coagulates in my stomach. Virginia is a tropical paradise compared to mid-Michigan. "Just tuition and books. The dorm was only partial."

"Still," he says.

"It's a done deal, okay?" I step back, well as much as I can with the people crowded behind us, while fighting back tears. I've kept a lid on my disappointment all day, but I'm about to erupt in a mess of emotion. "I'll be right back. Going to hit the bathroom."

"You're going have a bitch of a time getting back through."

I shrug then squeeze through the mass of people. Somehow I keep it together all the way down the stairs. Ignoring the bathrooms, I head out the side door into the smokers' area. Fenced off between buildings and space that was once an alley, the area is dark. Strings of lights line the ground along the bottom of each brick wall. Obviously, you don't need light to smoke—just to walk. I pass smokers huddled together, conversing amid their smelly haze. In the back, where it's the darkest, I lean my head against the rough brick and let the tears flow while my stomach rolls.

I hate this stupid shit. I hate crying. But the more I try to control it, the more the tears fall.

This is why I don't hang with my friends very often anymore. Their concern, though touching, breaks my heart. I spent four years working toward my goal of a scholarship. To have achieved that goal, give it up, and then be continually reminded of it just plain sucks. Yet I'm also aware that if Chloe and Marcus had gone off to college, I'd be a total wreck. That my friends are still here is something. Actually, at the moment it feels like everything.

I attempt reigning in my tears. I'm breathing deep, letting air out slowly, when what looks like a folded bandana comes into my blurred vision.

"Looks like you need this," someone says in a deep voice.

Embarrassment runs through me as I glance at the tall guy holding the bandana. His mop of dark hair blends into the night. He's wearing baggy shorts and a white T-shirt. In the darkness his face is mostly a shadow, though the lights strung along the ground highlight his ragged flip-flops, the most defined thing about him.

He jiggles the bandana in my face. "It's clean."

Mortified at my public breakdown, I reach for the triangle of fabric. "Um . . . thanks."

"No problem." He falls with a thud next to me on the brick wall, lifting one knee as he plants a foot behind himself. While I wipe my eyes, the zip of a lighter sounds in the darkness. "Boyfriend?"

A miserable laugh escapes before I can stop it. "Sort of . . ." I'm not about to explain my life to a stranger. I can't even explain it to my friends.

"Guys can be dicks." I hear the grin in his words.

"Yeah . . ." I finish wiping my eyes while wondering why *this* guy is talking to me. Why he won't let me cry in peace.

He lets out a stream of smoke. "Trust me, it will get better. And one day you won't even remember what you saw in such an ass."

Though I wish he'd go somewhere else, the conviction in his tone has me saying, "Sounds like you have experience."

His teeth flash white in the darkness. A large hand splays across his chest. "Thought my heart was shattered. Thought I was dying. Later I realized she wasn't worth such a response."

I dig my Vans into the cement. "Actually, I don't want to be disrespectful. He isn't a dick. He . . . just doesn't like me enough to continue our relationship through college. I can't hate him for that."

My shadowy bandana man is silent.

"Sorry," I mumble. "Too much stranger information."

He shakes his head. "No. I was just stunned. That's some mature thinking for someone who's . . . What's the cutoff for getting in here? Sixteen?"

"Eighteen," I mutter with irritation lacing my tone. "I'm eighteen. Nineteen in a little over two months."

He chuckles.

My face warms. And the red's probably noticeable since at five feet four inches, I'm far closer to the string lights than he is. Embarrassed about crying and now my looks, I hold out the bandana. "Thanks. I should get going. I, uh, didn't snot on it or anything."

He stubs his cigarette out on the brick wall before reaching for the bandana. His warm hand brushes mine, causing me to drop mine with a yank. "You going to be all right?"

Though confused why he'd care, I nod.

"Here, you might not need it," he says, digging in his back pocket, then holding out a card until I take it. "But just in case."

Thoroughly confused now but not wanting to be rude, I take the card and stuff it in my front pocket, mumble a good-bye, and wander through the semidarkness. This time I stop in the bathroom. No one pays attention to me while I rinse my face and dry it with a rough paper towel. A quick look in the mirror shows slightly red, puffy eyes. In the dark of the theater, Marcus shouldn't be able to notice. Or at least I'm hoping not. If he even suspects I've been crying, he won't let it go until I spill everything.

I do have to squeeze my way back through the crowd, repeating "excuse me" multiple times. I even get a few dirty looks, but I make it back to Marcus.

"Cool," he says as I slide next to him. "They're just about to get started. Long line?"

"Very," I say, looking ahead and pretending to have a huge interest in the stage.

He shoulder bumps me again. "You're going to love this band."

Not enough to try out for them. I keep my eyes on the stage but give him a close-lipped smile.

The overhead lights dim as the stage lights up and the crowd grows loud. Amid shouts and claps and people going nuts like idiots, four guys step onto the stage. They don't say anything, just take their places. Of course, my eyes follow the drummer. But the singer and the guitar player start the song with low lyrics and a repeating riff. Instantly, I recognize My Chemical Romance's "Teenagers."

With loud music roaring through the theater, the crowd goes wilder when the rest of the band enters the song. I watch the drummer. He's good. The song sounds good too. Though they play it similar to the original, they also speed it up, which gives it a louder feel.

Next to me, Marcus does a fist-pump dance and sings with the song. "Good, huh?" he shouts at me.

I nod. However, the verdict is still out. I tap my fingers on the banister and watch with a critical eye, and ear, more than for fun.

The next song, "Gamma Ray" by Beck, is totally different. I recall Marcus saying they played a variety. Guess this major switch proves it. After I watch the drummer for most of the song, I check out the rest of the band. They're obviously all talented and the singer can sing, but the nonmusic part of me notices the muscled arms playing the instruments, the shine of the singer's muscular bare chest under an open vest, and the tattoos on his arms. Though I can't make out faces from this far, I have a feeling some of the girls aren't here for just the music. Eye candy just might have something to do with the large female crowd directly in front of the stage.

The third song is something I've never heard before. It's catchy, with a long repeating chorus, a fast beat—and a folk influence is evident. I nudge Marcus with my elbow. "What's this?" I mouth.

"This is theirs!" he shouts in my ear.

My interest goes up a notch. I don't want it to, but the fact they don't do just covers impresses me. I nudge Marcus again. "What's their name?"

"Luminescent Juliet."

I give him a look and a question with it: *What kind of dumb name is that?*

He shrugs and keeps up his fist pump dance. For a boy so into music, he can so not dance.

I mostly watch the drummer through the rest of the set until the thud and want in my chest has me glancing at the rest of the band, but my eyes always go back to the drummer. He really is good. While he isn't too flashy—which I don't mind—his rhythm is spot on. He also looks like he's enjoying himself, especially during the fills. Between songs, the singer says some stupid shit, but for the most part the band seems to be serious about the music. I like that.

Once the singer yells out, "Goodnight!" The band heads off the stage and Marcus turns to me as the lights come on. "What do you think?"

"They're good." I turn to leave with the rest of the crowd.

He puts a hand on my arm. "Think you'll try out?"

I press my lips together.

His fingers grip my arm tighter. "Tell me you're thinking about it."

"Probably not." He opens his mouth but I cut him off. "Can we go?"

He nods toward the people leaving below us. "Give it a minute. I want to introduce you to the band."

I scowl at him. "Why didn't you tell me you knew them?"

He shrugs the ire in my tone away. "I just know the singer. He gave me the tickets. He lives in my dorm, but we can meet the rest of them too."

I take a step back and bump into the banister. "No way . . . I'm not in the mood."

"Come on, Riley."

I shake my head.

His excited expression fades. "Okay, then just let me say hi." After another of my looks, he adds, "I told him I was coming."

"Fine. Just don't introduce me."

We follow the end of the crowd down the stairs, then wait to get into the main floor until it's almost empty. A few stragglers like us hang out near the stage. Well, Marcus is near the stage. I'm a few feet back, resting against a rail.

He's talking to some guy about the performance when I remember bandana man from outside and the card in my pocket. I give the room a quick peek for a guy in a white T-shirt and shorts. No bandana guy in sight. I dig the card out. Since I thought the guy gave me his number—not that I'd call him—I blink at the black and green ink. One word stands out the most: *Suicide*. Then *free* and *help*. Slowly, like at the pace of a waltz, I realize he gave me a card for the Suicide Hotline.

My face warms. Looking around and still not finding the guy from outside, I stuff the card back in my pocket.

Just because a girl's in a dark alley crying doesn't mean she's suicidal. Yet beyond the embarrassment burning inside of me, I'm touched someone would try to help me, even if he got it wrong.

Like *way* wrong.

Still, I can see where bandana man was coming from. I probably looked pretty pathetic out there, crying alone. Major loser. The weight of my life just pulled me down for a moment. That's all. I'm okay. My palm presses the card in my pocket. I've never thought about *that*. However, crying alone in a dark alley does point to the fact I may need a change in my life.

Adrift in thought, I'm startled to notice the band has come out. The singer stands with an arm around some girl's waist and a beer in his other hand while talking to Marcus. This close—and even though he has a shirt on now—I can see that his body matches his face. He's quite good looking, with dark blond hair, deep dimples, and a crooked white smile. Tattoos cover his arms and an eyebrow ring catches the light. Chloe would be whispering "smoking hot" in my ear if she were here. More guys come out onstage and start packing up while they talk. The tall drummer starts tearing apart his set. The bass player talks within another group a few feet away. Stocky and energetic, he exudes fun with his buzzed hair and wide grin. He's all boy cuteness, still bouncing a bit as if onstage.

I'm watching the drummer and thinking about being able to pack up drums when the guitar player comes over to Marcus and the singer. Chloe wouldn't *whisper* "smoking hot"—the words would tear loudly out of her mouth with an F-bomb. While the singer is eye candy, the guitar player is walking lust. Dark hair. Dark eyes. Muscled body in a tight, dark tank top. Everything's dark about him except the row of small, silver hoops rimming his ears. The girls waiting behind him practically pant.

He brushes the angled flop of hair out of his eyes and looks up. Our eyes meet. Shit. He's caught me staring. His eyes narrow. My face flushes as my gaze finds the floor. He probably thinks I'm panting after him like the other girls. Doesn't know I'm just musically interested.

Feeling like an idiot, I find the nerve to glance up at the stage. Out of the corner of my eye, I can see both the guitar player and singer still talking with Marcus. No one looks at me. I cross my arms, stare at the old torn wallpaper on the far wall, and mentally will Marcus to shut up and come on. Behind my irritation, drums beat in my head.

I study the frayed wallpaper like it's displayed art until Marcus comes up to me. "You ready?" he asks.

"No, I thought I'd stare at the wallpaper for another five minutes," I say sarcastically, spinning away. Marcus catches up with me in the theater lobby. "Shit, Riley, slow down." But the whirl in my head has me moving fast. Maybe if I keep moving, the thought that's entered my brain won't come out.

"Why is the drummer quitting?" I ask as we step onto the sidewalk.

"He's transferring to another university." Marcus digs for his keys even though we're several blocks from his car. "He's good but you're better."

I don't respond. Instead I imagine playing again. Excitement churns in my gut.

"So?" Marcus elbows me in the side.

I don't want to play onstage. I'd rather be in the marching band. But I want to play. Bad. "You have their playlist?"

A grin breaks out on his face. "I can load it on your iPod. I already told my mom you'd be practicing in the garage."

I glare at him. This time I give him an elbow nudge. A hard one right in his ribs.

Chapter 3

The guitar player stares at me from across the huge dusty room, eyeing me with a bewildering contempt. Three naked lightbulbs hang from the high open ceiling. One above the drum kits scattered everywhere and the group of us waiting to audition. One above the instruments in the middle of the room. And one above the band standing at the far end of the room.

Boxes covered with dust line the wood-slatted walls, and there are tall windows at each end of the room. Covered with grime, which has probably been accumulating over the past hundred years, the windows let in little of the late-afternoon light. Though he's more in the shadows, I can feel the guitar player's gaze through the dimness.

He needs to find something else to look at.

My nerves are already in overdrive. Nerves are usually a good thing. My competitive streak mixed with nervousness takes my drumming to the next level. But that dark stare produces a different kind of nervousness. The kind that has my stomach in knots.

And I can't decide why he's staring at me. I'm assuming he doesn't remember me from last weekend, especially with all the other girls who panted after him. But the contempt in his stare might have to do with the fact I'm the only female in this muggy room above an antique store on the edge of downtown. Or maybe he's staring because after Chloe's makeover I look like a groupie.

I should have rubbed off more eyeliner. I should have refused to wear the top that makes even *me* look like I have cleavage. Maybe I shouldn't have come.

I move closer to Marcus as my gaze finds the nervous tap of my shoe. He puts an arm around me and squeezes my shoulder. I attempt to ignore the stare across the room and go into my competitive zone while Marcus talks with my competition, the other three drummers. It's kind of hard to get in that zone as Mr. Dark and Sexy stares at me while I don't feel like myself, more like Chloe's punk Barbie doll.

Chloe had estimated time perfectly. It took five flipping hours. She cut and dyed my hair. Now I have a thick fringe of bangs highlighted with white-blonde and a layer of blonde underneath my dark brown hair. I'm wearing a tight black top and tight knee-length shorts. Chloe's original choice was far too short, like lift a leg and show my underwear with every beat short. Though I let her go wild on the makeup, I refused the fake eyelashes. Hello? I'm going to be moving a lot, Chloe. For footwear, we met in the middle with a pair of black ballet-looking shoes. I wanted to wear my Vans. She wanted me to wear black high-heeled boots. Um no. Drummers use their feet, Chloe. She also had a beauty school buddy tattoo my arms with henna while the blonde in my hair set, since I refused the plethora of bracelets she planned on to complete her rock makeover.

"We're going to get started."

I look up to find the guitar player standing in front of Marcus. He's wearing a dark T-shirt and jeans. Nothing that screams hot. But he somehow does with that angle of hair across his face, the muscles noticeable under his shirt, and those full lips. My heart rate matches the jerking rhythm of my nerves. The guitarist nods toward me but his dark eyes stay on Marcus. "Sorry, but your girlfriend can't stay."

Ah, bingo. He does think I'm a groupie.

Marcus grins and pulls me closer until the side of my face is smashed against the *Pinterest* across his chest. "She's trying out, not me."

The guitar player's eyebrow arches, giving him a quizzical look. Otherwise, the angles of his face remain stoic. "Then I guess *you* need to leave."

"Come on," Marcus says. "I know Justin."

His placid expression doesn't change. "I don't give a shit if you're his long-lost brother."

Marcus's lips form a tight line as the guitar player stares him down. Luckily, the singer comes over and gives Marcus a fist bump. "Dude, you trying out?"

"I wish. But no." He turns to me, smiling wide. "Justin, this is Riley."

Justin looks me up and down. His gaze pauses two seconds too long on my cleavage. "You play?"

Marcus laughs. "She was supposed to play at—"

I nudge him in the ribs and nod.

"Cool." Justin grins and dimples groove his cheeks. "We've never had anyone so hot audition before."

The guitar player rolls his eyes. "We've never had a girl audition, so who exactly are you referring to?"

Justin's dimples disappear as he scowls at his bandmate before looking back to me. "We're waiting for at least one more guy, but we're going to start without him."

The guitar player nails me with an irritated look and crosses his arms over his plain T-shirt. "Why don't you go first, Riley?" His tone is smooth, but I catch the undertone of sarcasm in his voice. He doesn't think I can play. Because I'm a girl?

Justin raises a pierced eyebrow at his bandmate. "She doesn't have to go first, Romeo."

Romeo? What kind of asinine name is that? Anger and confidence straighten my spine as the knots in my stomach untangle. "I can go first," I say firmly.

Romeo's hard chin lifts as he nods. "We don't want to waste time."

Who is this douche bag? First, he stares. Now he judges based on my sex. "Hopefully I'm not wasting mine."

Justin looks at Romeo and then me before asking, "Do you need to warm up?"

"No," I answer while my eyes burn into Mr. Dark and Asinine.

His lips thin before he looks past me to the other waiting drummers. "Listen up," he says. I hear the conversation behind me instantly die. "We're going to get started in a few. We're assuming you've practiced. You'll be playing two songs with us. Two, maybe three, of you will make it to the next round for a longer set. You'll have five minutes to warm up"—he glances down at me—"if needed."

"What are the two songs?" I ask, my jaw tight.

Romeo continues to look above my head. "'Midnight' and 'Trace.'"

Huh. Good choices. Lots of range. From basic to fast to soft. And both songs are among their originals.

Romeo gestures to me. "Riley here is going to go first. The rest of you can wait in that adjoining room." He points to an open doorway.

"What the hell, Romeo?" One of the drummers behind me whines. "First this cattle call bullshit, but the competition on the other side of a wall?"

Romeo's expression stays flat. "We lost a drummer without warning. Bullshit breeds bullshit. If you want to try out, deal with it. But we need to get started, so get your kits partially set up and against the wall."

The pansies behind me grumble as they prep their kits, but from my time in the marching band, I'm used to playing head-on with my competition. Who cares if we hear each other playing? Their listening isn't going to change my skill.

While the late guy brings his kit in, Marcus and I set up the kit I rented this morning. I thought about asking to borrow his, but Marcus is a bit attached—more like a whole hell of a lot—to his set. I could care less. As far as I'm concerned, drums are drums.

After I'm ready to go, Marcus plops down in one of the chairs across from where the instruments are set up. Romeo gives him a level look, strapping on his guitar. Under that irritated gaze, Marcus is up in seconds and following the other drummers into the side cave.

I yank my sticks from my back pocket, and Marcus gives me a cuff on the shoulder as he passes. "Go get 'em, Rile."

Ignoring him, I sit on the stool. "Which one are we doing first?"

Justin stops adjusting his microphone and glances over his shoulder. "How about 'Midnight'?"

Since I couldn't care less, I'm about to agree but Romeo says, "No, 'Trace' has the slower transition in the middle. Drummers have a harder time with that." Though his expression appears smooth, I can detect the hint of a smirk.

Asshole.

Justin and the bass player watch him with bewildered faces as if he usually isn't a dick, which I find hard to believe.

I choose to ignore his attitude. "Okay. After four?"

With one raised brow, he nods.

I hit my sticks together four times and together we break into "Trace." Their flawless entry has me recalling my original impression of their talent. But soon I'm not recalling anything or anyone. Just dialing in as every beat from the kick drum vibrates through me. In my own drumming bubble, I nail the fills—damn I love playing fills—and roll into the bridge effortlessly. I'd been worried about my nervousness screwing me up, but within the song, I'm rhythm to my bone marrow.

After the song is over and I'm out of my zone, I notice the faces around me. Surprise etches expressions. Even Romeo appears a bit shocked. With wide eyes, Justin grins at me.

I hold in a smirk as the bass player lets go of his instrument and holds out a hand to me. "Sam."

"Riley," I say tightly, still holding in that smirk.

His bright blue eyes roam over me. "Yeah, I'm not going to forget anytime soon."

I let go of his hand while resisting an eye roll.

Romeo clears his throat. The shock is gone from his face. "Why don't you start us off again, Riley?" His sarcastic tone communicates he still isn't impressed, which is completely different from the look on his face seconds ago.

I've never had good aim, but he's only about five feet away. I imagine one of my sticks whacking his forehead with a loud thud. "'Midnight' then?"

"That would be the other song."

Hitting my sticks together, I wonder if my sorry ass aim could hit him twice. "Midnight" is fast and full of energy. As I crank out the beat, I forget about my anger and just enjoy playing the song.

At the end, Justin whistles in a low tone. "Damn, that was some straight playing."

Sam shakes his head as if to clear it. "Um, after you break down your kit, send the next one out."

Romeo gives my rented kit a sneer, setting his guitar on a stand before they all move to the far end of the room. While I break the set down, the hushed hisses of an argument hit my ears. That low hush has me breaking down the kit in record time, moving it against the wall and racing into the adjoining room.

The small attic-like room with a low slanted ceiling has chairs around the edges and rough wood-slatted walls. Amid the stunned gazes, I can feel an almost tangible jealousy in the air. It's more than obvious the other drummers didn't think I would be much competition and are shocked by my talent.

Piss off, boys. I'll outplay you anytime.

Marcus nudges my shoulder as I lean against the wall next to him. Probably feeling the resentment in the air too, he doesn't say anything. Just grins at me. I have to stop myself from grinning back.

I yank my sticks from my back pocket. "They're ready for whoever wants to go next."

The guy sitting closest to the door slowly gets up.

Tapping on my leg with the beat going on in the other room, I stand there listening to the other drummers for the next hour. One is absolutely awful. Two okay. The only one who comes close to me is the guy who showed up late. But he's not close enough.

After everyone plays the two songs, we wait together in the tiny room. One guy talks on his phone, bitching nonstop about the way the audition is going. Another taps on the chair next to him with his sticks. The last two argue about digital drumming.

Marcus leans closer to me. "I'll be surprised if they even go on," he whispers.

Unless they're idiots.

About twenty minutes later, Justin pops his head in the room. "We'd like everyone to come out." When we're all in the main room, he runs a hand through his dark blond hair, and the glare of the lone lightbulb above catches the assortment of ink on his arm. His posture makes it evident he's having a hard time spitting out his announcement. "Really, it's great you all came but we'd only like Matt, Gabe, and Riley to stay for the next round."

A murmur goes through the small crowd in front of me.

Justin didn't meet my gaze when he spoke and he still doesn't while the two drummers file out in a huff. My eyes flash to Romeo. His gaze meets mine and his lips twist in a sardonic smile. My eyes narrow. His lips twist more.

I look away in my own huff.

They are idiots.

Even though I'm sure this is Romeo's doing, they're letting him. I'm split in two. Part of me wants to follow the other drummers out. The other part wants to prove myself. But I already did. Within my crossed arms, my hands clench around the drumsticks until my knuckles whiten.

Marcus bends close to me and says under his breath, "Relax, Riley. You're in the final round. Plus it's more fair. Right?"

I glare at him but stay silent.

Once the other drummers are gone, Romeo picks up his guitar from its stand. "So who wants to go first?"

We're all quiet. Whoever goes last will have a major advantage hearing the band perform two sets with the other drummers. My chin goes up a notch. I don't need an advantage. "I'll go."

Romeo has been adjusting his guitar, but his dark eyes rise to me as the other drummers file into the room. There's a challenge in them that strengthens my resolve.

After resetting up my set, I slide onto the stool. "What song?"

Justin and Sam look to Romeo. "'Gone Baby,'" he says as if throwing down the gauntlet.

Another of their originals. Of course, he picks the one with the knife-edged timing. I have to be exact. Too fast and they'll fall over themselves, too slow and it'll drag like a funeral march. As Romeo stares at me, I give him a nasty smirk. "This one starts with a riff, right?"

His nod is tight before he strums out the loud riff.

Sam and I break in like we've been playing together for years. Justin starts the first line of vocals and I enter my bubble. Lost in the energy of playing, I'm almost startled when the song ends.

"Damn, that was fucking perfect, Riley!" Justin says as soon as we're done, bouncing in front of his microphone.

I grin at him.

Romeo's lip curls before he turns to me. "Okay, you've mastered that track, but can you do anything to add your own creativity?"

Does he want me to walk over hot coals too? "Sure," I say, keeping my tone light even though I'm about to lose it on this guy. "Same one?"

Appearing indifferent while he challenges me, he adjusts the guitar strap on his shoulder. "Let's try 'At the End of the Universe.'"

He's trying to trip me up, but I almost let out a snicker. The song may have several changes in dynamics, but this is my favorite of their originals. It's like he just gave me a present.

I count them in and we break into the slower tune. I keep it light, little things here and there to back up the vocal. I'm all about the melody, letting it stretch the beat and giving it room to breathe. Until I ease into a stronger beat, leading the band into the chorus with a half-time fill that complements the change. As we head back into the verse, I double the kick drum at the beginning of every measure, which fits the feel of the song better. Even in my own little world, I notice Romeo's look of surprise.

Obviously, he thinks so too.

When the final chorus kicks in, I bring my drums down low, pounding out eighth notes on my floor tom and quarter notes on the kick. It drives the band. They follow almost instantly, bringing the sound down low, insistent, yanking the volume down like the cops just showed up at the door. I slowly bring the volume up and again they follow my lead. Guess this is one way to get Romeo to join the Riley club. The contrast in volume ends the song with a powerful bang.

Sam turns to me. His thick eyebrows almost reach his buzzed hairline. "Man, Riley, you got it going on."

"I think that's enough," Romeo says tightly. "Move that piece of shit kit out of the way and send the next drummer in."

I should be angry about his snide remark, but I just conquered this band. I tear down my shitty kit with a smile.

While I lean on the wall next to Marcus, I listen to the other drummers play. But their playing doesn't worry me, though Romeo does. Everyone done, the band leaves us to wait in the cave. But we can hear the low hum of arguing through the thin door. And there's only one reason they could be arguing.

In the chair next to me, Marcus folds his arms across his chest in obvious irritation. He might finally understand the issue here. While Marcus's anger simmers, I wonder if Romeo loses the argument whether I can work with him. I recall the excitement of being behind the drum set. Is that feeling worth dealing with him?

"This is bullshit," Marcus says under his breath.

I don't respond.

The other drummers are quiet and appear shell-shocked. Yeah, they're aware there's really no competition here.

The words "Drop it, Romeo" come through the door before
Justin pops his head in. His ever-present grin shines at me. "So,
Riley, you want the job?"

Listening to Romeo's grumbling beyond the doorway, I recall
the feeling behind the drums. The feel of being in my own bubble,
away from the world. "Yeah," I say, returning his grin.

Chapter 4

"Riley!"

The coffeepot in my hand jumps at my mother's screech and dark liquid spills on the counter. I yank out my earbuds. "What?" I snap, reaching for a paper towel.

She comes around the kitchen island and points at my arms. "Are those tattoos?"

"They're henna." I throw the towel in the trash and finish pouring her coffee.

Her brown eyes widen on the red-ink swirls around my little biceps while fingers with gnawed-on nails rub a temple. "What does that mean?"

I push the coffee toward her, smiling at her obvious shock. "They're not permanent."

She doesn't reach for the cup. "Then what's the point?"

Drumbeats echo throughout the kitchen until I dig out my iPod from my pocket and slide the power to off. "Because I didn't want to wear a bunch of bracelets," I say as if that explains everything.

Her expression remains perplexed as she reaches for her coffee. Like usual she looks tired. Though it's after nine in the morning, she's still in her robe. Her shoulder-length brown hair is damp, so at least she took a shower. There have been several days this summer when my mother stayed in her robe and lay around in bed until it was time to get ready for work at two in the afternoon. The change from part-time day employee to nighttime manager at the department store she's worked at for years has been challenging for her, and then there's the divorce, of course.

My fingers drum on the counter. "I . . . um, joined a band." I hadn't wanted to discuss the whole band thing with her unless I made it. "Chloe wanted me to wear a bunch of bracelets, but I can't drum—" My mother's startled expression has me pausing.

"A band?"

"You know, with guitars and a crowd." I open the dishwasher and grab a stack of clean plates.

"Really?" She doesn't wait for a response. "Do you have time with your classes?"

"Mom," I say over my shoulder as I stack dishes in the cupboard, "I didn't even take a full semester. I already earned credits for calculus and senior AP English. Just for the fall, I went light."

"What about Jamie?"

I'm aware this is what's really bothering her. Mostly, she doesn't want Jamie with sitters, but I know money's on her mind too. "We only practice three times a week. By next month, it will be just two, and Chloe said she would watch Jamie on the nights you're not home."

"Hmmm . . ." She takes a sip of coffee and looks past my shoulder toward the sliding glass doors that lead to the yard and pool. The lines of her forehead are tight as she glances back at my arms. "What kind of band?"

"They play mostly alternative rock."

"Girls?"

I shake my head and open the silverware drawer. "Just me."

Worry lines her pensive expression. "Where will you be playing?"

"I saw them at the old movie theater downtown. So probably there. Maybe some bars," I add with a shrug as I drop in a pile of forks.

She leans on the counter as if she's too tired to stand on her own. "Riley, you sure this is a good idea?"

Several thoughts run through my head. Foremost is the fact that if I were away at college like I should be, she wouldn't even know what I was doing. Then there's the fact I'm almost nineteen. But I don't want to be disrespectful to her. "Mom, this is my chance to still play and be part of something."

Jamie runs into the kitchen. "Mommy!" she squeals, and wraps my mother in a hug around her waist. Now that my mom works full-time instead of part-time in the mornings, Jamie sees a lot less of her, which saddens me. When I was eight, my mom didn't work at all.

Squeezing back, my mom says, "Pancakes for breakfast?"

Jamie nods into my mother's narrow waist. My mom was always working on losing ten or twenty pounds, but over the last seven months she's become too thin. Both Jamie and I take after her though: petite, dark brown hair, and brown eyes. Jamie's are a rich, warm brown. Mine are light like toffee.

"Help me make them?" she asks, and Jamie nods yes. "Get the mix?"

I'm ecstatic my mother's actually doing something other than watching TV with my sister. Jamie bops over to the pantry while I pull out a mixing bowl.

Looking worried, my mother slides her coffee cup back and forth over the counter. "I'm not sure I get it, Riley. This change from marching band to rock band. But I know you're old enough to make your own decisions. Just . . . play the music. Don't get sucked into anything you normally wouldn't do."

Sex, drugs, and rock and roll, here I come. "Mom, you know me better than that."

She sighs. "I do. You're far more responsible than I was at your age. But everyone can become desensitized."

My lips press together to stop a response as I shut the dishwasher. If anyone has become numb, it would be my mother.

"You're rushing again," Romeo says for about the fifth time. "How many times do I have to tell you to slow us down on the bridge or we're all going to crash?"

I bite the inside of my cheek. He has been hounding me since I sat behind the drum set. First, lighten up on the fills and now slow down. I'd like to use his skull for a drum. We're back in the same space as when I tried out. Apparently, Sam's aunt owns the antique store beneath us, and this is where they've always practiced.

With a hand choking his guitar strap, Romeo asks, "Do I need to get you a metronome?"

What a dick. His insinuation I'm a beginner and need help keeping time pisses me off more than anything he's said or done thus far. Though my sticks are clenched in one palm, I keep my tone even. "Ah, no."

He lets go of his strap. "Really? Because so far you can't seem to count."

"Back off, Romeo," Justin says. "She's not going to be perfect the first practice."

"Thought she was superdrummer?" Romeo says snidely.

"She is." Sam winks at me. "Cute too."

"I'll get it this time," I say in a calm tone, ignoring Sam's flirting. I've refused to let Romeo see how much he's riling me up. I'm not going to cave now. It's hot up here, even in a tank top and shorts. I wipe my brow before counting off the beat with my sticks.

We do another round of "Paint It Black" by the Stones. I nail it. Romeo doesn't say anything, but Sam offers compliments and Justin a fist bump.

After a few more cover songs, Sam yanks off his bass and sets it against the boxes lining one wall. "I need a smoke." Disappearing down the stairs that lead out to the street, he yells, "Be back in ten."

Romeo turns to Justin, running his hands through his hair until he clasps the back of his neck and the muscles of his arms bulge. "We're not going to be ready for U-Palooza."

"Why? Riley's doing great." Justin tosses the sheet music he'd been reading from onto one of the chairs across from us. Pop cans, fast food bags, and other papers litter the space underneath. Ugh. Sloppy boys.

Romeo's chin lowers. "With six songs."

"So we'll do a shortened set. Who cares?"

Irritated, I roll my sticks across my thigh while they argue like I'm not here, like I'm not part of the band.

Romeo's arms drop and he gazes at Justin with visible irritation. "I care. We're not some garage band."

Justin rolls his eyes. "Don't get your perfectionist panties in a twist. We should be able to get three more done."

"It's still not enough." Romeo turns to me. "Can you read music?"

I nod. Although drum notation is a bit different, reading music isn't too hard after five years of piano lessons.

"Take the sheet music home and be ready for next practice."

"Will you fucking stop?" Justin pulls his phone out. "We're going to be far more ready than we would have with that ass-wipe you wanted." He turns to me and his expression softens. "Just ignore him and take a quick break, Riley. You're doing great. Looking good too," he says with a wink. Enough with the stupid winking. Pressing the screen on his phone, he walks to the far side of the dusty room. "Hey, Jessica, you busy tonight?"

"What is your problem?" I say under my breath when Justin is across the room and, I'm hoping, not paying attention to us.

Romeo's dark eyes pin me to the stool. He stands facing me with his sleek black guitar hanging from his neck. "I think it's pretty obvious."

His irritated gaze stabs at my confidence. "Just because I'm a girl?"

A tic twitches under a cheekbone. "Mostly . . ."

The sticks clenched in my hand smack against the stool seat. "That's a bunch of bullshit."

"It's not what you think," he says as his gaze continues to stab me while his hair flops at an angle that almost reaches his tightened cheekbone.

My lids lower and my upper lip curls. "I think you're a chauvinist pig."

That tic becomes more pronounced before a smirk curves his sensual lips. "Think whatever you want, but a little more aggravation and I'm sure you'll break, then your little ass will be gone."

My brows drop low. "Don't ever refer to my ass again, asshole."

His smirk widens. "What a dirty little mind you have, Miss M. I'd like to say I'm delighted with the knowledge, but I'm not."

I knew he was going to be a pain. I told myself to ignore him, but I really, really want to use his skull for a drum at the moment. Instead of jumping up and tapping on his head, I smile sweetly at him. "I can guarantee I won't quit. Obviously, me in the band pisses you off. And I'm finding that I like to piss you off."

His perfect face twists into a scowl. I hate to admit it but he even looks hot wearing a scowl. He opens his mouth, but Justin comes over in time before I have to listen to more of Romeo's crap.

I roll my sticks between my palms and give him the evil eye. Why is it if a person looks like they stepped off the cover of a magazine, they're usually a certified dickhead?

Chapter 5

I had imagined my first day of college completely different. I envisioned an eclectic group of friends, a new and different location, and a plethora of stimulating classes. Not one of my visualizations came true. And to top it off, I'm having lunch in a packed cafeteria with a classmate from high school.

"Aren't you dating that one band guy? What's his name?" Kendra Dobson asks, shoving her empty salad bowl away.

I blink at her. As soon as she saw me coming down the aisle of Philosophy 101, she was nodding and waving me toward her. Though we spoke less than ten words to each other in high school, seeing a familiar face had her overly friendly on the first day of college. Cliques in our high school were never tight, but neither Kendra nor I were members of more than one. She hung with the popular crowd and was one of the reigning beauty queens. I hung with the band geeks. Yet all through class, she'd been whispering and writing stuff in her notebook for me to read like we were the best of friends. Not wanting to be rude, I pretended interest while trying to take notes on the lecture. Once she saw my schedule, she decided we should eat lunch together. I went along with her because otherwise I'd have to sit by myself since Marcus is in a class right now.

All the way to the cafeteria, in the long line, and through most of lunch, I heard about parties with drunk people I barely know, about who hooked up with who over the summer, including several of her own flings. And now that Kendra has finally asked something about me, I'm startled.

"Aaron Dregski." I push away the other half of a club sandwich. "But we're not dating anymore."

She looks up from digging in her purse. "Really? You two were the cutest couple."

I glance at the table of guys next to us, wondering how she can ignore their ogling her. "Um, thanks, but he went to college in another state."

Kendra's long-lashed eyes constrict as she slams her purse on the table. "I hate that shit—people breaking up because they can't do long-distance relationships. Like did he date you last year because it was convenient or something?" My stunned look has her frowning. "Sorry, I . . . Hey, didn't *you* have a music scholarship to some major university?"

This is the real reason I didn't want to hang out with Kendra. Her blasé attitude I can handle. Her questions, not so much. "I changed my mind and decided to stay home."

She gives me an odd look. "So you're in the band here?"

I reach for the other half of my sandwich. Music is better territory than Aaron or my parents' divorce. "Not the marching band. I'm in another band."

She pauses, opening her lip gloss. "What band?"

"Luminescent Juliet." I take a huge bite.

Her eyes round. The lip gloss stays closed. "Get out."

Nodding, I finish chewing. "For the last two weeks." And playing has been awesome. More than I thought it would be. However, putting up with Romeo, the rock drill sergeant, has sucked.

"Wow. I wondered about the new look you've got going." I pause, lifting my sandwich. My expression must tell her she hit a nerve, because she adds, "You look better." That nerve now being hammered. "I mean older, more college looking. Not that you weren't cute before . . ." She trails off but my irritation dissipates.

Unfortunately, I'm used to the "cute" thing. I've never been referred to as beautiful or even pretty, always "cute." Like I'm a frickin' kitten or something. But Chloe's makeover *has* forced me to pay attention to fashion more. My normal sloppy look of loose T-shirts and baggy shorts or jeans looks odd with my wild hair and red-brown swirling tattoos. Today I'm wearing low-riding tight jeans, a black tank, and flip-flop wedges.

She leans across the table. "You know, I saw them once. That guitar player, holy-yummy-fuck-fest."

Sandwich bits almost spray from my mouth at the thought of sex with Romeo. I swallow and push my plate away again. "Ah, fest?"

She nods while glossing her lips, then throws back her blonde curls. "Come on, you have to admit he's beyond hot."

And a total dickhead, which is best kept to myself. I shrug. "He's good-looking but so is Justin, the singer."

She grins. The curve of her sparkly lips looks devious. "It's hard to notice anything, even the music, with that guitar player in your face. He, like, sweats images of hot sex. What's his name?"

I kind of get why the sight of Romeo shocked her out of noticing Justin. Justin's like sunshine. A day at the beach with the wind catching your laughter and sand between your toes. Romeo is darkness. The floating feeling between awake and dreams that holds a mysterious captivation.

"Romeo," I respond, hoping to end the conversation. Visions of Romeo and hot sex are the last things I need in my head.

"Like as in Shakespeare?"

I shrug. "I guess."

"Does he go here?" she asks, with excitement lacing her tone.

"I think so." I reach for my backpack. To be honest I don't know much about Romeo other than he's a chauvinistic jerk. And yeah, he's hot.

She grabs her own bag, some huge over-the-shoulder designer thing. "You *have* to introduce me."

Other than practice, like I'd hang out with that tool but I agree to introduce her as we dump our lunch trays. She follows me out the side door even though her next class is the other way.

"Rush week is coming. I want to pledge for Gamma Pi Omega," she says as soon as we step outside. "You interested?"

In a sorority? No. Especially here. I glance at the sleek lines of the fountain in the middle of the outdoor common area. This university was built in the seventies. Every building and piece of construction reeks of modern. No ivy-covered architecture here. In fact, the college just gained university status about eight years ago. The fraternities and sororities don't even have houses. But I wouldn't have joined a sorority in Virginia either. Over-the-top social is not my thing.

"I'm too busy with the band," I say tactfully.

"Oh yeah, I can see that." Her glossy lips press together in a tight frown. "I just thought it would be cool to pledge with someone I knew."

"I'm sure you'll get accepted. Make it. Whatever they call it."

"As long as my GPA is a two-point-eight or higher at semester. I may need a little help in philosophy."

Really, I should have seen this coming.

Kendra makes sure to get my e-mail address before we part ways. Between my philosophy notes and my connection to Romeo, I'm guessing she'll be e-mailing a lot.

JEAN HAUS   45

Calculus is in another building across the small campus. Since I'm early and expecting the class to be hard, I sit up front at a corner table. The room is much smaller than the auditorium used for Philosophy 101. And instead of desks bolted to the floor, this room has tables.

Other students stream in as I pull out a new notebook, a graphing calculator, and my thick calculus text. Waiting for class to start, I absently drum my pencils—erasers down—on my book. I have a new beat going when someone plops down beside me. Horror, instant and angry, flows through me at the sight of my tablemate.

Oh just . . . hell no.

"Fancy meeting you here, Riley," Romeo says, leaning back with an arm around his chair. "I thought you were a freshman."

This cannot be happening. I look around the room for another seat. The room is almost full. "I am."

"Then what are you doing in my class?"

"Didn't know you owned the class," I snap as someone takes the last empty seat. I whip open my notebook. Generally, I'm a nice person—Chloe often says *too* nice—but around Romeo, I become superbitch with a trademark sneer. "I took Calc one and two in high school."

He lets out a low whistle while yanking a binder from his bag. "Too smart for your own good, aren't you?"

I ignore his stupid smart question. I'm more of a hard worker than anything else. I had to do Calculus II as an online course, which blowed. Got a B in that one. "Aren't you a senior? Shouldn't you be done with this class?"

"I'm a junior, and this class didn't fit into my schedule until this semester."

"Huh?" I kind of assumed Romeo was years older than me.

"I'm twenty-one," he says, understanding my confusion. "I . . . ah . . . missed a semester of high school and graduated late. Not that it's really any of your business," he adds in a snide tone.

"Why are you sitting here?" I ask through clenched teeth. Dealing with him at practice is one thing. In class, it's intolerable.

"I find that I like to annoy you," he says in a sickening sweet tone before his full lips twist into a mocking grin. Because he is mocking me. With my own words.

My angry retort dies as the balding professor walks through the door. He welcomes everyone, introduces himself as Professor Hill, and hands out a syllabus for the semester. Romeo instantly turns serious and attentive as the professor reads over the syllabus.

With his profile visible, I study my bandmate. Strangely, I've never been this close to him before. All of Kendra's comments have me assessing him. Long, dark hair lies over his forehead in a swoop while thick shorter hair covers the back of his neck. His winged brows arch over full lashes. And the slanting cut of his jaw and cheekbone is in severe contrast to the angle of his straight nose. All right, together his features do paint a yummy picture.

But not perfect. That straight nose is a tad too long. A sprinkling of dark scruff covers his jaw. And those ears lined with silver hoops stick out just a little too much. Okay, I could be desperate to find faults. He's close to perfect. Yet Kendra's right about one thing. Romeo exudes sex. I'm not sure if it's the scruff or those full pouty lips or his dark gaze—probably a combination of all three—but I've never met anyone so hot. Sweaty images tumble through my mind while I stare at him. If I'd known Kendra was going to put these images in my head, I never would have eaten lunch with her. How the heck am I supposed to pass this class with him sitting next to me?

He glances at me and those dark eyes, so brown they're nearly black, meet my stare. I refuse to look away. As if not breaking our gazes means I wasn't checking him out. He arches a brow, then smirks at me. That smirk says he's guessing my deviant thoughts. I give him a scowl, then attempt to pay attention to the professor. Focusing with Romeo next to me is harder than dealing with Kendra.

Shit. I'm going to flunk out of both classes. If only I was where I should be, in Virginia.

After going over the syllabus, the professor takes roll, walking around and filling in a seating chart. I pay close attention. Not only for my name but also for Romeo's. There's no way I'd ask him for his last name, so this is my chance to learn what it is. I almost miss it because the professor says, "Justin Romeo." I'd been expecting Romeo Something. Once it finally sinks in that Romeo is his last name and Justin his first, I lean toward him and whisper, "J.R., huh?"

His lids lower but he doesn't look at me. "Romeo works fine."

"So where's your Juliet?" I ask, and the name of our band finally makes sense. If naming it after him makes any kind of sense. Then I realize they probably call him Romeo because there are two people named Justin in the band.

His eyes darken as he leans closer to me. "Did you want to try out for the part?"

"No," I snap more loudly than a whisper.

"Probably for the best." He nods. "I'm not sure you'd make it past the first cut."

Okay, I never expected His Hotness to be attracted to merely cute me, but his blatant proclamation is not only nasty, it pisses me off. Keeping my anger in check, I shrug. "I'm not the harem type anyway."

Those dark eyes round slightly before he laughs. Loud.

Since we're in the first row, the professor gives him a long look.

Romeo clears his throat and sits up.

I take vigorous notes once the lecture starts, writing down any-thing the professor says or does on the board. Every example from the whiteboard is perfectly copied into my notebook. However, not all of the information enters my brain. In fact, very little. Between the hotness radiating off the person next to me and the anger inside of me, the professor might as well be teaching underwater basket weaving.

After two hours of lecture, Professor Hill announces a much-needed fifteen-minute break before the next two hours of class.

I'm not surprised at the horde of girls surrounding Romeo as soon as he steps into the hallway. Walking past them toward the exit, I don't restrain an eye roll. Outdoors, I sit on a bench, listen to my iPod, and tap the beat on my knee. When I come back to class a few minutes early, I'm surprised to see Romeo and just one girl talking at the end of the hall. They stand close together, speaking quietly.

Pausing, I lean against the wall across from the door to class with several other students. Though I blame hanging in the hall on taking full advantage of the break, curiosity has me watching Romeo and the girl from the corner of my eye. From the back, the girl is tall and lean, with straight blonde-brown hair. She turns slightly and smiles up at him. I'm looking at one of Jamie's Barbie dolls. Well, sort of. Jamie likes to cut their hair then color the strands with marker. He smiles back but not as wide. Finally, she gives his chest a playful push before taking off.

It's obvious they know each other. Wondering how well has my curiosity pulsing in overdrive as I go to my assigned seat.

Romeo waltzes in with a wicked grin in my direction, but the girl who sits at the table to the right of us stops him with an interro-gation about the band. I doodle on the cover of my notebook while I listen to him answer her questions. Though her initial question was about Luminescent Juliet, most of her inquiries after that are about him, not the band.

"Did you enjoy watching me?" Romeo asks, plopping down next to me.

I continue doodling on my notebook. I'm not entirely sure why I was watching him—both with the girl outside and then the one inside the classroom—but my cheeks heat up. "Conceited much?"

"Interesting, I thought you were looking for ways to get under my skin. I never considered you might be into me. How . . . cute."

My scribbling becomes aggressive. I refuse to look at him. "Yes, since you've been a dick for the last two weeks and now are being one in class too, I've become infatuated with you. I'm a closet masochist."

He leans close enough for me to catch the scent of his woodsy-smelling shampoo. "If you dress the part and bring a whip, you'll definitely get past the first cut." The words are low and spoken near my ear.

My head snaps back and I almost collide with his chin. I lean away, not too much, refusing to back down from his smug expression. "It's official. You are a chauvinistic pig."

He just grins.

Jerk.

The professor starts class again. I take incomprehensible notes again. Sex drips off my table partner the entire time. Ugh. Kendra should have kept her piehole shut. I already internally admitted he was hot, but now my brain's swirling with unwanted images. If I were in Virginia, I wouldn't be dealing with him or the sweaty, naked pictures in my head.

Chapter 6

Every Tuesday night Jamie and I meet my father for dinner at five thirty. On Saturdays my father comes over at six and watches Jamie while my mother works. This is their interaction because until the divorce is final, my mother will not let my sister go to his apartment. The girlfriend is there. My mother claims allowing new people into Jamie's life during the upheaval of the divorce could be detrimental, especially if my father's new relationship doesn't last. My mother is looking out for her daughter, but I'm aware there's a bit of spite laced into her demands.

Unfortunately, the girlfriend is sitting across from me at the moment. With her sleek dark hair and the black blazer she wears, she's attractive in a slick modern way I find annoying. My mother has more of a cardigan-and-turtleneck mom persona. I've seen the girlfriend from a distance before but never met her until today, and though it's not her fault, I'm fuming that my dad brought her. I'm not even sure what I just ordered. I just pointed at the menu.

"Can we go watch them make pasta," Jamie asks me as she twirls the ponytail I gathered her hair in this morning for school. My sister thinks watching noodles coming out of a machine is one of the most exciting things in the world.

I smile sweetly across the table. "Could you take her to the lobby?" I ask Ms. Husband-Stealing Girlfriend. "I need to talk to my dad for a minute." Though I don't really want her around my sister, the urge to talk to my dad outweighs my dislike of her.

"Sure." She slides out of the booth and wobbles for a second in her ridiculously high heels. "Come on, Jamie." She holds out a hand that is at least ten years younger than my mother's. While the girlfriend's dressed in somber black, my sister is girly cute today in a pink shirt and matching tennis shoes.

Most likely thinking of them bonding, my idiot father watches them go with a wistful look on his face before he loosens the tie around his neck. I consider his dating someone so much younger. My mother used to tell him he grew more handsome every year. Although he's forty-seven and his hair has gone salt-and-pepper, he's thin and fit from running every morning.

As soon as my sister is out of hearing distance, I snap, "How could you?"

My father leans back against the booth. "Riley, it's just dinner. I could bring a business associate. What would be the difference?"

"So you're assuming I'm not going to tell Mom?"

"Yes. I'm assuming you're going to act like an adult. Sara is part of my life. Whether your mother wants it or not, she's going to be part of Jamie's and yours."

Bitterness has me gripping the table between us. I've tried, somewhat successfully, to stay out of my parents' bickering. My two cents won't change anything. However, internally I've always been on my mother's side. My father left us just days after the New Year and started dating the girlfriend in January. Obviously, their connection started long before he left the house.

"They say it takes a year for people to come to terms with a divorce. Those people include the children," I say, sounding like a pamphlet on the effects of divorce.

"We're getting married, Riley." He reaches for his drink. "Hopefully, the divorce will be final in February, so we're planning on March."

My mouth falls open.

He sets his glass down with a soft thud after taking a long drink. "I'd like you and Jamie to get to know her before the wedding."

Astonishment has me compressed into the vinyl of the booth. "Are you trying to destroy Mom? After twenty-one years of marriage, does she mean nothing to you?"

His jaw tightens. "Riley, I know this isn't easy for anyone. But Sara and I are in love."

I snap back up and lean across the table. "What does that mean? Because you're in love, you can stomp over everyone else? Did you even love Mom?"

"Your mother and I . . ." He sighs. "Things were never right after Maggie miscarried. She became severely depressed." My teeth clench. Of course, she was depressed. She'd carried the baby for almost seven months. "After Jamie was born we thought things would mend, but they never came together. I know this seems sudden to you, but for the last ten years we were trying to make it work."

"Are you telling me half my childhood was a lie?"

"No marriage is unflawed, Riley. Ours just slowly deteriorated over time."

"For you," I say stubbornly.

A muscle twitches in his cheek. "Perhaps your mother isn't as pragmatic as I am."

"Or maybe it has something to do with how you went about it," I snap again.

"Let's not—"

"And maybe you shouldn't be so selfish and should wait at least a year after the divorce to marry your girlfriend."

He places his elbows on the table and leans forward. "What about Sara? Maybe she wants a family. Whether you like it or not, she's part of this too."

My stomach rolls at the thought of my father having another family. Half siblings? Something so ridiculous never occurred to me. Forty-seven-year-old men should not be starting second families. "You can't be serious," I hiss.

"I'm getting married, Riley, whether you like it or not." I open my mouth but he cuts me off. "Your car's in my name. I still pay the insurance and put money in your account for gas."

"Are you threatening me financially?" I ask in a tone laced with repulsion. Yes, he pays for my insurance. Yes, I drive the old family sedan. But who watches Jamie four times a week? Who takes care of the house and yard? Who cooks dinner for *his* castoff family?

"You're almost nineteen. Pretty much an adult." He raises a gray eyebrow at me. "If you're going to be disrespectful, why should I continue supporting you?"

Obscenities catch in my throat, but lucky for him the girlfriend and Jamie return and slide into the booth before I lose it on my father with a torrential storm of disrespect. When I notice the diamond on the girlfriend's ring finger, I almost do lose it.

Our food comes. Everyone else talks. I eat. Or rather, push cannelloni around my plate. Jamie seems to like the girlfriend, which upsets me some more.

On top of my father's awful matrimonial news and asinine threats, I have band practice tonight, and this is one night Chloe can't babysit. I was going to ask my father to take Jamie to the movies or mall or somewhere, but there is no way in hell I'm letting my sister go anywhere with the two people sitting across from me.

Once Jamie's done eating, I use homework as an excuse for leaving early. My father looks skeptical, but he doesn't argue. He gives my sister a hug. He doesn't push the issue with me when I step back from his waiting arms. Jamie tells the girlfriend good-bye while I tug her away by the hand.

After a trip home for Jamie supplies, I make it to practice only a few minutes late. As soon as we get up the stairs, Justin asks while looking at my sister, "What's going on?"

"My sitter fell through."

He looks back and forth at each of us while his forehead creases. In deep discussion behind him, Romeo and Sam lean over a sheet of music.

"My mom works nights."

Justin crosses his tattooed arms and his lips turn down. "Okay, but you really think a kid belongs up here?"

Jamie steps closer to me and I put an arm around her shoulder. "Well, I'm not about to leave her home alone." His expression stays irritated. "She has her Nintendo DS, books, and homework. She'll stay quiet and busy for the next couple of hours."

"What about you? You going to be practicing or babysitting?"

My hand tightens on the strap of Jamie's bag. If anyone was going to be an ass about this, I expected it to be Romeo. Boy was I wrong. "I can do both. But if it's such a big issue, maybe we should skip practice tonight."

At that Romeo comes over and gives Jamie a quick smile. "The kid will be fine, Justin. Quit acting like an assho—jerk. Riley's already late, so let's get started. We only have two more practices before the weekend." He turns his attention to me. "You look over the music?"

"Yeah," I say, tapping my temple. "I got it."

"What about the rule?" Justin asks loudly. "*Your* rule. No one's allowed to watch us practice."

Romeo's brows lower. "That was made for the distracting girls you used to bring who were looking to get la—uh, busy. Not for ten-year-olds."

"She's eight," I say.

"Whatever," Romeo says, staring down Justin.

Justin gives him an indignant look but goes over to his microphone. Before I can thank Romeo, he's back talking with Sam. Jamie's expression is worried as I try to get her settled in the chairs across from us. This is the first time I've wanted to give Justin a whack with my drumstick, usually it's Romeo. I'm crouched in front of her telling her everything is okay, but she keeps peeking at Justin. If she doesn't get comfortable soon, I *am* going to leave.

"Hey, that looks cool," Romeo says, sitting two chairs over from Jamie and pointing at the Nintendo DS. "What games have you got?"

Jamie blinks up at him. "SpongeBob and Barbie dress-up."

"Huh, SpongeBob sounds good. Barbie might be a bit girly for me." He rubs his chin as if in thought. "Or would I like it?"

My sister giggles. "It's probably too girly."

Romeo nods while I watch him dumbfounded. "You may be right, but could I check out SpongeBob during our break?"

She nods. "You'll like it. *All* the boys like it."

"Cool," Romeo says with a grin, then takes off.

Who would have thought I would be thankful to Romeo twice in one night? Never me. I remind my sister to do her homework first, and I make sure she's aware the music will be very loud— like when she listened to me practice my snare in my room all last year—before I move to the drum set.

In between songs, I keep an eye on Jamie. She mostly does her homework, but every now and then I catch her watching Romeo. Obviously, females of all ages are drawn to him.

At the break I check her homework while Jamie shows Romeo how to work the DS. His playful banter has her giggling in overdrive. He's even kept his usual hounding to a minimum, and has yelled only when Sam and Justin cussed. His whole demeanor—100 percent different this evening—has me considering, for about two seconds, bringing Jamie to all of our practices. If only Romeo were like this all the time.

Wait a minute. Scratch that.

If Romeo were like this all the time, I would be obsessed with him.

Enamored with our guitar player, Jamie spends the rest of the practice playing her DS and peeking at Romeo.

Done practicing, I'm bent over, packing up Jamie's stuff when Justin comes over and places a palm on my lower back. "Hey, Riley." I stand but he doesn't remove his hand, only shifts to the side of me. "I want to tell you sorry for earlier. I'm not sure why I acted like a jerk. Maybe Romeo's rubbing off on me," he says with a smirk. "But it's okay if you bring your sister."

Holding her bag while still sitting on the chair, Jamie watches us.

I'm not sure if he's being genuine or just trying to maintain his leader persona. Even *I've* noticed how Justin likes to act like the front man, but it was obvious from the start Romeo runs the show. "Well, thanks. I won't make it a habit, but I may need to bring her again."

He nods. "You should come out with us sometime after practice." He glances at Jamie. "Obviously not tonight, some other time though."

I joined the band to play. Not to hang out or—from the obvious invitation in Justin's green eye—to hook up with anybody. A band member hookup would definitely create hostility among all the egos in the room, and could possibly land me out of the band. Not that I'm interested. I always leave right after practice. In fact, Romeo's usual attitude has me practically running out the door. Along with the fact that Chloe babysits for free.

I don't want to cause friction, so I say, "Yeah, some other time."

He finally removes his hand from my lower back but doesn't move away. Over his shoulder, Romeo and Sam stare at us. Sam looks angry. Romeo disgusted. Great. Just when I thought Romeo might lay off. Sam could be jealous. He does like to flirt. Not that I reciprocate.

But who knows what dickhead's problem is.

Chapter 7

After four years of playing high school band, I learned to enjoy watching football. The fans, the crowd's excitement, and of course, the band became nostalgic. Even though I grasped only the basics of the game—like what a first down is or the purpose of a thrown flag—I usually enjoyed watching the sport. Not so much today. Nostalgia has me feeling ill and wanting to be more than a spectator crunched between fans on steel bleachers. I want to be at the far end of the stands with the band every time it plays something. However, I'm here for Marcus so I suck it up.

"I saw on Facebook that Aaron's coming tonight," Chloe says offhandedly.

Sitting between us, Jamie says in a whine, "I want to see Aaron."

Of course, she wants to see Aaron. What with almost a year of movies shared on the couch, trips to the park, and countless dinners at our house with him, she's grown to care about him. But with Chloe's news, I ignore even Jamie. I'm already nervous about performing tonight at the U-Palooza. Aaron in the crowd is the last thing I need. "Why is he home?"

Chloe shrugs. "Homesick?"

My eyes narrow on her profile. "It's the first week of school for me. The second for him."

"Oh no, don't look at me. Maybe this is your new buddy Kendra's doing. She's been posting all week on Facebook about Luminescent Juliet and you." She rolls her eyes. "Why would I invite that douche bag?"

True. Ever since Aaron broke up with me because he couldn't do a long-distance relationship, Chloe, who once liked him, hasn't been too forgiving. And I've been staying away from Facebook. After all the questions and comments about Aaron and me from all of our friends, I couldn't take rehashing our breakup every time I logged on.

"But you can bet he'll be drooling a puddle tonight," she says with a smirk before turning to the game.

While the Hawks football team lines up for a field goal, I hold in a groan at the thought of becoming Chloe's Barbie doll in a few hours. But that's exactly why I suspected she might have invited him. Her idea of rubbing my hot new look—her words not mine—in his face. "Think he'll want to get back together?" Her gaze of fury snaps to mine. I laugh. "Just kidding."

Chloe doesn't laugh. "You'd better be."

Sensing the animosity in the air, Jamie looks back and forth at each of us. "I like Aaron."

"We do too," I say with a smile, and straighten one of the barrettes in her shiny hair. Chloe lets out a huff. I ignore her. "He's just not my boyfriend anymore."

Jamie frowns at me.

The kicker makes the field goal and we cheer with the rest of the crowd.

With a glance at the scoreboard—we're still down by four—and the time, I turn to Jamie. "It's almost halftime. Do you still want a hotdog?" She nods her head vigorously. "Chloe, you coming?"

"No, but I'll take a roll of sweet farts."

As expected, Jamie giggles.

"Be right back with those farts," I say for the purpose of adding more giggles.

Hand in hand, we make our way through the packed crowd in the bleachers, then down to the concession stand. While we wait for two hotdogs—at least I didn't have to make lunch today—a Sprite, popcorn, and one roll of SweeTarts, I notice someone standing amid a bunch of girls. Unfortunately, so does Jamie. Her hand tears from mine before she rushes to the end of the concession stand line.

"Romeo!" she yells, and waves.

He smiles at her and waves back, standing in the circle of his adorers. Flinching, I almost knock down the box of napkins on the counter. His warm, open smile competes with the brilliance of the afternoon sun. I've never seen him smile like that. So startled by the radiance of it, I blink before turning back to the counter.

Romeo's already talking with Jamie by the time I collect our food. When I get to them, she's asking him to sit with us. Great.

He slides his hands into his pockets, looking from me to her—probably deciding if he can contain his inner dick throughout half of a football game—before he agrees. During the last two practices, he was as relentless as ever. So much so that Justin didn't have a chance to offer his invitation again, because I hightailed it out of there faster than ever. But now on his best behavior around Jamie, he helps carry the food to our seats. Once again I consider bringing Jamie to all of our practices. But no, Justin was right. She doesn't belong there.

Chloe's eyes almost pop out of her head as we sit down. While I introduce them and reveal he's the guitar player, her mouth could catch flies as she stares at him. She nudges me hard with an elbow when my sister and Romeo start talking Nintendo.

I give her a look and unwrap my dog.

She mouths, "Holy fuck." Stomps one high-heeled foot, then mouths, "Why didn't you tell me?"

"Asshole," I mouth back, and take a bite. I haven't shared Romeo's attitude toward me to anyone. I'm hoping that if I ignore him being a jerk, he'll give it up.

She twists around to look at Romeo in conversation with Jamie, whose giggling is starting to annoy the people behind us.

"You've lost your mind," she says aloud, and Romeo looks up.

I give him a weak close-lipped smile while chewing and wait for Jamie to get his attention again before I kick Chloe's high heel.

"You're nuts," she says under her breath.

Ignoring her, I finish my concession stand lunch.

The first half ends and the players leave the field.

I hand Jamie a hotdog. "The band's coming on."

She looks up at Romeo. "You like watching the band?"

He grins at her. "I love watching the band. It's the best part of the game."

I stare at the slight crinkles in the corners of his eyes. Who is this alter Romeo around my sister? Chloe nudges me again. I refuse to look her way. I can imagine the expression—one that conveys I'm nuts again—on her face.

A whistle sounds, then the beat of a drum. The announcer's voice booms with the introduction of the band as it forms a line on the other side of the field. My breath hitches at the sight of white-and-red uniforms edged with shiny brass. Another whistle blow, and the band begins marching across the field, with the percussion line leading and pounding out a drumroll. The brass section follows in a V. One more whistle blow, and the percussion line drills out a fast beat until the band stands in front of the home audience. Quiet for a few seconds, the band is colorful and bright in the afternoon sun while anticipation hangs in the bleachers.

Suddenly, the drums roar until the entire band breaks into blaring music—and my chest tightens into a knot.

Chloe, Romeo, Jamie, and my nervousness about the performance tonight are forgotten as want and regret swirl inside of me. Marcus is in the second line of the drums. I used be in the line ahead of him. In the center. The leader. I crouch down with my hands splayed at the sides of my face. I didn't think watching him was going to be this hard. My eyes and ears stay riveted to the scene and the tune, but my body is frozen want as they play.

Music booms as they march and change formation into a visible *H,* for *Hawks.* Brightly colored flags fly behind them. Horns blast as they change formation again and the drumline comes back to the front.

I can't help imagining being out there with them playing and marching. My fingers dig into the skin above my temples. They're good. The marching band I should have been in would have been better. On another field, in another state, I should be playing and marching right now too.

Instead, I'm in the bleachers curled up like an insane person.

At the end of the performance, I finally notice my heavy breath, Chloe's hand rubbing my back, Jamie curled next to me, and the audience cheering. After two more whistle blows and another drumroll, the band marches back to its spot in the stands on the far left.

I slowly sit up.

"You all right?" Chloe asks gently.

I gulp in air and nod.

Jamie's hand tightens around my arm. "Marcus was good, huh?"

Her eyes question me. Though she doesn't understand my re-action, she knows something is off. "Marcus was great," I say as warmly as possible. Above her head, Romeo stares at me. The strik-ing lines of his face crease with apparent confusion.

Chloe lets out a laugh and leans across me. Her gaze locks on Romeo. "She's not a freak. Just a band geek. She was supposed to go to Virginia. Scholarship and all."

His dark gaze bores into mine. His mouth hangs slightly open before he asks, "Then why aren't you there?"

"She has to watch—"

"I'm needed at home," I say, cutting off Chloe. I never, ever want Jamie to feel responsible or guilty for my decision.

Romeo still looks confused, but my tone or a ding from his phone, which he digs out of his pocket, helps us drop the subject.

I give Chloe a look while he reads a text.

"I'm an ass. Forgot. Sorry," she says under her breath, then looks to Jamie, who's watching us. "Want some SweeTarts?"

Chloe keeps handing SweeTarts over my lap as the second half begins. Romeo's busy texting until he stands and waves to someone in the aisle. The girl from the hallway waves back. Within seconds she shuffles her way toward him. Dressed in a white polo and a navy skort, she looks tennis preppy. I realize as he shoves the phone back into his pocket that she must be who he was texting.

After she gives him a quick hug, he introduces us to April. Al-though he explains I'm the new drummer, he doesn't give her a title, but she has to be his girlfriend. Though Romeo is beyond hot, I can't understand why someone would date him. Girls follow him like he's the Pied Piper. And April's constricted smile as she offers Chloe and me a quick hello conveys the jealously she must harbor all the freakin' time.

With Romeo *and* April here, I grow more uncomfortable. But I watch the game for the most part. Chloe and I chat every now and then on our end. Romeo and April converse between themselves. Jamie, seated in the middle, is the only one who talks to everybody.

The Hawks end up losing by two points. Shuffling out, Romeo quizzes me on the time and place for our gig tonight like I'm a simpleton who can't remember the simplest of directions. His girlfriend watches me with a hooded expression as I answer him in a tight tone. I resist rolling my eyes in response to her look.

Even if he found me attractive or if I were in the running for a boyfriend, he's the last person I would hook up with. Even if they drip with sexual allure, chauvinistic jerks don't appeal to me.

Chapter 8

After meeting Marcus in his dorm room—appropriately praising his playing and saying good-bye to Jamie, because Marcus was giving her a ride home—I survived Chloe's ministrations for over two hours. Lucky for me, Marcus's roommate had gone home for the weekend, because Chloe had me try on more than four different outfits and we argued the entire time.

When Marcus returned, his eyebrows about reached his hairline as he stared at me in my outfit: a tight, thin-strapped dark red top that complements the tattoos on my arms, a black flared skirt (I added shorts underneath), and knee-high combat boots. Chloe lined my eyes heavily and split my hair, leaving the long underneath blonde down and the brown in a high ratted-out ponytail. Marcus's long whistle had Chloe somehow smiling and frowning at the same time.

Now I'm standing behind the stage in a small cement-floored room without Marcus and Chloe while fighting a strong urge to vomit. The U-Palooza is held—annually after the first week of school—in a park with an outdoor amphitheater along the river downtown. The nine fraternities and sororities of our university put it on together and split the proceeds after giving a percentage to charity. Everyone is invited and tickets are cheap. Five dollars or something. Local bands always play, and for the past two years Luminescent Juliet has been the major draw and the last band to play.

Though I'd heard about the concert before, I've never been to it. But the students' talk working the concert has my stomach rolling. Last count, over a thousand tickets had been sold. Over a thousand people, including Aaron and other kids from high school, will be watching me. The music from the current band rumbles around me. Nervousness has me past the point of really hearing it.

From nowhere it seems, Justin comes and puts a tattooed arm around my shoulders. "Riley, you're looking a little pale."

I stare at him and sway in his grasp.

His mouth turns into a thin line. "Don't tell me you're scared."

My eyes widen. I can't answer because I'm freakin' terrified.

His fingers tighten around my shoulder. "You're an awesome drummer. You'll be fine. Just do your thing."

Do my thing? What does that even mean?

Leaning against the wall on the other side of the room, Romeo watches us with a scowl puckering his lips. His constricted gaze makes my stomach churn more. I never had stomach problems until my father left. Right now it feels like my gut is going to clench until it caves in on itself.

"You can do this," Justin says. When I don't respond, he adds, "Riley, you've got less than twenty minutes to pull yourself together."

I flinch. Twenty minutes is not long enough. I'm going to puke. The absence of music—which means the other band is done—along with the crowd's shouts and whistles cause dread to crawl down my spine.

"Riley . . . ," Justin says while he studies me with wide eyes. I've probably gone from pale to green.

The other band files into the room. I barely notice them. A student tells us the stage will be ready in fifteen.

I weave, even with Justin's support.

After several long minutes of watching me sway under Justin's arm, Romeo shoves away from the wall. His eyes burn into me, but he says to Justin, "Hate to tell you, but I told you so." His expressions burns with condescension.

I flinch again. This time from anger at his arrogant look. The last thing I need right now is Romeo being a dick.

"You're not helping," Justin says between clenched teeth.

Romeo shrugs. "Not sure she can be helped. Told you she was a bad idea."

I wiggle out from Justin's arm and lurch toward Romeo. "You're such an asshole." I spit the words up at him.

His grin is cutting. "You shouldn't have joined the big boys if you can't handle the heat."

I grab my sticks stuck in the waistband at my back and poke his chest where the metal swirl of a symbol on a leather string always rests. "Screw you."

Sam walks in. "Ready?" He pauses, reaching for his bass case leaning against one wall. "What's going on?" he asks, eyeing the sticks at Romeo's chest.

Romeo's brow arches as he looks down at me. "I'm not sure. On both counts. Why don't you tell him if we're ready, Riley?" His tone challenges me.

My eyes narrow as my sticks lower. "I'm ready."

Romeo smiles. Though the smile doesn't hold the brilliance from earlier, it looks authentic for once. "Good. Let's go."

Justin gives me a surprised look, but I whirl around and stomp toward the stage entrance.

I step into the dying light of the coming night, and the lights at the front of the stage flick on. The crowd goes wild. With the other three at my back and Romeo's words ringing in my ears, I march to my seat. The yells, claps, and whistles grow louder. Replaced with anger, my frayed nerves are gone.

"You shouldn't have joined the big boys."

Justin goes to the microphone in the center of the stage but faces me. Sam hangs in the back. Romeo walks to the edge of the stage, raises his guitar, and breaks into a riff. Six seconds later Justin whips around while Sam and I break into "Check Yes Juliet" by We the Kings. The song's a little overly pop compared to most of our stuff, but Justin talked the other two into the song because of the play on words with our band name. Bizarrely, he thinks it's beyond cool. For all his swanky clothes and tattoos, Justin can sure be a dork sometimes.

My anger fades as I play. I go into the zone. Music and drums fill my head and drive me into a satisfied thumping machine. Dickheads and over a thousand people watching barely edge my consciousness. I need this. Marcus was right. I can't be happy unless playing is part of my life. And here onstage is even better than practice. An odd clash of energy blended with excitement and serenity merged with pleasure flows through me. With each strike and rotation around the kit, all my anxieties drift into the night air. I become mindless energy while playing. I'm hot and sweaty by the second song, and feeling on top of the world.

For almost forty minutes, we're four people in tune with one another. Romeo's grueling pace in practice pays off. Communication, even in the form of nods or glances, isn't needed. We roll through ten songs like a professional skateboarder on the half-pipe. Six covers and four originals. From classic rock to punk to alternative to bluesy folk—whoever writes our original stuff has a thing for this mix.

I'm in my own drum bubble in the back, but Justin, Romeo, and Sam move around, share microphones, and interact with the crowd at the front. They actually rehearse that crap in practice. Lucky for me, being a girl, they dismissed me as a backup singer. Though I can carry a tune, my voice isn't too great.

The beat of my heart, the rush in my veins, and the natural high of playing for a crowd decreases when I step away from the drums, but the crowd, wild and vociferous, keeps the pump of my heart accelerated as Sam, Justin, and I step to one side of the stage.

A student brings out a stool and lowers the microphone while Romeo switches guitars. Because we haven't had enough time to practice, he's finishing our set with two acoustic songs. I've never heard him play. In fact, I don't even know what he's going to play.

The lights on the floor dim. The crowd quiets to a low murmur. Sam slings an arm around my shoulders and leans on me. Justin gives him a look, but I ignore them both as Romeo's fingers strum the first notes. When he starts singing, I recognize "Remember Everything" by Five Finger Death Punch. Of course, he plays beautifully. His long fingers move over the instrument in a graceful dance, but his voice has me clenching my jaw so my mouth doesn't fall open in astonishment. Deep with a resonation of gravel, his singing has me shocked. Obviously, he doesn't have the range Justin does, but the emotion woven into the vocals takes the song to a different level.

He's magnetic, sitting in a small circle of light on the dark stage. His profile is shadowy carved lines as he leans toward the microphone. His body a tight coil, from his bare forearm over the guitar to the glimpse of his hard, curved chest showing between the open folds of his shirt. He's dark and sexy, but his music overpowers his physical allure.

His voice glides into the night, over the audience, and pulls us with him and into the song. The crowd is transfixed by him. I'm transfixed. This song obviously means something to him, and it's impossible not to be touched by the emotion pouring from him, even though he sits almost still, with eyes hooded and foot slightly tapping. As he sings about regret and guilt, raw pain pours from him and I can't look away. It's like we're getting a glimpse into his soul. The beauty of it has me clenching my sticks within my crossed arms and restraining my body in a tight line. When he holds the last note and strums the last time, I let out the breath I'd been holding in and my shoulders sag. His performance leaves me feeling exhausted.

A stunned then slowly thunderous building of applause ricochets around the amphitheater.

Sam gives my shoulder a squeeze as another student hands him an acoustic guitar. He goes and stands next to Romeo, who taps his foot four times, and they break into a fast bluesy tune that tries to wipe the raw emotion of the last song, but nothing ever will. At least from my mind.

"What is this?" I ask, still baffled by Romeo's performance.

Justin leans close to me. "'Gold on the Ceiling' by the Black Keys," he says in my ear, with his lips brushing the lobe before he turns back to the stage.

Wow. I feel stupid. Though it sounds a bit different acoustic, the song is on my iPod. The tune is so catchy and rhythmic, I get why Romeo picked it—but still exhausted from the emotion of his prior performance, I couldn't recall the song.

They finish the song and the crowd goes wild again. Justin yanks me out on the stage, and we all bow in a line several times. My musical high had died into awe while I was watching Romeo, but shouts, claps, and whistles, though somewhat embarrassing, pump a tittering elation through my veins. I'm in such a fog of exhilaration, Justin has to yank me off the stage.

Back in the cement-floored room, I breathe heavily as Sam gives me a fist bump. "You kicked ass, Riley."

Justin gives me a hug. Once again his lips brush my earlobe as he says, "I knew you could do it."

A new elation hits me hearing their congratulations. Reality. I just performed in front of a thousand people. On a stage. With a rock band. Me.

Setting his acoustic guitar in its case, Romeo grins. I recall him pissing me off before we went on. His smirk has me wondering if he did it on purpose, but I don't have time for reflection as Marcus and Chloe rush through the door. Of course, the students standing guard wouldn't be able to stop *them* from coming in.

Chloe envelops me in a hug. "You were the shizit!" She steps back to let Marcus in while her eyes roam over Justin.

"You were effing awesome!" Marcus suffocates me before lifting me and twirling me in a circle. When he sets me down, I'm stunned by the harsh expressions each of my band members wears. All dressed in ripped jeans and different types of black shirts—and with scowls on their faces—they look rocking tough and angry.

Chloe breaks the silence. "So who's ready to party?"

Chapter 9

After packing everything into Romeo's ancient van—giggling at the vehicle, Chloe asked if Dewey Finn from *School of Rock* sold him the van and, surprisingly, Romeo laughed at her joke—we rushed back to Marcus's dorm and I changed into jeans but kept the rest of Chloe's crazy look together. The university is in a township outside the main city, surrounded by fields of corn and newer homes. So from the dorms we walked across a country road to the off-campus apartments where Sam lives. Knowing that Marcus's roommate would be gone for the weekend, Chloe and I had already planned to spend the night in the dorm.

Still on a high from the adrenaline onstage, I let Marcus give me a piggyback ride through the apartment's parking lot. Though we're goofing around and having fun, I'm somewhat nervous about going to the party. Romeo better not be a dick. Handling his attitude during practice is one thing. I'm not willing to put up with his shit at a party. I'm also nervous about meeting people after being onstage, and wondering if they'll just like me because I'm the drummer or like me for me.

When we walk into the living room, some people offer fist bumps or raise their drinks to me. Most of them are strangers. Yeah, being in a band has suddenly made me popular. I'm not sure if I like the hollow attention. I shouldn't be surprised though—how else would Romeo, the superdick, be so popular?

The small apartment is nearly full of bodies, and even more people spill out of the sliding glass doors onto the lawn in the back. Loud music from outside spills in. From the tiny kitchen, Justin spots me. He unwinds his arm from the girl next to him and calls me over. People part as much as possible while I make my way to the counter bar. Sam and Romeo stand inside the U-shaped kitchen along with as many girls who can fit. Some of the girls look at me with envy. But with girls wrapped around them, neither Sam nor Romeo notices me.

Justin yells something to Sam, then four shot glasses and a fifth of Absolut appear. Justin raises his own shot after pushing one toward me. Shots in hand, Sam and Romeo follow. The loud conversation around us quells quite a few decibels as he waits. "To a great set and our new kickass drummer Riley!" Justin shouts and downs the alcohol.

People cheer.

Beside me, Chloe and Marcus grin.

Vodka burns down my throat into my stomach, but I stop myself from coughing. I'm not much of a drinker. Three wine coolers usually have me past giggly and over my limit.

Another shot appears in my hand.

Sam lifts his glass and we follow suit. "To another great fucking year of music!"

More shouts echo around us. The liquid doesn't burn as bad the second time around.

At the third shot, Romeo lifts his little glass. "To Justin and me not strangling each other this year," he says loudly but doesn't shout.

Justin rolls his eyes before tossing back the vodka while Sam throws his head back, laughing.

Must be a story to that one. I'm imagining the dusty practice area destroyed in a long, drawn-out fistfight as Chloe grabs my shot and downs it before anyone can say anything.

When the fourth shot appears in my hand, it takes me a few seconds to realize it's my turn. I lift the glass and think of being onstage. "To drums beating through my veins."

Romeo's surprised eyes focus on me as he drains his shot. Caught in his stare, I almost choke as liquid falls down my numb throat. The image of him onstage baring his soul suddenly flashes through my mind as Justin reaches for the glass in my hand. I shake my head. "You trying to kill me? No more."

He just laughs while he fills the small glass on the counter.

Chloe pushes me outside.

Surprisingly, or maybe not, dancing people move out of our way.

Three steps into the shadowed yard, someone's yelling my name. I spot Kendra waving and dancing on a picnic table. More people from my high school stand around her—including Aaron.

My head whips toward Marcus.

"Hey, he asked. I wasn't going to lie to him about a party," he says defensively.

"Dumbass!" Chloe hisses. "Like she wants to see him."

Marcus shrugs as we move through the people dancing, talking, and drinking toward the table at the back of the yard. Toward Aaron.

"Riley!" Kendra squeals, then jumps down and hugs me as if we're besties from way back. "You have to introduce me to the band," she slurs in my ear, but I'm aware she's only interested in meeting one of them.

"Later," I whisper. My head's already buzzing. I'm not going back in until that bottle's gone. Though I'm trying not to, I notice Aaron over Kendra's shoulder.

Kendra releases me from her grip and the rest of her posse welcomes me. Some with a "hey," others with eager compliments. Most of them belong in the Kendra category. I spoke less than ten words to them during high school. But Marcus seems to know them better, judging by the number of fist bumps he shares.

The music is loud even back here by the line of trees, so I don't catch all of the conversation around me. I just stand there like an idiot until Aaron steps before me. Looking like he's unsure whether to hug me or run, he settles on a grin and a "Hey, Riley."

"Aaron," I say with a nod while a bittersweet longing rushes through me. Tall and lean with sandy brown hair, he has one of those boyish faces. Yet with his height, he comes off manly. Remembering my hands in that hair and my mouth on that smile, I step back—suddenly overwhelmed with memories.

He steps closer. "The band was awesome. *You* were awesome," he says, then takes a sip of the beer in his hand.

I force myself to appear calm and collected. "Thanks. Why are you home?" I blurt. Obviously, the three shots are already affecting me.

He shrugs. "Don't have classes on Fridays. I might be coming home a lot on weekends."

One of Kendra's buddies is handing out beer. I snag one. Why is he telling me this? "That's almost a five-hour drive." I crack the beer open while recalling his position on long-distance relationships: They never work.

He shrugs again but his eyes roam over me. Though it's dark out here, I recall the color of his eyes. Hazel with just the tiniest specks of green. He has lovely eyes. I take a huge gulp of beer.

Never one of my favorites, it doesn't taste too bad after three shots of vodka. "Thought you said the drive was too long to come home, except for holidays."

"I said a lot of things that have turned out to be bullshit."

My heart lurches at his words.

Chloe, who had been talking to our former classmates, steps next to me. "If it isn't Aaron, back from the big, huge, major, far-away, out-of-state college."

"Hey, Chloe," he says lightly, like he's drunk, a moron, or purposely disregarding her attitude. He doesn't appear drunk and he carried a 4.0, so the last would be my guess.

I gulp more beer. Aaron watches me. With a hostile glint in her eyes, Chloe looks back and forth at the two of us.

Kendra appears. "It's later."

"It is," I agree, winding my arm around Chloe's. "Come on," I say to Kendra, and nod to Aaron. "See you around."

He frowns.

"Don't tell me you're even thinking about it," Chloe says as we get closer to the house.

I down the rest of the beer.

"Oh fuck. You are."

"Aaron said he made a mistake," Kendra slurs.

Chloe gives her a murderous look.

I step between them and face Chloe. "Relax. Thoughts and actions are *totally* different," I say, and step back inside. For once I'm searching for Romeo.

He's leaning against the far cupboards. A girl is pasted on each side of him. Justin's nowhere to be seen, but Sam's still in the girl-filled kitchen too. He's playing quarter bounce with a bunch of people at the peninsula counter.

People once again part for me. Romeo gives me a surprised look when I step in front of him but smiles at Kendra and even shakes her hand after I make introductions. *Is he only an ass to me?* Kendra ignores the stares from the girls at his sides and shamelessly flirts. Chloe joins in on the quarter bounce.

While I stand there like an idiot, leaning against the fridge, Sam hands me a shot of something amber colored and I down it. Ugh. It burns even after the vodka and beer. Some of the girls ask me questions about drumming, but most are intent on Romeo and Sam. Kendra hasn't said a word to me. She just keeps talking and creeping closer to Romeo. I get why the girls are giving her—dressed in a skirt, a tube top, and a little jacket, with her blonde hair curled in ringlets—dirty looks, but their continued looks at me are irritating.

I'm just the drummer. I'm not in line for some band lovin'. Not even close to the end of it.

While I think of Aaron waiting outside, Sam keeps giving me shots. Chloe intercepts most of them. Yet I down at least two more. Or maybe three.

Surrounded by scantily clad college girls, Romeo barely looks at me. Other than handing me booze, Sam's preoccupied with slapping quarters on the counter. And Chloe's obviously determined to get wasted from the number of shots she's intercepted.

The room grows warm. The voices become too loud. The images of people begin to overlap. Hoping fresh air will help, I stagger back outside.

On the patio, music roars inside my head and dancers knock into me while the world tilts and spins. Some guy—who looks like two—I've never seen before tries to grind against my ass. About to vomit for various reasons, I push through the people and wobble down the row of apartments until I find a dark one with lawn chairs on its little patio.

For quite some time, I sit there with a numb mind while the echo of conversation and music comes from the direction of the party. My stomach slowly settles as time passes. I just might have been nodding off when my phone vibrates in my pocket. It takes me forever to fish it out and read the text.

Marcus: Chloe is shwasted. I'm taking her back to the dorm. Will be back.

I'm about to text him back—a feat that might be beyond difficult in my current state—saying to wait for me, when a shadow hangs over me. My body jumps but as Aaron's face materializes out of the haze, I slump back into the chair.

"I've been looking all over for you," Aaron says, and plops down in the chair next to me.

After blinking several times, I slide my phone closed. "Why?"

"I miss you, Riley."

I lean forward and point. "You broke up with me." The words come out slightly slurred.

He sets his can of beer on his knee. "People make mistakes."

I close one eye so there is only one shadowy Aaron across from me. "It's been a month," I say slowly, then in an unusual whine add, "You haven't even called or even texted me."

"I wanted to. Five hours away, I thought breaking up was for the best, but when I saw you tonight, you looked so damn hot . . ."

Annoyance breaks through the alcohol fog of my brain. "I never looked hot before?"

Oblivious to my horrified tone, he grins white into the darkness. "You've always been cute, but you were beyond sexy onstage tonight."

I'm speechless. I'm crushed. And sick. I'm going to be sick. Though I'm still buzzed, his words bring lucidity to our past. His pronouncement ruins the memory of every kiss, every caress, and every sigh. The intimate moments deeply treasured in my heart dis-integrate at the realization of how he regarded me. The only per-son I'd ever slept with never found me sexually attractive. Kendra's question—"Did he date you last year because it was convenient or something?"—comes back to haunt me, because yes, evidently he did.

Mistaking my silence for something else, Aaron leans closer and raises a hand to my cheek. I resist the urge to punch him in the nose, then leap up and slide across the dewy grass. "I'm sorry but you were right. Five hours away is just too much."

"Riley!" he calls out from behind me. I run through the people partying outside, past the other darkened apartments, and into the parking lot. Once I get across the street, angry tears start falling. I ignore my wet face until I'm in front of Marcus's dorm. Then I take a deep breath and wipe my cheeks. Lucky for me, a girl steps on the porch and slides her card in the lock, so I don't have to wait to get buzzed in. She gives me a look when I follow her into the building, so I mumble something about my friend Marcus living here and my staying the night. She shrugs before ascending the stairway.

Walking down the hall, I'm hoping Marcus hasn't left yet or that Chloe isn't passed out so I can get into his room. To my sur-prise, Marcus's door isn't closed all the way. I wipe my eyes one more time, but before I push the door open, a soft groan sounds followed by the moan of, "Yes. Yes. Oh, fuck yes."

Confused, I freeze.

Who is in there with Chloe? Is it even Chloe? It sounds like Chloe. But maybe it's Marcus with a girl from the party. I hadn't noticed either of them in hook up mode with anyone.

"Slide up, Chloe," Marcus pants.

Realizing Marcus and Chloe are in there—together!—I stum-ble away from the door with my hand over my mouth. My heel crashes into the opposite door, but I somehow keep my yelp to a whimper before whirling toward the entrance.

Five shots—or maybe six?—and one beer, and I've landed in the fucking Twilight Zone.

Chapter 10

In the span of one night, my world has gone crazy. Okay, maybe *crazier.* And I have nowhere to go to escape the madness. Semidrunk, I sit on the curb next to my car in front of Marcus's dorm. The keys are in my bag in his room. Though I wouldn't drive after drinking, at least I could curl up in the backseat if I could get in, but no, my night just keeps getting better. Between Aaron's horrendous hot flash and my two best friends who can't stand each other having a screw fest, I can't imagine things getting worse.

"Riley?" someone asks from behind me.

I turn to find Romeo staring down at me. Yup, things just got worse. The last thing I need right now is dealing with his shit.

He kneels, resting his elbows on his knees. "You okay?"

My bottom lip quivers. Maybe it's the craziness of the night. Maybe it's the consumption of too much alcohol. Or maybe it's the concern in his gaze, but suddenly I feel like bawling all over again.

His brows lower. "Why are you sitting out here?"

My lip quivers again but somehow I hold in the tears. "Um . . . I'm waiting for Marcus and Chloe." That's kind of the truth.

He glances at the phone in his hand. "It's past two o'clock. You shouldn't be out here alone."

I shrug while holding in a second round of tears.

His dark eyes become more concerned. His fingers reach for my arm. "Why don't you wait in my room?"

"You live here too?" I ask, surprised. I'd expect Romeo to live in some kind of swanky apartment where girls come to be seduced. Or maybe to seduce.

Nodding, he pulls harder and we stand. I'm thinking about telling him that I'll just wait here. Extra time around Romeo isn't on my agenda, but the idea of Marcus finding me out here waiting and then explaining why doesn't hold much appeal. So I let Romeo tug me inside. His door is the second from the entrance.

For a few seconds we're engulfed in darkness, then he flips a lamp on and soft light fills the space. Of course, the room looks very similar to Marcus's. Two twin beds. Two desks and two dressers, with an industrial tiled floor beneath them. But the thing that sets the room apart from Marcus's is the two halves of the space. On one side, the walls are covered with movie and band posters, like any other dorm room. The walls on the other side are plain, except for a long shelf over the bed filled with musical instruments.

Romeo drops his keys on a dresser while I stare at the shelf. There's a banjo, several flutes, a violin, and even a thin drum. The sight of the shelf has me forgetting the problems that were overwhelming me while I sat on the curb. After his acoustic performance tonight, I don't even have to ask if the instruments are all his. "Do you know how to play *all* of those?"

He falls onto a chair in front of a desk. "Some better than others."

Entranced with that shelf, I tug off my boots, kneel on the bed, and reach for the drum, then pause. My glance to him is questioning. He nods stoically. I sit on the bed with the instrument on my knees. The wood is slightly warped. A faded, knotted design fills the center. And the fastenings are made of wood. The drum is obviously old and homemade. My fingers trace the painted knots. "Where did you get this?"

Romeo's gaze rises from the motion of my fingers. His brown eyes are liquid chocolate. He lets out a short breath. "It was my grandfather's. His father's before that. Someone down the line even farther made it."

I smile. "It's beautiful."

"It's called a bodhran," he says softly. Most likely thinking I'm a sentimental drunk girl, Romeo just stares at me.

My eyes shift away from his gaze and back to the shelf. I'd like to reach up and grab the beater for the drum, but despite the care the instrument needs—I still feel the cloudy effects of one too many shots—it is late. Pounding on a drum in the dorm during the wee hours probably isn't a good idea. I turn and put the drum back, but the sight of all those instruments has me yearning for the sound of music. "Which do you play best?"

His now-hooded eyes hide what he's thinking. "The fiddle."

I tilt my head and glance at the instruments.

"The violin," he says, clarifying.

"Oh," I say, reaching for the instrument and its bow. I hold them out to him. He raises a brow that slips under the ever-present wedge of hair angled across his forehead. I extend my arms. "Play something for me. Since it's late, something soft I guess."

With an expressionless face, he slowly reaches out and takes the fiddle from my grasp. Tucking it under his chin and lifting the bow, he watches me with dark eyes. But at the first note, his lashes sweep down.

The tune is soft and haunting. with long notes as his dexterous fingers move on the stem. My breath catches at both the melody and the sight of him. The angled muscles of his neck are tight from the effort of holding the instrument under his chin. The light from the lamp shines off one high cheekbone. His full lips are slightly open, and the sweep of his lashes creates shadows on his skin.

He plays with a deep-felt emotion, like he did with "Remember Everything." I sit frozen and captivated. Drunker on him than alcohol.

Done, he lowers the fiddle to his lap and his gaze finds me.

I let out the air I'd been holding in. "That was beautiful." I don't tell him I mean both the music and the sight of him.

He gives me a half smile.

"What was it?"

"Some old Irish folk tune," he says with a shrug.

"Your grandfather taught you?"

"Years ago."

My foggy brain puts two and two together. "You wrote all our original music?"

He nods.

Thinking of the band, I point at him like a little kid. "You're not being a dick to me. Why aren't you being a dick?"

He glances at the wall of posters across from us. "Not the time. I found you sitting on a curb looking lost and sad. Not your usual warrior self."

I flinch. He's referring to superbitch. "Okay, but why are you usually such a dick?"

"I told you." He sighs and runs a hand through his dark hair. "I want you to quit."

Shit. I feel my lip trembling again. "Why?" I say in a desperate-sounding whisper, and embarrassment rushes under my skin.

He stands and lays the fiddle back on the shelf before plopping next to me on the bed. He clasps his hands together and rests his elbows on his knees. Looking at the floor, he says, "When it comes to the band, Justin and I rarely get along. Sam picks sides every other day. I'm fucking sick of it. I formed the band. I write the music. I set up almost everything. Do most of the work. I had three meetings with those fraternities and sororities over the last two weeks so everything would go smooth tonight. Justin likes to play at being the front man and I don't really give a shit in public, but when he tries to call the shots behind the scenes"—he finally looks at me—"I get pissed."

My phone buzzes in my pocket. Most likely Marcus, I ignore it. I'm trying to understand what Romeo's saying but it isn't clicking. "So you didn't want me for a drummer because Justin did?"

His mouth turns down as he nods. "That's part of it. If I say go, Justin says stop, and vice versa."

"What's the other part?" I ask with dread.

"Like I said, we don't get along. And . . . having a girl in the band just seems like a bad, bad idea. Especially you."

I stare at him totally confused. What's so wrong with me?

"It's not just that you're good looking."

Me, good looking? Though far from obsessed with my physical side, I accepted my little-girl cuteness a long time ago. I could be plain or even unattractive. Cute isn't so bad, but good looking? Coming from His Hotness? My head swims, and it definitely isn't from the alcohol.

His gaze finds the floor again while his clasped hands tighten. "When you play, you're so focused, so driven, so damn beautiful." His voice breaks on the last word.

My breath catches. I go from swimming to drowning. No one has *ever* called me beautiful. Much less the hottest man on the planet. And after Aaron's revelation this evening, that Romeo called me beautiful probably means more than it should.

"They're already flirting. Soon one of them is going to make a move and . . ." He glances up and stops at my openmouthed stare. "What?"

I'm humming inside. I could blame it on the alcohol but it's him. His eyes so dark they're almost black. Lips so full they draw me to them. The sexiness always dripping from him somehow hums into me. And that word. *Beautiful.* I want to kiss him. Badly. Desperate for him, I lurch forward. Completely uncoordinated within my rush of desire—and perhaps too much alcohol—I collide with the side of his head.

"Ow!" I rear back, holding my forehead.

"Shit!" Romeo says at the same time. "What the hell was that?" Leaning away, he rubs his temple. "You trying to kill me?"

My face burns as he watches me. My deep blush must give him a clue at what I was trying to do, and comprehension slowly enters his gaze.

Still rubbing his temple, he says, "I can't figure you out. Every time I think I have . . ." His eyes cloud with indecision.

Turning redder by the second, I'm about to jump off the bed and run from the room when he reaches out and catches my chin in a tender grip. I freeze. My skin tingles under his touch. He gently pulls me closer and leans forward. My heart threatens to thud out of my chest as our gazes lock. Mine has to be a picture of shock and wonder.

"You do something that blows my opinion upside down," he whispers, tracing my bottom lip with a calloused finger.

Those full lips come closer and I'm lustful energy, trying to throw myself in his lap and attack him, but he holds me back with a gentle hand at my shoulder and kisses me softly. Once, twice, three times. My heart still thuds wildly yet I catch the rhythm he sets. A rhythm that wants to savor our kiss. Savor me.

I thought I was drowning, but I'm floating. Upward and into him and his slow, burning lips.

He builds the tempo, pressing his soft lips harder against mine while his hand gently slides up my neck, digs into my ponytail, and loosens my hair. His fingers tangle in released strands, gripping my head while his other hand curls around my waist. He gently drags me closer and his tongue sweeps, slow and delicious, across mine. His mouth's sensual and slow exploration has my hands gripping the skin of his shoulders, left bare from his sleeveless shirt. As he delves deeper, I suck at his tongue and he groans into me. My nails dig into his skin.

That groan was hot.

Suddenly, I'm lying on my back. Romeo kneels over me, hands pressed into the bed on each side of my head. He bends, his hair brushing my forehead, and slowly draws my lower lip into his mouth in a sensual tug that has me both drowning and floating. Though I can feel the warmth radiating from his body, I want to feel all of him. I curl a leg around the worn butt of his jeans and attempt to pull him down, even yank at his leather necklace with its attached Celtic knot. My body is screaming for the contact.

Letting go of my lip with a tender tug, he rolls to my side. Not what I was aiming for, but the line of his hard body against mine has me turning my head. Once again, we kiss slowly until the rhythm between us builds. His calloused fingers find the bottom edge of my top and skim across my stomach. My body's jolt tears our mouths apart. He chuckles —the sound echoes inside of me—but his hand stills.

"You okay?" he whispers, and nips at my ear.

Unable to speak with his mouth on my skin, I nod.

His lips slide along the line of my jaw while his fingers swirl a pattern on my stomach and ribs. By the time his lips cover mine, I'm panting. Hard. The kiss is frantic and hot and nothing like I've ever felt. A mere kiss has never gotten me so worked up. Between more searing kisses, he tugs at my top and I eagerly help him shed it from my skin. His mouth and weight press me back into the bed. When his hand slips under my sports bra and his rough palm grazes my skin, I moan into him.

His arm trembles. His tongue pauses its movement with mine. Slowly he pulls back and I almost whimper as his hand leaves my skin. "Damn. This is going too fast," he gasps. Drawing back, he longingly gazes at my body before quickly yanking a blanket across my seminakedness.

My fingers grip his arm as my eyes question his.

"We're just starting to become friends," he says, his lashes sweeping down so I can't read his eyes. "We're not ready for this."

"You don't want me," I blurt out miserably, still raw from Aaron's revelation earlier and the memories of countless girls surrounding Romeo.

"No." He shakes his head. "That's not it."

I look at the wall while my lower lip trembles again. What the hell is wrong with me tonight? I want to put my trembling lip in a straitjacket.

"Riley," he says softly. But trying to get my emotions under control, I stare at the painted brick wall. He tugs my hand gently and places it *there*. "Does that feel like I don't want you?" he asks hoarsely.

My gaze flies to his. With a shudder and a reluctant look, he drops my burning hand. It curls in remembrance.

I try to explain my reaction. "I just . . . my ex . . . he didn't . . . he said . . . ," I ramble weakly, my voice breaking. A sob builds in my throat while he frowns and stares at me. Still a bit buzzed and depleted from our blast of lust, I'm falling apart into pieces of anguish. "He admitted . . . he never thought—"

"Shhhh," he whispers, pulling me closer to him by the waist and cradling me against his shoulder while his fingers stroke my hair.

The weight of the night settles on my chest. I slowly release a shudder and my body calms. He keeps gently stroking my hair. My eyes flutter closed. His thumb at my waist creates a soothing pattern. I let out another deep breath and drift into the cocoon he creates until dreams and darkness engulf me.

Chapter 11

Something keeps buzzing and vibrating against my hip. But content and snug, I try to ignore it. Stay asleep. I float back into a nest of warmth before the irritating buzz comes again, and I slowly become aware I'm lying on a muscled chest. Stomach muscles rise under my palm. An arm pins me against a hard body. And my leg is curled around a muscular thigh. These things more than the buzz wake me up. My eyes fly open with last night's memories.

I'm in Romeo's bed. With Romeo.

Detangling myself quick as lightning, I paste my body to the wall with my knees still on the mattress.

Below me, his face is soft in sleep, almost boyish. His beauty freezes me. I simply stare at him until his arm slowly sweeps across the bed as if searching for me.

Shit.

He's going to wake up.

Grabbing my top from the headboard, I leap over him and frantically search for my boots while tugging on my shirt. One lies on the floor but the other one is nowhere to be seen. My head is almost under the bed and my fingers reaching for the boot—How the hell did it get so far back?—when Romeo softly says, "Riley?"

Double shit.

"Yeah," I say weakly, yanking the boot out.

"You leaving?"

His voice sounds confused. Whether because I'm leaving or he's still half asleep, I'm not sure. I don't look at him but instead plop down on the end of the bed. I could sit in the chair but then I'd have to face him. "I need to get home."

I hear him sit up. When his hand touches the bare skin of my shoulder and my body imagines it as a caress, the mortification rushing under my skin bursts. Beneath the mortification, the darker fear of rejection pulses. "I'm sorry about last night. About coming on to you. I . . . my ex wanted to get back together. Then I found Marcus and Chloe going at it and . . . between the alcohol and everything else, I just wasn't myself. I was in shock. It was a messed-up night. I was messed up on more than just alcohol." Oh, hell yes. Score. If that wasn't a perfect save face, it doesn't exist.

His hand drops with an echoing thud on the bed. "I thought you were waiting for Marcus and Chloe?"

Oh, triple shit. "Naw." I knot a lace. "I was kind of waiting for them to ah . . . finish?" I can feel my face burning. "Please don't say anything about it to them."

"Why would I?" Tension tightens his tone.

"I'm just saying. I'd be beyond embarrassed if they found out I knew." I peek at him through my hair. His eyes are hard. His face rigid. His mouth an angry thin line. He looks like he's about to combust. My gaze finds my feet again. Is he really *that* pissed I lied about Marcus and Chloe last night? "I've got—"

"To get going," he says sarcastically.

At his tone, I'm desperate to escape. The turn of the lock sounds as I push off the bed.

Romeo is up and past me in two seconds, holding the door open just a crack.

"What the hell?" I hear Justin yell from the other side of the door.

My hands slap against my cheeks. My eyes round. Justin is Romeo's roommate?

"I'm busy right now," Romeo says through the crack.

The skin under my hands burns.

"What?" Justin says incredulously.

"You heard me."

The door groans from a push. "Are you fucking with me?"

"No. Give me a half hour."

"The last time I brought a girl—"

"Just go!" Romeo says angrily, then turns and slams his back against the door.

My fingers dig into my cheeks as this new revelation threatens my spot in the band. "This can't be happening."

Romeo smacks his head against the door and closes his eyes.

My eyes shift to Justin's messy side of the room. "You're not going to tell him about last night, right?"

His eyes snap open. "Yeah, because I want to destroy the band."

That hits a nerve because obviously Justin was out all night with somebody, but somehow I can't be. Or maybe just not with Romeo. Or Sam. But the bigger problem would definitely be Romeo, who I *was* with all night. My hands finally drop. "Okay . . . um . . . we'll just pretend last night never happened."

Romeo's eyes narrow before he nods. Letting out a long sigh, he cracks open the door. "He's gone." He opens the door wider and I fly out into the hall without a good-bye.

Down the hall and two knocks later, I'm collecting my stuff from all over Marcus's room while he, still dressed in flannel pajama bottoms and an *I Love My Baby Bump* T-shirt—his thing for collecting free T-shirts goes a little too far with that one—stands over me.

"Where were you all night?" he demands.

"I slept in my car." He doesn't know the keys were in my bag.

"Huh?" He rears back from leaning over me. "I checked it early this morning."

"Must have been when I was on a walk. Bit hungover. Way too many shots." Keeping my gaze on my clothes strewn everywhere as I collect them makes it easier to lie.

"Why didn't you respond to my texts?"

"Phone must be on silent."

"Shit, Riley." He shakes his curly head. "Look at the thing once in a while. You had me worried like a sick bitch."

"Where's Chloe?" I ask, trying to change the subject.

"Left in the middle of the night."

"How'd she get home?" I ask, since I was her ride.

He shrugs but tightly grips his neck from behind. "Must have called somebody when I was out looking for you."

Since he's not being up front with me, I feel just a little better about lying to him. Just a little.

"Um, Riley?"

"What?" I snap, settling three heavy bags on my shoulder. Wanting to have options, Chloe packed way too much.

"Your shirt's inside out." His expression is startled. "And backward too."

Air rushes from my lungs as he stares at the tag above my chest. My face burns. Last night my lip was in tremble mode. Today my skin is in flame mode. My face needs to gain some damn control. Finally, I come up with a somewhat plausible excuse. "I used it for a pillow."

His frown is knowing. "Wouldn't be much of a pillow."

"Better than nothing," I say through clenched teeth.

He nods, but the knowing gleam in his eye stays.

Both slightly hungover—and with my mom and sister out on their usual Sunday-afternoon library trip—Chloe and I decided to make it a pool-lounging day. We rarely hang out at Chloe's house. She and her single mother live in a tiny apartment. She's always said she's living it up at my house.

My father has a decent job in an engineering firm, but we were never rolling in the dough. Now as the divorce looms, I wonder if my mother will be able to afford living in our two-story, four bedroom home even if my father continues paying the mortgage. Scared of a huge electric bill, she's only run the air-conditioning this summer when the temperature has hit over ninety. Though it's nowhere near ninety today, the sun is out and it's hot for September.

"What's for dinner, Mom?" Chloe asks from under her hat. Long white ribbons hang off the wide brim, trailing over the back of her pool chair and into the water.

I take a long sip of iced tea before responding. "Mexican casserole. It's in the slow cooker." I drag a foot through the pool water and rest my plastic glass on my bare stomach. Chloe hates this suit even though it's a two-piece and says the short bottoms make it look like I should be out running instead of swimming. My opinion of her tiny suits is that she should stop getting them from Victoria's-Slut-Secret. She finds my opinion amusing.

"You and that stupid Crock-Pot."

"I'd die without a Crock-Pot and the Internet." I let out a weak laugh. "I swear recipes are the only reason I go on the Net anymore. But you just throw a bunch of stuff in and presto, four hours later you have dinner."

"Ugh. Riley, you're beyond butt-ass-lucky you joined that band because otherwise you'd be the most boring eighteen-year-old in the universe."

The band. The best and worst thing about my life lately. I've been holding last night in all day and waiting for her to tell me about Marcus, but she hasn't brought him up. Needing to get out my own secret and hoping she'll share too, I say, "Something happened last night."

She pushes the brim of her hat up. Her eyes are so wide her fake lashes rise above her plucked brows. "What? This better not be about Aaron."

I shake my head. I haven't told her about that yet either. He's been texting me all day. I've been erasing them without even reading. His words last night stabbed to death what we had together. I take a deep breath and blurt, "I spent the night with Romeo."

Her mouth drops open, her chair wobbles, and then—*splash!* She's underwater and her hat is floating by me. I kick it back her way. Coming up, she spits out water and sputters, "Holy shit! Are you trying to kill me?"

What's with everyone thinking I'm out to annihilate them lately? "Ah, no . . . just sharing my sexual escapade." And hoping she'll share hers too.

Chloe never goes underwater. Irritated, she wipes at her running makeup and slicks back her wet platinum-blonde hair. "You didn't think telling me you had sex with Romeo might be a *bit* shocking?"

"We didn't have sex," I grumble, and fish out an ice cube from my tea.

She stares at me, then reaches for her chair. "How could you sleep next to *that* without going into attack mode? Did Aaron kill your sex drive with his lameness?"

I'm not going to admit I did attack Romeo. I finish chewing the ice cube while she settles back into her chair. "We . . . things got a little heavy, but it's complicated with the band thing. We work together and neither of us plans on repeating last night."

She wrings out her hat over the water. "So you don't like him?"

I blink at that. Do I like Romeo? Not so much. Do I want him? Hell yeah. I clear my throat. "I'm attracted to him. Who wouldn't be? But he's still an asshole."

"Huh," she says, plopping the wet hat on her head. "Never thought you'd be one to fall for the bad boy type."

"I'm *not* falling for him."

Her mouth twists in an open O. "Is he a good kisser?"

My eyes open big and round at the memory of his lips on mine, and of him sucking my bottom lip into his mouth.

She laughs.

I chuck an ice cube at her.

We float some more. She teases me. I chuck more ice cubes. But she never reveals whom she slept with last night. Though I'm betting there wasn't much sleeping going on in that room.

Chapter 12

Between Kendra and Romeo, I'm starting to detest Mondays. Though my Ancient Roman History class on Wednesday mornings is super boring, at least its drama free. However, dealing with Kendra is not as bad as dealing with Romeo. I'm dreading going to calculus.

"So the party was awesome, huh?" Kendra says, dipping a fry in the huge ketchup pool on her plate. The red of the condiment and the bright blue of her nails clash in the bright cafeteria light.

I force a nod. I was relieved during philosophy when Kendra didn't bring up the weekend. Guess my relief was short-lived. I reach for my milk. Ever since I began cooking because of my mother's nightly absence, I've been more in tune with nutrition for Jamie's sake, but it's rubbed off on my own choices. Iced tea instead of pop. Two-percent milk at least once a day.

Kendra continues rolling her fry through the ketchup. "The show was pretty good too."

Of course, Kendra would like the party better than the concert. "I was nervous, but yeah, we rocked."

"Can you tell me something?" Kendra asks, obviously not interested in discussing the concert.

"Sure," I say, dreading her question. I'm sure it's about a particular bandmate.

She tugs a long strand of blonde hair behind an ear and leans forward. "Does Romeo have a girlfriend?"

My eyes widen and milk catches in my throat. I cough and cough while Kendra stares at me with a suspicious look. "Sorry," I say, and let out one last cough. "I think it went down the wrong pipe."

Kendra's gaze stays in skeptical mode.

"Um, I'm not sure, but I think so," I say. "I met her at the football game. Though he didn't say she was his girlfriend, they acted like they were together. Her name is April." How the hell had I forgotten about his girlfriend? Milk curdles in my stomach at the thought he cheated on her with *me*.

Kendra's eyes lose their gleam of doubt. "Well, that explains it."

I give her a questioning look as expected, try to ignore the sick feeling in the pit of my stomach, and hold in my building freak-out.

"He flirted with me all night. More than any of the other girls. It didn't make sense when he left and didn't even ask for my number." She finally pops the drowned fry into her mouth.

Ego much?

Kendra reaches for another fry. "Is she pretty?"

I take a huge bite of my chicken sandwich and nod vigorously. Kendra's pushing the irritating scale. She might be worse than Romeo today.

"Well, that sucks." She dabs her fry. I want to smash that fry on the table or maybe grab it and another one to stuff in my ears. Kendra lets out a long sigh. "I'm really, really attracted to him."

I make a point of looking at the time on my phone, strap on my bag, and grab my tray. "If they break up, I'll let you know." I give her a weak smile. "See you next week."

Though I'm early, I race across the campus and into the science and math building. Lucky for me, the bathroom is empty. Inside a stall, I lean on the door with my forehead against the metal and let my freak-out commence.

I'm such an idiot. Idiot. Idiot. Idiot. But I only met April once. The girl hardly talked to me. I forgot Romeo had a girlfriend. She should have made a bigger impression. Not just given me jealous looks. Buzzed or not, I would have never hit on him if I had remembered. Plus, why wasn't she there Saturday?

My entire face smashes against the stall door.

Get a grip. Get a grip. Get a grip. It's mostly Romeo's fault. He should have stopped it from happening. He's her freakin' boyfriend. Right? Maybe they're just dating. Aren't in a full all-out relationship. But I'm betting *she* is why he stopped. Still, to let it get that far then let me spend the night? His assholeness goes up a notch.

I push away from the door.

Okay. Okay. Okay. I made a mistake, an awful, huge mistake. I need to face reality. If they are dating exclusively, I'm an accidental semicheater. And Chloe thinking I'm falling for Romeo? Um no, I do not fall for cheaters. Cheaters suck. Ugh. So I kind of suck. Inadvertent suckage though.

I take a deep breath.

Freak-out finished. I need to move on and learn from my mistake. *Pay attention to who you're kissing, Riley, regardless of how hot they are.*

As usual, I'm early for calculus. Though I went over the assigned sections last night and did the work, I skim the material while waiting at my table. I don't want to think of Romeo, April, or Saturday night—excepting for playing—ever again. Unfortunately, he plops down next to me within minutes and tosses an envelope onto the open pages of my book.

At the sight of him, those soul-filled eyes and full lips, memories of Saturday night rush into my brain. His lips, his hands, and the gentle slide of his fingers in my hair pass through my mind's eye like a lush silent film. I lock the images out with the clench of my jaw. "What's this?" I ask, reaching for the envelope.

"One hundred and seventy dollars."

"Huh?"

"Your share of the payment for U-Palooza." When I continue to stare at him, he says, "You don't think it's enough? We usually do get more but for that one we get just a percent."

My fingers reach for the envelope. "More?"

He leans back and the angle of hair that falls across his forehead shifts. "You do realize we get paid for gigs?"

No, I didn't. Compensation never occurred to me. I just wanted to play.

At my bewildered look, he says, "You think we play just for fun?"

My brow lowers. It's more than fun. It's music. It's drumming.

The indecisive look he wore Saturday night changes his gaze. The one that accompanied his words about not figuring me out.

Professor Hill walks into the room and sets his briefcase on his desk with a thud. I tuck the envelope into the back pages of my book, and we both give him our attention. Soon I'm scribbling notes about vectors and dot products. I try concentrating on the professor. Attentiveness is easier said than done, but at least I force my gaze from going to the left.

The sight of April and Romeo talking at one end of the hall has me hanging out at the other end during break. I'm sitting on one of the standard couches near the entrance and scrolling through my phone when someone plops down next to me. I give him a slight glance as I read Chloe's text asking if Romeo hit on me during class. I'm about to explain the girlfriend thing in a text back, but the guy next to me asks, "Aren't you the drummer from the last band on Saturday?"

I lower my phone and meet an amazing pair of light blue eyes. "Yeah, Luminescent Juliet."

He grins at me. "They were good but you rocked."

"Thanks," I say, trying not to blush. With wildly spiked hair, a lopsided smile, and ear gauges, he's stylish and cute.

"Really, you were one of the best drummers I've ever seen, and I've been to a ton of concerts."

Impressed I made such an impression, I murmur another thanks.

He puts out a hand covered with silver rings. "Mike."

I shake his hand. "Riley."

"So when's your next show?"

"Three weeks at the Razor," I say, then stand.

"I'll have to catch it," he says, standing and grinning again.

"Yeah, you should. Sorry but I have to get back to class." I take a step toward calculus and he follows.

"I'm on my way to chemistry, but ah . . ."—he rubs his chin— "I'd really like your number." He nods to the phone still in my hand.

"Oh, um . . ." Shit. I have no idea how to deal with this. At age fourteen, I was a bit popular with some of the skateboarders since I could outtrick most of them, but refusing a make out—okay I didn't refuse all those offers—at the top of the curvy slide is worlds away from this. Recently, I've witnessed Kendra dealing with guys hitting on her at lunch. She tells them to eff off. Not such a great idea for this guy since he seems to be a fan of the band. Yet the idea of some guy calling that I hardly know freaks me out.

I decide to lie. Beyond lame. But I can't think of another tactful way to dodge his request.

"Actually, I would give it to you, but I'm kind of seeing some-one right now."

"Yeah, I figured as much." Walking next to me, he shakes his head. "If your *kind of* doesn't work out, I pass through here every day."

I reach to open the door to the classroom and notice Romeo not only walking toward us but also intently watching us. The evil bitch inside of me, who only he seems to bring out, smiles flirta-tiously at Mike. "I'll have to remember that."

Romeo's eyes narrow on us. His mouth thins to an angry line.

"Great." Mike gives me another grin as I walk into class.

I grit my teeth when Romeo sits down. I can feel his indignant stare, but I don't acknowledge him. Several examples from Professor Hill later, I've almost forgotten he exists. *Almost* is the key word.

After class, I whip my books and calculator into my bag in an effort to escape without any more communication with my table-mate. Before I can stand, he asks, "So have you thought about it?"

"What?" I snap.

"Quitting."

"I'm not quitting," I say through clenched teeth.

"It's going to be harder now, you know."

"What does that mean?"

"After what happened on Saturday."

"We are pretending that didn't happen," I snap, beyond angry he would bring up Saturday, especially after his minidate with April during break.

"Well, it did."

I can't keep my expression from turning horrified. "So you're going to tell Justin and Sam about . . . it?"

"No. But between us, I'm not going to pretend." His eyes roam over me.

I ignore the sultry look. "Why?"

"I told you I want you to—"

"Quit. Yeah, that's becoming crystal clear. How's April by the way?"

Except for the ghost of a frown, he doesn't miss a beat. "She's fine. If you think I was hard to deal with before, I'm going to become your worst nightmare."

Snatching my bag from the table, I hiss, "Bring it on, asshole." Then I stomp out of the room.

If he wants a war, I'll give him World War III. Though I'd never admit it to him, playing in the band is the one thing in life I look forward to lately. I'm not giving it up just because he wants me to quit, three boys can't keep their egos in check, or because a particular one keeps my hormones in overdrive.

Chapter 13

The past two weeks of practice have been awful. Though we tend to ignore each other during calculus—except the times he looked smugly from my eighty-five- and eighty-three-point quizzes to his ninety-five- and ninety-nine-point quizzes—Romeo and I are at each other's throats during practice. I used to ignore him. Now I point out his flaws and argue whenever he's overly critical. And he's overly critical all the time. It's gotten to the point that Justin and Sam tell us both to shut up several times each practice.

Tonight when Justin asked me to go out after practice for the thousandth time and Romeo scowled at us, I agreed. After texting Chloe for permission first, of course. The wonderful girl does sit for free.

My agreeing had to do with Romeo's announcement at the beginning of practice rather than with his scowl. He announced he was tired of looking at my lame-ass drums. Sam and Justin had seemed uncomfortable when he further explained that my kit sent the message of suck. Musicians are judged by their instruments. And the beat-up appearance of mine said I couldn't play worth shit.

Though somewhat true—I've noticed Romeo and Sam regularly cleaning and shining up their instruments with folded bandanas—this was obviously a new tactic to get me to quit.

Smiling sweetly, I told him I'd have a new set by the next practice. I'm going to look like a total ass if Marcus doesn't agree to let
me use his set. I'm planning on going into the heaviest mode of
begging possible. However, Marcus's deep love for his drum set has
me worried.

So after practice, I'm sipping on a beer that Justin bought me.
His dimpled smile at the waitress eliminated her need to see my ID.
Apparently, his dimples equate to Jedi mind tricks. We sit in the
back of the bar by the pool tables and dartboards. A few feet away,
Sam, Romeo, and several girls throw darts. Sam introduced the girls
to everyone, so he must be the one who invited them.

I tear my eyes from a girl—clad in a top with a plunging neck-
line—flirting with Romeo and catch him grinning at me. I turn
toward Justin. He asked me to come. He's the one sitting here with
me. I force myself to concentrate on him and not what's going on in
front of the dartboards. "So I take it you guys come here a lot after
practice."

Justin leans back and drapes his arm along the back of my chair.
"Yeah, at least once a week." He takes a long swig of beer, then
watches me over the rim of his bottle. "So how long have you been
playing drums?"

Ignoring his sultry gaze, I honestly say, "Eight years. I took piano lessons from six to ten." Jamie took lessons too but when money
got tight, those were one of the first things to go. I pick at the label
of my beer. "When I said I wanted to quit, my mother told me to
pick another instrument. She was determined for me to be a well-
rounded child. Music was part of the equation." My mother used
to read parenting magazines constantly. She used to be the perfect
homemaker. I hold in a sigh. "Marcus played drums, so that was
my instrument of choice. We were very competitive as kids. So she
reluctantly found someone to give me lessons."

He leans closer. "How'd Marcus take it when you were better than him?"

I grin at the memory. "When I beat him out for first chair in band the first week of sixth grade, he didn't talk to me for two days, which was forever to an eleven-year-old. But he kicked my ass at skateboarding, so things evened out." I take a sip of beer. "What about you?"

He gives me a questioning look.

"How long have you been singing?"

"With the radio? Forever." He laughs. "Onstage? Only since the middle of freshman year here."

"Really?" Justin is a pretty damn good singer.

He nods. "I was shocked too when Romeo asked me to join."

"Why would he ask? Why would you agree?"

Justin shrugs. "We were roommates. He must have heard me singing. Like I said, I was always singing with the radio or my iPod. I'd always been into music. And what eighteen-year-old wouldn't like fronting a band? Everyone knew me after our first gig." He grins. "Especially the girls."

I ignore the girls comment. "Huh. So you just got in front of a microphone and that was that?"

"Ah, no. Romeo had his work cut out for him. After we found Sam and Gary,"—I'm assuming Gary is the former drummer—"we didn't perform for a couple of months. I was the major issue. Romeo was a lot more patient then."

Patience and Romeo? "I find that hard to believe."

Justin laughs again and his dimple grooves. "He was. Taught me how to read music, how to breathe right during vocals, about pitch, and even how to frickin' stand correctly."

Romeo the supermusician.

At my eye roll, he adds, "Hey, I didn't come to him as fully formed talent. However, I looked as pale as you did before my first time onstage. Romeo had to bully me to go out too."

So Romeo had challenged me on purpose that night. I glance over my shoulder. Showing her how to throw a dart, Romeo's wrapped around cleavage girl from behind. No wonder April looks jealous most of the time. Her boyfriend is a major player. Ugh. How did the conversation turn to the cheating asshole?

I take a sip of beer and return my attention to Justin. "So the whole tattoo, piercing thing you have going," I say, gesturing to his eyebrows and arms. "Did that happen before or after you joined the band?"

The waitress comes before he can answer. Justin orders two more beers. I'm not even half done with my first.

Once he's done flirting with the waitress, Justin points to the tribal design on his left biceps. "This was my first one. Got it in Cancun during spring break senior year of high school. My dad, who's a doctor, about flipped. Not over the tattoo but the thought of some dirty parlor in Mexico," he says with a smirk.

He continues describing his tattoos, when and where he got each of them, before moving on to the "stories" behind his eyebrow and nipple piercings. He even lifts his shirt to show me the ring in his nipple. None of the stories are too deep.—"I was drunk and decided it was time for some ink." "A girl I dated was into nipple piercings."—As he talks, I'm getting a complete picture of Justin through his body art. He's not a bad guy. Maybe a bit of a man whore. But he's just out to have fun. Carefree and cool seem to be his main life goals. And with his obviously rich father, his aimless lifestyle isn't too hard to maintain. While Sam and Romeo wear plain T-shirts and regular jeans—except for onstage, where Romeo dresses more like his roommate—Justin wears designer T-shirts and expensive ripped denim daily.

If Chloe were here, she'd be whispering "hot but major douche bag" in my ear.

But really, I can't be overly judgmental. It's not like I'm Miss-Wanna-Do-Something-Awesome-with-My-Life. My goals of wanting to play drums and simply go to college aren't exactly lofty. I haven't even decided on a major or minor yet.

When Sam and the girls sit at our table, Justin's describing how he didn't flinch as the needle hit his nipple. Romeo's at the jukebox. The girls gaze coolly at me until Sam makes a comment about me drumming. Their eyes grow a bit less icy. Wow. I'm getting sick of this and wonder if they give each other bitch looks. Or maybe because I'm inside the secret, prized circle of band hotties, the looks are reserved for me.

The conversation turns to our upcoming gig while I peel away the rest of the label on my beer.

Romeo comes over, flips a chair backward, and leans his elbows on the back of it just as the music starts. The girl—Anna, I think—at his end leans over, showing him her cleavage at a better angle, and says something that brings a slight smile to his face. Of course, Romeo's nice to everyone but me.

When he sings along with the song's refrain, his gaze pins me to my chair. The song is "Dirty Little Secret" by the All-American Rejects, and from the twinkle of his eyes it's obvious he picked the song to piss me off. And yes, I'm pissed. Fuming actually.

Draining half of my second beer, I angle my chair and scoot closer to Justin. The girl on the other side of him pauses whatever she was saying and gives me a dirty look. I give one back. Justin grins. She starts up again, something about her poetry class, and I pretend to be part of the conversation.

About half an hour later, Romeo announces he's leaving. Though he claims he has to study, his voice is tight. The girls all frown as Sam gets up, and Justin looks to me. "Give me a ride?"

A trip to the dorms is out of my way and I'm positive Justin plans to hit on me, but the recent image of Romeo singing about me being his dirty little secret has me nodding.

"Justin," Romeo says, his teeth clenched, as he leans across the table, "have you forgotten the agreement?"

Justin meets Romeo's hard stare. "Relax. I'm just in the mood to party."

Romeo gives him another stern look—actually, he looks quite pissed—before telling the girls, who watch him with wide eyes because they've probably never seen his dick side, good night and motioning for Sam to follow him. Watching him leave, I'm piecing together the agreement, which of course has to be about me.

True to his word, Justin parties. He downs several tequila shots with the girls. He tries to order me one. I remind him I'm driving. The girls play more music on the jukebox. They dance. Within minutes, they pull Justin out to dance and rub all over him. He tries to pull me out to join the clothed orgy. I decline and sip water. The night goes on in this vicious, boring cycle until the waitress finally announces last call.

Predictably, one of the girls offers to take Justin home after they down their last shots. Before I can gladly concur, he wraps an arm around me and squeezes my shoulder. "Got my ride right here."

Lucky me.

The ride to the dorm feels like forever as Justin searches through songs on my iPod and belts lyrics into the night from the open window. Never thought I'd grow sick of his voice, but with every passing street, it grates more on my nerves.

Finally, I pull up to his dorm.

Of course, he doesn't get out. I don't turn the engine off. And although my stomach churns—my upcoming rejection is probably not going to go well—I take advantage of the silence and his buzz. "What's this I hear about an agreement?"

He lays his head back on the headrest and looks at me through his lashes. "It's about you."

"I figured as much. What exactly is it?"

He scoots closer and leans an elbow on the console between us. "He'd be pissed if I told you."

Though Justin likes to act the front man, his buzzed-up honesty makes it obvious he knows who runs the show. "As if I'd tell him."

In the dim light from the dashboard, his twisted grin brings out his deep dimples. He obviously likes my bitch attitude toward Romeo.

"We're not supposed to hit on you or anything. That's why he finally agreed to let you in the band. If anyone seriously hits on you or tries to hook up with you, then you're out. That was the deal."

My hands clench the steering wheel, but his explanation is pretty close to what I guessed.

He leans closer to me. "But what happens when we can't resist? What happens when you draw us like a moth to a flame?" He reaches out and runs a finger softly down my cheek. "Like a dying man to heaven?"

If this is the normal shit he spouts, the girls he's with are either as drunk as him, seriously blinded by his dimples, or really horny. Guess if you're looking for a lay, Justin's the perfect no-strings-attached.

I cover the fingers caressing my cheek and pull at his hand. "Oh, I think you can resist me."

He shakes his head, leans even closer, and looks at me through his lashes again. "I don't think I can. I'm falling and you're the parachute that will save me."

"What?" I shriek before my laughter escapes at the ridiculous image of me bloated wide above him as we fall through the air. His soft, sultry expression turns hard as I giggle. It takes me a moment to rein in the laughter. "I'm sorry, but that was the lamest line I've ever heard." Another giggle escapes. "A parachute!" I gasp and then dissolve in another round of hilarity.

Justin leans against the headrest as I try to control my laughter. "Guess I should go."

I can only nod. I'm afraid if I try to say anything, I'll burst into giggles again. He slowly gets out of the car and goes to the main door of the dorm. While I wait to make sure he gets in, Justin looks over his shoulder. I offer a wave. He waves back, then tumbles through the door of his building. Five seconds later, I can't hold it in any longer. With my head nestled against the steering wheel, I'm laughing like crazy. Part of my uncontrollable laughter is from trying to hold it in so long, but really—a parachute?

Chapter 14

The next day I sit on a bench in the center of campus at the edge of the outdoor common area. Marcus agreed to meet me for a late lunch. Pissed and confused about the whole Chloe thing, I haven't seen him in a while, but I need to ask—beg—him about using his drum set, and I'd rather do my begging face-to-face. But his class ends over an hour after mine. So I listen to my iPod, shuffle through music, and read from *The Life of Julius Caesar,* my latest assignment in Ancient Roman History.

Taking a break from the tedious account of Mr. Caesar, I set the book in my lap. Although the day is sunny and warm, the leaves are beginning to turn. Soon autumn will flow into the cold days of winter. Days like this are little treasures that demand to be stored up before the cold keeps me from the outdoors. The pool needs to be closed up soon, but I have no idea how. My father always bought the chemicals and took care of the pool. Between Google and the salesman at the pool store, I hope to figure it out.

Beyond the circle of benches and down the circle of cement steps, a dark blond head catches my eye, standing out among the many people enjoying the weather. Justin sits on the edge of the wall circling the fountain. The black ink on his arms gleams in the bright sun. A girl with long strawberry-blonde hair sits next to him. Actually, she's almost in his lap.

I let out a laugh and the person sitting on the bench across from me gives me an odd look. I shrug and glance back at Justin. So much for me being his parachute. Looks like he found another string to tug. Any guilt I had for using him to piss off Romeo—then rejecting his advances with laughter—fade as I watch him flirt.

Strangely, Justin's womanizing ways don't bother me. It's not like he has a girlfriend, and it's obvious he's a player. But then Romeo and Sam are too. However, Romeo—hot jerkface cheater—is the one with the girlfriend.

Suddenly, Marcus plops down next to me, breaking me from my thoughts of Romeo. I give him a smile. Perfect timing.

He grabs my iPod from my lap and looks at the song playing while I pull out my earbuds.

"Do you ever listen to anything slow?" he asks with a smirk.

I shrug. When it comes to music, I love the drums. For some people it's the riff of the guitar or the vibration of the bass. For most it's the words of the song and the vocals. But the drums speak to me. They boom into my chest and spread to my fingers and toes. Maybe it's because I play them, but that doesn't matter. Music speaks to me through the beat of the drums. "Slow usually means less drums."

He shakes his head and stands. "Come on. I'll buy. I'm starving."

While we walk to the cafeteria and move through the line, he asks me about my mom and Jamie. I tell him they're fine. I ask him about the marching band. He tells me it's great. I feel a twinge of jealousy. The marching band can't be anything like the drama of being in Luminescent Juliet. But then, being onstage in front of a wild crowd is a rush that performing on a football field can't compete with.

We find a table near the window in one corner. The seating area is nearly empty compared to when I'm here near noon some days with Kendra.

He's dousing his hamburger with ketchup and I'm cutting the chicken of my salad when I say, "I have something important to ask you."

His face tilts defensively. "Then why don't you just ask?"

The set of his chin throws me for a second, until I realize he must think this is about Chloe. "I really need to borrow your drum set."

"My set?" he asks, confusion changing his guarded expression.

"Please? Besides my having to pay for the rented kit, yours is better," I say simply, instead of telling him how Romeo tried to get me to quit using a different tactic.

"Sure. Of course you can use them." He reaches for his burger and waves a hand. "It's not like I'm home much."

Well, that was way easier than I thought it would be.

"Thanks," I say, relieved. Two summers of lawn cutting went into those drums. "Saturday should be cool. We're doing a full line-up at the Razor." He frowns while chewing. "You're coming, right? Saturday's are eighteen and over."

He shakes his head and swallows. "We have an away game. It doesn't start until four and it's almost two hours away. Shouldn't be back until after midnight."

I drop my fork loaded with chicken and salad. "Well, that sucks. Chloe's not going to be there either. She's got a date," I say before I can stop myself.

Marcus pauses, reaching for his burger. I'm trying to determine if that means anything, but he breaks my concentration by asking, "Why doesn't Supertramp bring her date to watch you?"

My head snaps up. I'm very tempted to admit I know about him and Chloe. "Don't call her that."

He shrugs. "If the condom fits . . ."

This is an argument we've had several times. The first was sophomore year when he tried to warn me about destroying my reputation if I kept hanging around with Chloe. As if I had a reputation. And like her dating two guys from the football team one month apart was that big a deal. Though I'm sure their mouths made it sound like a huge deal. "Tell me something. Do you think the guys in the band, especially Justin, are slutty? Because Justin doesn't have a flavor of the month. More like a flavor of the night."

"Well, he's a gu—"

"Don't even say it, or—," I warn, and start to raise my bag of croutons. Marcus never talks about other girls—girls more promiscuous than Chloe—like this, which has me wondering why he is now.

He smirks. "Or you'll kill me with croutons?"

I lower the bag slowly. "Her first date with the guy shouldn't be in some loud bar. He wants to take her to some fancy restaurant."

Marcus scowls. "Then the backseat of his car?"

I'm about to chuck the croutons at his forehead, but the sight of the group coming in the cafeteria causes the bag to fall from my fingertips. Romeo leads a group of what looks like twelve-year-old boys to the chalkboard menu. He points at the first item. "What group do burgers fall into?" he asks loudly.

Several boys yell out, "Protein!"

"Good job," he replies.

"What's he doing?" I ask, gesturing toward Romeo with my fork.

Marcus glances over his shoulder and watches before turning around. "I know he gives private boxing lessons or sessions or whatever it's called as a part-time job." He shrugs. "Must be doing it as class."

"Boxing?" I ask incredulously, remembering his gentle fingers dancing over the fiddle then my skin. However, I have noticed the impression of dominance he silently exudes. What girl wouldn't?

Marcus nods and speaks through a mouthful of food. "He won the state championship twice. As a kid, then during his senior year. Was on the team here freshman year but quit to do the band thing." He takes a gulp of his chocolate milk. "How do you not know any of this? You're with those guys all the time."

Romeo points to pizza and several boys yell, "Carbohydrate!" Others yell, "Protein!"

I pull my eyes from Romeo, dressed in a university T-shirt and gym shorts. No surprise, he has nice legs. Very muscled. The last thing I want is Marcus noticing me salivating over him. "I'm kind of busy at home. I just go to practice, play, and leave right away."

He raises a brow.

"The house needs to be cleaned. The lawn cut. Jamie has homework now. And there's always laundry." I sigh. "I hate laundry. It multiplies like rabbits or something. But I'm getting good at cooking."

An onion ring drops from his fingers. "Shit, Riley, I know your mom's working full-time, but so do lots of women."

"She's depressed."

"So that makes you the Mom, Dad, and cleaning lady?"

I shrug. "It's just hard for her to . . . do things sometimes."

"You're enabling her depression."

Sadly, I'm aware of this, but I slap the table, annoyed. "What am I supposed to do? Let the house fall down around me? Let my sister take care of herself?"

Romeo and his group are now at the dessert section.

"Your mom needs to step up."

"She's working full-time. She's trying to adjust after more than twenty years of marriage."

"Even though they're getting divorced, your dad should help more."

I'm not going to explain that my mother won't let him because of the girlfriend. It's none of his business. "He's busy."

"Never thought your dad would become a deadbeat."

My chest tightens. My gaze finds the zigzag pattern on the carpet. Part of me, the part that spent eighteen years with my father before he left, wants to defend him. The other part is starting to agree with my friend. My father's financial support isn't enough, but he gives into my mother's demands—like only seeing Jamie at our house on Saturdays—too easily. "Just drop it, Marcus." I look up to find the boys scribbling on scraps of paper and Romeo watching me. Our gazes lock before I spear a clump of chicken and salad. Suddenly, I'm very interested in lunch.

"One more thing," Marcus says.

"I said to drop it," I growl.

"I don't think Mags is aware she's using you, Riley. But she is."

"Marcus—"

Suddenly, Romeo is above us. "Hey, Marcus," he says, then looks to me. "Riley. You two doing okay?" He leans over the plants on the half wall next to our table. His tone is casual, but his gaze constricts on Marcus, who looks confused.

"We're fine," I say lightly. "Everything's fine. You coach boxing?" I gesture to the scribbling boys to get his attention away from Marcus, who looks like he might soon pee his pants or something under Romeo's gaze.

He nods. "More like train, but yes."

I tilt my head as if in thought. "Does working with kids wear you down? Is that why you're such an uptight asshole?"

Marcus's mouth drops open.

Laughing, Romeo pushes away from the wall and his biceps bunch. "Nope. Someone else tends to make me that way." He gives me a pointed look before glancing at Marcus. "See you two later." He hauls his tight ass back over to the group of boys.

When Romeo is out of earshot, Marcus asks, "What was that about?"

I should have kept my big mouth shut, but I'm so used to arguing with him at practice, my snide questions just came out. "Obviously, we're not too fond of each other."

"Really? You're one of the least-confrontational people I know. And it doesn't seem like he dislikes you. In fact, it seems like he's worried about you. Eyeballing me, like he was pissed I was upsetting you or . . ." Marcus's expression becomes pensive as he studies me.

I have a sick feeling he's remembering my backward shirt and putting two and two together. "Trust me. We don't get along. He wants me to quit the band."

Marcus's eyes grow huge. "What? Why?"

Once again, I should have kept my big mouth shut, but I'm sure Marcus was thinking I was with Romeo that night. Unfortunately, things tend to grow bigger the more people know about them. I wave a hand. "Don't you remember tryouts? He wanted another drummer."

"Then he's an idiot."

I give Marcus a wide smile. "My thoughts exactly."

Chapter 15

The first set went perfectly. It ended with "Bullet In My Hand" by Redlight King. With the build then drum explosion, I love playing that song. The next set will start with two originals, "Blood on Snow" and "Trace." Energy from playing for almost an hour buzzes inside of me while I gulp down water. The club isn't huge but it's packed. I've been here with Chloe before. Two days after she turned eighteen. People usually come here to grind against one another on the dance floor. This Saturday night they're here to listen to us.

Surrounded by jars of olives, maraschino cherries, and boxes, we take a quick break in the stock room. There's no area behind the small stage here. High-energy music—I'm guessing Pong—echoes from the main club. Justin and Sam are drinking a quick beer. Romeo's talking to some guy about adjusting the lighting. I'm leaning against the wall and trying to catch my breath. Drumming for almost an hour is a workout.

Reaching in my bag for another water, I notice my phone flashing with a message probably from Chloe giving me an update on her date. I grab for the phone wondering if the text is going to read *awesome* or *douche bag*. But the message isn't from Chloe. It's from my dad, and when I read it—*your mother's in the hospital*—my heart drops.

I ignore all the voice mails he left, step farther into the stock room, past shelves of cocktail napkins, and hit his speed dial number with a shaky finger.

He answers on the second ring. "Riley—"

"What's going on?" I ask in a frantic tone.

"Settle down. Maggie's doing better. She's in stable condition."

His words don't kill my panic. "Why is she there?"

I hear him sigh and imagine him running his hand through his gray hair. "Apparently she overdosed on sleeping pills."

"What?" If I thought my heart dropped before, now it's on the concrete floor.

"I said—"

"I heard what you said. But did she . . . do it on purpose?" The question comes out in a whisper as fear threatens to explode and turn me into a raving lunatic.

"At this point, they don't know."

Air rushes out of me. Deflating, I lean against the wall next to the shelves and let myself slide, landing with a plop on the floor. "Where's Jamie?"

"Sara took her home a little while ago. She rode here in the ambulance. She's the one who called 9-1-1."

My eyes close as visions of what Jamie must have gone through flash through my mind. "Is mom . . . awake?"

"She's in and out of it, but I think Jamie needs you more right now."

"Okay, okay, okay," I keep saying, but the urge to see my mother safe and talk to her is overwhelming. "What's her room number?"

"Three-twelve."

"I'll be there in a bit."

"Riley—," my father starts.

I end the call. Lifting my head, I notice all three of my band members staring at me from the far end of the stock room. I push myself up on wobbly legs. "I have to go."

"What?" Justin asks incredulously. "We have another set to finish."

"What's going on?" Concern etching his expression, Romeo steps past Justin.

I reach out and hold a shelf for support. "My mother's in the hospital."

Sam's blue eyes turn huge. "Is she okay?"

I blink. "I think she's going to be all right." At least healthwise. Mentally she's falling apart.

Justin's confused face turns hard. "Then you should finish the set."

Romeo watches me with a growing frown but says to Justin, "Shut the fuck up."

"What?" Justin points at Romeo. "You're the one who always worries about our reputation. Says we have to look professional. What the hell will it look like if we don't go back on?"

Romeo's fists clench at his sides as he steps inches from Justin. "You think she can go out and play with her mother in the hospital?"

"She said her mother was going to be okay . . . ," Justin says weakly.

Romeo's jaw tightens. "Get. Out. Before I knock you out."

Justin blanches, but one look at Romeo's hard expression and clenched fists has him spinning toward the door.

Romeo reaches for my arm. "You look like you're going to collapse. Where are your keys?" I gesture weakly to my bag on the floor. He snags my bag and drags me by the arm down a short hallway. Sam follows and Romeo tosses his keys at him. "Get your acoustic, explain an emergency came up, and apologize. Play as many songs as possible. Justin should be able to keep up with the vocals. Tell the owner I'll call him as soon as possible. And I'll call *you* for a ride later."

Sam nods at the directions as he follows us out. He heads straight for the van in the alley while Romeo pulls me to the parking lot.

He pauses at the edge of the car-filled lot. "Where's your car?"

Mentally, I'm still sitting in the stock room. "Why?"

"I'll drive you to the hospital."

"I can—"

"You can barely walk. Where's your car?" he repeats.

In defeat, I point to my gray sedan.

On the way to the hospital, except for Romeo telling me not to worry about the gig, the car is silent as I clench my thighs in a silent scream. I'm not sure if Romeo is upset about leaving or is giving me space, but I don't care. In a daze, I only want to see my mother.

My stupor continues until I get to the third floor of the hospital. Romeo steered me across the parking lot, around the hospital, and into the elevator. Without him, I probably would have gotten lost.

My father hugs me as soon as I get off the elevator. "Riley, I'm sorry but there's nothing you can do right now. She's . . . the drugs are still wearing off."

I don't hug him back. Though I may be wrong, though it may be unfair, I can't help blaming him for what has happened. I step away from him. "Then why are you still here?"

His expression is pained. "Sara took Jamie and my car."

Anger destroys any remnants of the haze I'd been in. I whirl away from him. "I'll be back in a bit," I say to Romeo, who offers a curt nod.

My father follows me down the hall. As I pass the nurses' station, I hear him explaining who I am, but I just march on.

My mother's room is quiet except for the beep of what I'm assuming is a heart monitor. She lies still, looking small and fragile in the hospital bed. She's desperate sorrow lying before me. And so alone. The divorce has left her isolated. Or maybe she's isolated herself.

My lip trembles as I reach for her hand. At my touch, her brown eyes flutter open for a second, then close again. Watching her lie there, I want to shake her awake and demand answers. I want to hug her and tell her my father isn't worth this. I want to wheel her and the entire bed out of here. Mostly, I want to go back in time and make sure this never happened.

After I stand there for several long minutes, holding her hand tightly—she doesn't move—I give her knuckles a soft kiss, then gently lay her hand on the blanket before exiting the room. I don't go into the waiting room, just hover at the door. Romeo and my father sit across from each other but both are quiet.

"Let's go," I say to Romeo, then to my father, "Sara should be here within the half hour."

My father stands. "Riley, don't look at me like that. I still care about Maggie. I sent Sara home with Jamie because I couldn't leave until I knew Maggie was going to be okay. I plan on being here in the morning."

"Care or guilt?" His face pales at my question. Before he can answer I hiss, "And don't come in the morning. Do you really think she wants to see you?" Turning, I stomp toward the elevator.

Romeo stays silent as we leave the hospital, but worry and despondency build a lump in my throat. As soon as I get in the car, my sobbing starts. Romeo doesn't say anything, just pulls me into his arms.

"She overdosed. Because of him," I say into his shoulder. Not because I want to share but because I need to say the words, need to hear reality, even if it comes from my own lips.

He stiffens for a quick second, then rubs my back as I continue to sob. "You know that stupid commercial is true," he says. "Depression hurts. It's an illness. Your mother needs help."

Realizing he's right, my mother is truly ill, I sob harder. He continues holding me, offering support without words. Finally, nearly spent, I pull away from him. "I need to get home."

He nods, starts the car, and asks for directions.

I dig through the glove box for a napkin while he drives, then use the paper and the slow leak of falling tears to wipe the stream of mascara and eyeliner running down my face. Once we pull in my driveway, I say in a nasal tone, "Um . . . guess you should come in until Sam gets here."

Romeo quietly follows me onto the porch.

Jamie flies off the couch and into my arms the moment I enter the house. Falling into the nearest chair in the living room, I just revel in the feel of her small arms around me. Behind me, I hear Romeo tell Sara my father is waiting for her to pick him up. Good, because I don't want to talk to the woman. I'm super annoyed she's in my house. Then I hear his one-sided conversation with Sam about a ride and directions.

"Did you see Mom?" Jamie asks, sitting up in my lap. Her worried eyes search mine. "Is she okay? Daddy told me she was okay, but she wouldn't wake up."

"She's okay. We'll go see her tomorrow morning."

"She wouldn't wake up," she repeats. "She just laid on the hallway floor. Why wouldn't she wake up, Riley?"

"She's . . ." I look above Jamie's head and catch Romeo watching us from the chair opposite mine. "She's sick, but she'll be better soon." My throat tightens at the lie. My mother's depression isn't going to get better overnight. Noticing Jamie's in pajamas, I say, "It's almost midnight. You should be in bed."

"I . . . Can't we sleep down here? Like a slumber party?"

She's scared to be alone after what happened. "Okay, go get your blanket and pillow."

Jumping off my lap, she finally notices the person sitting in the chair across from us. "Oh, hey, Romeo!" She looks back and forth at the two of us with a confused expression. "Is Romeo your new boyfriend?"

The sight of Romeo's startled expression has a laugh escaping me. "No, we're just friends." Not really. "Go get your stuff."

"Huh, well he should be," she says, looking at him and then me again, then running upstairs.

"Sorry about that." I reach for the remote. Romeo shrugs but his expression stays startled. I flick on the TV. With his black shirt, black boots, and the silver hoops lining his ears, he looks out of place in my mother's pastel living room. "You have siblings?"

"Only child."

I start pushing buttons. "Well then, I'm even sorrier about this then."

He raises a dark eyebrow and crosses his feet.

I cue in Jamie's favorite show, some Disney Channel sitcom, and use the remote to gesture to the screen. "Prepare to be annoyed."

He frowns at the TV.

His silence is starting to freak me out. "How soon until Sam gets here?"

"Within the hour."

Hoping to get away from his loud quietness, I ask, "Do you need anything? Pop? Water? Iced tea?"

"I'm fine."

Okay, maybe my gratitude is long overdue. "Um . . . ," I say. "Thanks for tonight. Not only for shutting Justin up but for driving me to the hospital and here. You were right. There was no way I could have driven." I take a deep breath. "And thanks . . . for all the other stuff," I add, thinking of him holding me.

"You're welcome. But no problem," he says stiffly, and his gaze flicks to the TV.

Jamie comes down and she and I move to the couch. She settles her pillow and head on my lap, but before the first commercial break, she's fast asleep.

It's kind of weird sitting and watching a Disney sitcom with Romeo. I turn the TV over to regular cable. "Anything you interested in?"

He shakes his head. "No, but could you turn it off. So I can say something?"

"Ah, okay." I'm suddenly filled with apprehension as I click off the power.

With a pensive expression, he scoots to the edge of the chair. "I . . . want to apologize for the way I've been treating you." His full lips turn down. "For the way I've pretty much always treated you. I've been a complete ass."

I'm stunned then angry at the contrite look in his eyes. "Is this because you feel sorry for me? Because of my mother?"

He sluggishly rubs the dark scruff on his chin. "Not exactly. I do feel sorry for you, especially because of what you're going through with your mother. If our roles were reversed, wouldn't you feel sorry for me?"

Thinking of him having to deal with what I did tonight and what tomorrow will bring, I can't help but nod.

He takes a deep breath and lets it out. "Tonight I saw you as a real person, instead of someone who has the potential to destroy what I've worked so hard to accomplish for the last two years. Even more, tonight had me realizing hard work and determination don't trump everything and everyone else. Life is bigger than Luminescent Juliet." He runs a hand through his hair. "Deep down I know that. I just—my ambition kept it buried."

I'm shocked and silent as his eyes search mine while he waits for a response. The chirp of bugs through the open window grows loud. "I . . . your behavior almost makes sense hearing it from your point of view. But you have been an ass, and all I ever wanted to do was play."

"I'm slowly getting that." His full lips compress into a thin line. "Maybe after dealing with Justin for so long, I tend to think most people want to be in a band for the social connections."

I glance down at Jamie. She looks peaceful sleeping in my lap. "You may get your wish after all."

He cocks his head, silently questioning me.

"I might have to quit."

"That's not what I want anymore," he says softly. "We'd never get another drummer like you."

I brush dark strands of hair from my sister's face. "I love drumming, yet my family's more important than playing."

Lights flash in the window and an engine sounds in the driveway.

Romeo stands and glances at Jamie sleeping on my lap. "I'd understand if you decide to quit, but I'm hoping you'll stay with us." His expression serious, he stops in front of us. "And if you need anything—help with Jamie, someone to talk to, or something else—call me. I want to help."

I'm stunned for the third time but manage to mumble, "Thank you."

He nods and disappears into the hall, then the door quietly shuts behind him.

The rumble of the engine fades away, but my shock at Romeo's words doesn't. Though he has been a jerk, he has always shown his true colors when push came to shove. Like when Jamie came to practice and with everything he did tonight. He may be a player and a cheater, but he's nothing like shallow Justin.

Chapter 16

J amie and I went to the hospital almost as soon as we woke up. Although the doctor wanted my mother to stay, he signed her release papers right away and we left the hospital before nine this morning. I'm not sure if my father ever came to check on his wife.

I haven't had a chance to talk with my mother. Jamie won't leave her side. They've spent most of the day lying in mom's bed watching TV. I took lunch up to them—soup and sandwiches—a couple of hours ago. But the need to discuss last night with my mom is plaguing my conscience and making my stomach roll.

I'd forgotten Chloe was coming over, dealing with all the turmoil going on in my head. When she showed up at the door, I was almost thankful for the mindless primping get-together. She'd come to fix my hair, nails, eyebrows, and whatever else she deemed necessary.

"How can I paint your nails with your hands clenched?" Chloe asks, holding the small brush dripping with black polish over the kitchen counter.

I look down at my curled fingers, then straighten them. "Sorry, I'm a bit tense."

Her expression turns mocking. "A bit?"

"Long night," I murmur, then think about a safe topic. "So how was your date?"

She swipes at my nails. "Pretty good. He's rather mature. Maybe too mature for me. I hadn't realized he's twenty-seven."

Staring at her platinum head bent over my hands, my eyes grow huge. "Twenty-seven? Where did you meet this guy again? And does he know you're eighteen?"

"He works in the garage across from my cosmetology school. And yes, he knows I'm eighteen."

My nose wrinkles as she finishes a pinkie. "Then he's skeevy."

She shrugs. "He's nicer than most of the tools I date." She gestures toward the stove and the boiling pasta. "You want me to drain that?"

I nod but the whole Marcus thing is at the tip of my tongue. She always calls Marcus a tool and she's been different since that night. Not her usual fun, sarcastic self. I'm thinking of the best way to voice my knowledge and get it over with when my phone bursts into a fast drumbeat. The name on the front has me almost falling off my chair. It's like my thoughts conjured up his call.

"You gonna get that?" Chloe asks from her spot at the sink.

My nails still wet, I carefully reach for my phone. "Ah, hello."

"What happened to your mom?" Marcus asks.

"Who told you?" My warm feelings for Romeo from last night instantly fade.

"Justin said you ran out in the middle of the gig to the hospital."

I get mad at myself. I should have known it was Justin instead of Romeo. "She's fine. She's home."

"Why was she in the hospital? What happened?"

I can only guess and I'm not sharing that with him. He's already dissing my mom. "I . . . don't want to get into it right now."

"Huh, well . . . okay. How are you doing?"

"I'm all right. Getting my hair done and cooking dinner. Can I call you back later?"

"Ah sure," he says. "She's okay though, right?"

"Yes. I gotta go before the chicken burns. Bye," I say quickly, and hang up.

Chloe glances at the already cooked, cooling chicken. "Who was that? And what was it about? Because you're beyond flustered."

"No one. Nothing," I mumble.

Chloe's eyes spit fire at me. "What the hell? What is with you lately? Everything is some deep dark secret with you."

I wince. I wouldn't call it keeping secrets. Just withholding information. My mom's issues are hers. And though I didn't tell Chloe about Romeo wanting me to quit, I did tell her about messing around with him. "Oh, and what about you?"

"What is that supposed to mean?" When I'm stubbornly silent, she reaches for her keys at the end of the counter. "I don't know if it's the divorce or the scholarship thing or what, but you're edging on the line of bitch."

"You're going to leave me with foils still in my hair?" I ask incredulously, pointing to my head. If it were up to me, I would have left the roots underneath brown.

"Wait another twenty minutes. You can take them out yourself," she snaps, and whirls toward the hallway.

"I know about you and Marcus," I blurt.

She spins around and keys fall to the floor, but she doesn't bend to get them. "He told you?"

I'm not sure which indicates her shock more, the screechy pitch of her question or her openmouthed expression. I shake my head. "I almost walked in on you two. One of you must have left the door open."

With her eyes downcast, she slowly slides onto the stool next to me. "He asked me not to say anything to you. So I didn't."

I'm not sure why he cares about me knowing, but at the moment I'm interested in her. "Do you like him?"

She sighs. "It doesn't matter."

"Why?"

She twists a glass of iced tea between her hands. "Because he's in love with you."

I instantly stop blowing on my nails and burst out laughing. "Trust me. He's not."

Her long-lashed eyes rise to mine. The pain in them kills my laughter. "He is and always has been."

I shake my head. Though I suspected he had a crush on me before I started dating Aaron, I haven't noticed that vibe from him in a long time. "He told you that?"

"He doesn't have to." Her sigh is longer. "Remember when we became friends?"

I go around the counter and reach for the drained pasta. "When you started coming to the skate park during eighth grade."

"I kind of used you. I set out to be your friend because of Marcus."

The strainer wobbles in my hands. "Are you telling me you've been my friend for the last six years to hook up with Marcus?" Finished dumping the pasta in a baking pan, I force myself to set the strainer, not slam it, on the counter.

She waves a hand. "No, that was just at first. Within a couple of weeks, I realized how awesome you were. It's just like I've always been mega-aware of him while he's always been mega-aware of you," she says with a frown.

I'm frowning too because it does sound like the past six years of our friendship have been for a hookup. "So *I've* been keeping secrets?" I snap, grabbing the butter dish from the counter.

She gnaws on her lip and lipstick edges her teeth. "I didn't want to make it difficult if you ever returned his feelings."

Anger fizzles out of me at her reasoning. Her self-sacrifice is actually touching. "Wow, Chloe, that's pretty amazing you'd do something like that." She blushes. I don't think I've ever seen her blush. "But I'll never be with Marcus. He's like a brother. But I think he may like you, even if he doesn't realize it." I cut slivers of butter into the pasta.

A hopeful gleam lights up her eyes, but she blinks it away. "He's always been into you."

Though I'm not sold on his undying love, I say, "Maybe he *thinks* he is, but the way he gets so worked up over you is almost ridiculous."

Her expression brightens. "What does he say?"

"Um . . . it's kind of like the way you treat him."

She frowns.

I open the fridge and reach for the chicken stock and milk. "You've been crushing for years but act like you hate him. Maybe he does the same thing."

She follows the trails of condensation on her glass with a bright red nail. "Sometimes I wonder if my feelings are a stupid rejection thing. Like Chloe the Testosterone Conqueror finally getting her way. Then I see how caring he is with you, and my heart goes all gooey and does this little melting thing." She snarls at her iced tea. "Sometimes I hate that little gush of melt."

After sprinkling Parmesan over the pasta, I start stirring. "Ah, please, please don't get too graphic, because I might hurl, but how was that night. I mean did Marcus seem into you physically?"

Chloe's gaze devours the motion of her nail on the glass. However, her lips curl into a slight smile. "It was good. He was into me and our drunken haze of lust. But almost right after, he started talking about not telling you."

My stirring turns vigorous. How could he? If Marcus were here right now, I'd bitch slap him with the wooden spoon in my hand. "That's why you left?" She nods and I imagine her spending the night crying her eyes out. "Marcus is an ass."

Her smile is wide. "So are you going to come clean with me?"

"No, not really," I say sadly. "It's about my mom. I'm not sure what's going on, but it's not really my problem to share."

"Oh," Chloe says, then points at me, "but it's affecting you."

I shrug and plop pieces of chicken over the pasta. "I'll get through it. I'm always getting through it," I say with a huff that causes my bangs and the foils in them to lift. "What about Neil? I thought you were in love with Neil. I thought he destroyed your heart when he broke up with you after prom."

"I did like Neil. Not as much as Marcus, but sometimes you take what you can get."

I can't help a frown. That is just plain sad.

Except for the crinkling of aluminum foil, the kitchen is quiet as I cover the top of the pan. "I guess I've been holding out on some band drama too."

She gives me a calculated look. "More Romeo stuff?"

"Sort of," I say, opening the oven and pushing the pan in. "It's not like I purposely didn't tell you. I just want to play. Not get sucked into male drama."

Chloe laughs. It's good to hear her laugh. "Male drama? That is wicked funny."

While she pulls the foils from my hair, I tell her about the night Justin hit on me—his lines have her laughing almost as much as I did—then about Romeo wanting me to quit, which has her in a pissed-off fit. She's still sputtering over what an asshole he is after I explain his reasoning and that he's over it. I don't tell her I might quit. I don't tell her about last night. Wishing I could, I remember Romeo offering to listen.

After rinsing my hair and torturing my eyebrows with wax, Chloe packs up her beauty equipment, gives me a long hug, and leaves.

I clean up the kitchen then wander upstairs and am relieved to see Jamie sleeping, curled against my mother's side. Part of me is terrified to face last night, but I have to know. I sit on the edge of the bed and my mother's gaze moves from the TV screen to me.

"Has she been sleeping for a while?" I ask, gesturing to my sister.

My mother nods, scoots up to a seated position, and holds the lapels of her robe in a stiff grip. She's small and tired looking but her posture is defensive. While her fingers whiten in their tight grip and fear pounds in my chest like a drum, I try to find the right words to ask her about why she spent the night in the hospital.

"Last night was an accident," she says as if reading my mind. "I would never do anything like that to you or Jamie. To myself. And I'd *never* want to scare you like that."

I want to believe her, but she's been so depressed lately that her actions override her words. "Then how did you . . ." I can't seem to get out *overdose.*

She looks away and clears her throat. "I don't quite remember. Before I told Jamie to get ready for bed, I took a couple sleeping pills. Then we read some books in her bed and I fell asleep. But when I woke up and went in my own bed, I couldn't fall back asleep. So I think I took some more. I don't remember how many.

Obviously too many." She rubs my sister's back. "I'm lucky Jamie woke up and found me."

My hands grip the edge of the bed while I try to believe her. "Do you usually take sleeping pills?"

She sighs and drops her hands into her lap. "Yes, Riley, sometimes worry keeps me from sleeping."

"Are you still going to take them?"

She shakes her head. Her face appears strained. It's an expression that has become part of her. "My doctor warned me about having behavior side effects. Obviously, that's what happened."

Finally, relief comes over me but not entirely. "Maybe you should see someone."

Her chin lifts. "Like a psychiatrist?"

I nod. "Or a counselor. The way dad left and with everything changing so suddenly, it's easy to see how—how you could be depressed."

She shakes her head. "My insurance only partially covers visits. We don't have the extra money."

"Your health is more important than money," I say firmly.

She looks away again. "My regular doctor already has me on antidepressants."

"Huh," I say, startled at the news because she's always so down. Then I blurt, "They don't seem to be working."

"They're helping. Things just take time, Riley." She reaches out and grabs my hand. "And you're always helping. I can't tell you enough how much I appreciate your help. How much it means to me."

I grasp her hand in return. "Mom, I just want to see you happy."

She gives me a weak smile but the expression behind it is tense. "I'll be happy again."

I nod and force a smile back but think, when? Next month? Next year? Ten years from now?

No matter how much I try, I can't imagine her happy ever again.

Chapter 17

I'm slightly nervous to go to calculus on Monday after Romeo's apology and his knowledge about my mother. Luckily, Kendra stayed off Romeo topics during lunch so her chatter was annoying as standard but didn't reach nails-on-chalkboard level. I feel like a tool eating with her every Monday, but I don't want to eat alone, and although I could just grab something quick and head outside or to a couch in the hall, Kendra would be mortified to eat alone. So to the cafeteria I go and let our grating friendship escalate.

Early to class as usual, I'm reviewing last week's notes as Romeo strolls in the half-empty room. Dressed in a gray T-shirt with a darker gray button-up flannel open over it, he looks like his normal dark and sexy self. Since I had to take Jamie to school today, I whipped my hair into a quick ponytail, brushed on a bit of mascara, and threw on the first jeans and sweatshirt my fingers found in the closet. Dressed this grungy, I probably don't even reach my normal cute.

Romeo leans over after setting out his books. "How's your mom?"

"Better," I say, flipping the pages of my notebook. When I meet his concerned gaze, I add in a hushed tone, "She says it was mistake. She took some sleeping pills but doesn't remember how many." Each time I think about her explanation, it grows conviction. But sharing it has my belief skyrocketing. My mother did *not* try to kill herself.

Romeo's dark eyes search mine. "*You* believe her?"

I rear back and snap, "Of course."

"Hey," he says in response to my angry tone, and leans closer, "you're taking my question the wrong way. I meant as her daughter you'd be able to judge if she was concealing anything."

My anger deflates. "The divorce has been really hard for her, but she'd never do that to my sister or me."

"Sounds like she needs help coping with the divorce."

I can't help a sigh from escaping, but I don't feel guilty revealing anything about my mother to Romeo since he was part of the drama that went down on Saturday night. "She thinks counseling is too expensive."

"A price should never be put on a person's mental health." He reaches for his notebook and scrawls across a clean sheet of paper. "Here," he says after ripping the page out. "They have a variety of therapists and offer services with a sliding scale, even free to some."

There's a phone number on the paper and over it the heading: Child and Family Services. "Thanks," I say, folding the sheet, then stuffing it into my pocket. I'm grateful for the information, but I'm wondering how he knows so much about the place. And the fact that he has the number memorized must mean something. Though I want to ask him about it, I'm aware of how invading that question would be.

"So you're not quitting?"

I shake my head. Playing drums keeps me sane.

He gives me a half smile. "Good."

Suddenly the girl—I think her name is Sharon or Sheena or something close to one of those—from the table over is directly in

Romeo's line of vision. A muscle twitches at Romeo's temple, but he smiles slightly and offers a greeting.

I pretend to review my notes while she leans over farther and turns chitchat into an informal request for a date. Romeo smoothly and regretfully explains how busy he is this weekend. Sharon/Sheena tears out a piece of his notebook paper and writes on it in pretty loops. Romeo takes the paper with a grin and a "thanks."

Professor Hill strolls in swinging his briefcase and *Sheena*—I caught the name and what no doubt was her phone number on the paper—stands, removing herself from our table. Without looking my way, Romeo shoves the paper into his calculus book while the professor silently takes roll. The normal flurry of note-taking commences within minutes.

The usual pings of lust—it's easier to ignore Romeo from behind a drum set than while sitting next to him and crunching the area of curves—that bombard me during class are almost absent. I'm too occupied with the thought of what he's going to do with that number. Then there's his knowledge about counseling. It's almost like he broadcasted he goes there. But what would this perfect specimen sitting next to me need therapy for?

After two hours—I knew a four-hour class would be a bitch—of note-taking, we're rewarded with the return of last week's quiz. I stare at my quiz with dread. A red seventy-three glares at me from the top. Each grade has been lower than the one before. This one is a major plunge. With the exception of a B in geometry and that stupid online course, I've always gotten As in math. Though most people find Calculus III easier than II, I'm finding out Calculus III is like Geometry on crack. I can handle a B. I'd rather have an A. But Bs are doable. Contemplating my downward trend and imagining what a graph of my future scores would look like, I'm envisioning a C or worse by the end of the semester.

Shit. Shit. Shit.

I glance at Romeo's quiz. A ninety-six shines from the top. The grip on my paper causes my quiz to crease. Why is this stuff so much simpler for everyone else? Guess I'm just not a 3-D girl. Two dimensions make more sense.

Romeo notices the crinkle of my paper and his eyes widen slightly at my score. I slip the quiz under my notebook and pretend immersion in the calculations of our last problem on my graphing calculator.

"I'm going to be studying over the weekend for next Monday's test," he says nonchalantly as he stuffs his quiz in a folder. "We could study together."

Thoughts tumble through my head. He didn't offer to tutor. He offered to study together. Knowing my pride, he probably phrased it that way intentionally. Studying with him would be torturous for my hormones. Getting a C or a D in this class would destroy my GPA and knock a chunk out of that pride. He's gotten high nineties on all of his quizzes. My quizzes show an apparent need for help. I suck up my pride, shove down my hormones, and say in a matching nonchalant tone, "I'm busy on Saturday, but will you be studying on Sunday?"

"Sure. I do laundry on Sunday though. So if you don't mind me running out to change loads, you could come by the dorm."

Visions of his dorm room—more like visions of us in his dorm room—almost have me backing out. But there won't be alcohol, it will be in the middle of the day—and most important, if I don't get some help, my test grade will blow. "I could come over around one?"

"That will work," Romeo says in an even more nonchalant tone than before, but his dark chocolate eyes look intense. My gaze goes back to my calculator.

Done handing out quizzes, Professor Hill announces the break. Swallowing my pride, I mumble "thanks" before hightailing to the bathroom. Coming back, a ping of jealously or guilt—I'm going with guilt—hits me in the hallway when I see Romeo talking with the beautiful April. I rush to my seat. I haven't stood in the hall and watched them since that first day. However, the more I get to know Romeo, the more I'm leaning toward the opinion that he and April are casually dating. He doesn't seem like the type to cheat. Now Justin . . . His name and the word *girlfriend* should never be spoken together. But still, why would April want to date a guy in a band? Surrounded by willing women, they're all players to some degree.

Recalling the two of them with their heads together out in the hall, I toy with the idea of coming up with an excuse—*something* that *somehow* slipped my mind—to back out of Sunday. But with the corner of my quiz sticking out from under my notebook and a strong determination to ignore Romeo's hotness, I decide to keep the study date. Really, what could possibly happen while doing calculus and laundry?

Chapter 18

Late Tuesday night after dinner with my dad and then band practice—which wasn't too bad because Romeo has toned himself down a bit—I'm sitting at the desk in my room and writing an essay for philosophy when my phone breaks out with Iggy Pop's "Lust for Life." Though it's one of my favorite drum-beats, I'd planned on adding more of my favorites, one for each of my most-used numbers—I just never have the time. I glance at the name and let out a sigh. Marcus has called me at least three times since Sunday. Having no idea about how to explain why my mother was in the hospital, I haven't called him back. I'm also still pissed about the way he treated Chloe.

Iggy's voice fades. Guilt pounds in my head. My phone beeps announcing a text. Releasing a sigh, I pick up my phone and read the text.

Marcus: What the hell? Why haven't you called me back?

Gnawing on my lip, I stare at my phone. I give in after finishing my essay. I've been putting the call off for too long.

"Shit, Riley," he answers. "What is with you and your phone?"

"I've been busy," I say, which is absolutely true. I'm always busy lately. "So what's up?"

"Ah, I've been worried about your mom."

"Mom's good."

"So what happened to Mags?"

"I'd rather not say. It's kind of personal but she's good." Perhaps not good but functioning.

"What?"

"Marcus—"

"Are you kidding me? We've been friends since second grade. Your mom has made me thousands of PB and Js. She's practically my surrogate mom, but whatever happened in the hospital is too personal to share?" Each word comes out at a higher volume than the previous.

"She overdosed on sleeping pills," I snap.

"Holy shit!"

"Stop. It was an accident."

"You sure?"

"She didn't remember how many sleeping pills she took. Listen, I didn't even tell Chloe so I'm expecting you to keep this to yourself."

"Like I'd tell anyone, especially Chloe. You know me better than that."

The way he says, more like spits out, Chloe's name has me thinking he doth protest too much. "I was talking about people like your mother. My mother would freak if your mom knew. People tend to assume the wrong thing." Myself included.

"Like I even talk to my mom anymore. Hey, is this why you didn't call back?"

"Kind of," I say, skirting the issue. "But I have been busy."

"Too busy for me?"

"Marcus, I've been too busy for *me*." Thinking of Chloe again, I add, "But I want to go out this weekend. You up for a movie?"

"When?"

"Saturday," I say, not revealing to him Chloe will be there too. He agrees enthusiastically and doesn't seem surprised at the midnight time, then we wander into talk about the marching band and Luminescent Juliet.

When I tell him I have to get back to homework, he says, "Yeah, I have a shitload to do too. But I've been wanting to say something for a while so . . ."

My heart starts thudding in panic remembering Chloe believing Marcus is in love with me.

"I wanted you to go to Virginia, but a part of me was like fan-fucking-tastic when I heard you weren't going. I would have missed you too damn much." There's a long pause of silence between us. "Forgive me?"

"Of course, Marcus," I say with relief. "A small part of me"—a very, very tiny part—"didn't want to go either. I knew I'd miss my family and you and Chloe. So maybe things worked out for the best."

"Maybe."

"Okay, I've got to go. See you Saturday." I set my phone on my desk with a new feeling of guilt. Neither Chloe nor Marcus knows the other is coming. I've turned into a sneaky matchmaker with one phone call.

Each October the only theater still showing movies downtown runs the *Rocky Picture Horror Show* at midnight on every Saturday of the month. And for the past three years, Chloe has hauled me to at least one showing. We've never brought Marcus. It's always been just the two of us amid rowdy costumed fans. Neither Chloe nor Marcus looked happy when we met up in the lobby, and neither of them have talked to each other, just to me.

Marcus and I are both dressed in T-shirts—mine is plain and his has *Reading Rocks!* across the front—and jeans. However, Chloe looks fabulous in a forties-looking red dress with a flared skirt and a matching hat. She always dresses over the top for this. I was count-ing on her flash, but Marcus hasn't seemed to notice.

We stand at our seats amid the loud crowd—fans dressed up like Dr. Frank-N-Furter, Brad Majors, Janet Weiss, Riff Raff, and other characters—with me in the middle, watching the movie and yelling the audience lines. Well, Chloe and I yell most of the lines. The only ones Marcus figured out are "Asshole!" and "Slut!" when-ever the main characters' full names are said. Between the popcorn and the profanity, he's having a good time. Unfortunately, whenever he says "Slut!" he glances at Chloe. With each yelled *slut* and glance her way, Chloe seems to get more introverted.

About halfway through, Marcus asks me to tell him the lines in advance. So I try to whenever possible. During the floorshow to-ward the end, he yells out the line I just told him—"Blow us a kiss slut!"—in Chloe's direction.

Chloe freezes. Marcus laughs. My stomach turns. When he keeps laughing, Chloe pivots the other way and walks out of the theater. I give Marcus a dirty look, then follow her out. Within the heavy press of bodies, some in the aisleway, I lose her. Once I'm out in the concession area, I spot her outside on the sidewalk.

"Chloe!" I yell, stepping outside, but she shakes her head and keeps walking. I run to catch up with her. "I'm sorry. I shouldn't have invited him."

She daintily wipes at a tear so it won't smear her makeup. "It's not your fault he's being an asshole."

"I shouldn't have invited him," I repeat. "I just knew you'd look good tonight and I wanted him to see you dressed up. And I just hoped . . ."

She smiles through her tears and gives me a hug. "Oh, Riley, he's seen me dressed up before. But thanks for trying," she says over my shoulder. "Oh shit, here he comes." She pulls away. "Catch you later," she says, forgetting or not caring we came together in her car.

I whirl around as Marcus comes up to me. "What the hell is your problem?"

His face scrunches in confusion. "What are you talking about?"

"Why were you such a jerk to Chloe?"

He shrugs. "I'm always a jerk to Chloe."

But that was before you slept with her! Oh, I so want to junk punch him into reality. "Marcus, you need to stop. Obviously, it's not rolling off her anymore."

"Maybe that's just her conscience."

Marcus and I have had our spats over the years, but this time I'm truly pissed. "Can you just take me home?"

"You don't want to watch the rest of the movie?"

"No, I don't want to watch the rest of the movie. It's something Chloe and I do together," I snap. "Since you pissed my ride off into leaving early, you need to give me a ride."

He digs in his pocket. "Sure. Fine. I'll give you a ride home. Maybe I'll just stay at my house tonight. At least my mom will be happy."

We walk to his beater of a car in silence, and other than the radio, the car is quiet on the way home. I sit with my arms crossed and fume the entire way. But when we pull into my driveway, Marcus says, "Look, I'm sorry I was a jerk to Chloe."

"You need to tell her that, not me."

He mumbles something under his breath.

"What are you mumbling?" I demand from behind clenched teeth.

"Chloe just gets on my nerves. It's like we can't do anything unless she comes."

"Okay, I'm not even going to listen to this." I reach for the door handle. "We're in college not kindergarten."

His fingers grip my shoulder. "Wait, Riley."

"What?" I ask within a sigh.

"I . . . Could you please let go of the door?"

I let the handle go and fall back against the seat.

He turns to me, bending a knee. "You had to know that I liked you junior year."

Oh hell no. "Why are you bringing this up?"

He takes a deep breath. So deep his chest expands. "Because I never stopped liking you," he says with the air he lets out.

Hell to the no. "Marcus—"

"I know it probably doesn't seem like it. Since I'm friends with both you and Aaron, I decided to bury my feelings. Even after Aaron broke up with you. But when you didn't get back with him last month, I started thinking about you and me again. And I'm tired of pretending."

Oh really hell no. "Marcus—"

He runs a hand down his face. "I think I'm in love with you," he says with a laugh as if being goofy softens the seriousness of the words.

"Then why would you sleep with Chloe?"

He rears back until he's pressed against the window of his door. "She told you that?"

"No, you moron. You left the door open. I almost walked in on you two."

He watches me before he slowly says, "It meant nothing. It's always been you. Never her."

"Oh, Marcus, that's not what I meant. If you love me, why would you be attracted to Chloe?"

"Because I'm a guy?"

"That's the lamest reason I've ever heard. It sounds like something Justin would say."

He groans with frustration. "Can we just forget everyone else and talk about us?"

I want to give him some excuse about my life being such a clusterfuck that I can't deal with this right now. I don't want to hurt him, yet I know if the truth isn't said, everyone will go through more hurt later. "No. You slept with Chloe, and whether you realize it or not, she has feelings for you. Beyond that, I love you as a friend, like a brother."

"Like a brother?" he repeats softly.

I nod, open the door, and tell him good night.

Walking into my house, I wonder what's going to turn to shit in my life next because I'm quite sure my friendship with Marcus is now on the rocks.

Just like everything else.

Chapter 19

The slow thud of a headache beats behind my eyes. It could be the math. Calculus III sucks. Or it could be the continuous clench of my teeth. Ignoring Romeo's hotness is entirely too hard.

We sit on the rug with our backs against his bed and our books in our laps. Crumpled papers covered in long calculations lie between us. Romeo's dressed in jeans and a T-shirt. He isn't wearing shoes and even the sight of his naked feet is sexy. Each time he leans over and explains something, I catch the scent of clean shampoo, minty mouthwash, and a subtle spice I'm guessing is body wash, which puts inappropriate images in my head. Beyond the fact that we're in a band together and he's a player is the fact that I shouldn't be thinking of him all sudsy in the shower while I'm studying for a class I could fail.

I'm starting to understand thirteen-year-old boys. I need to get a grip on my hormones.

"What'd you get?" Romeo asks.

I tell him the number on my calculator.

He shakes his head and shows me the screen on his.

Fuck. Whenever I'm wrong he gets close. And my head swirls. If it isn't his smell, it's the brush of his muscled arm on mine. Or the concentrated look in those dark eyes. Or the pout of those full lips while he thinks of how to explain something. I knew this wasn't going to be easy, but his close proximity is bordering on torture.

Of course, he leans over and points to the diagram in the book. The skin of his arm slides over mine. "I'm going to guess you missed the inner ledge here." A musician's finger traces the drawing in my textbook while his scent surrounds me.

Shower spray and muscles covered with bubbles flash through my mind. "Yeah, you're right. I keep forgetting those little surfaces," I say, keeping my gaze on the tubular drawing.

"Take a break while I go change laundry?" He shifts back to his spot and I allow myself to breathe again.

I force a weak smile and nod. "My brain's getting fried."

"The library would have been easier, huh?" he asks, standing and stretching.

I have to force a nod. His jeans ride low. Between his hipbones, ridged stomach muscles flex. Holy hell. I resist fanning myself with my notebook and gaze around the room. "It's kind of odd that you and Justin live here," I say, stupidly looking for anything to get my thoughts off his body.

He reaches for the empty basket on the bed. "You mean in the dorm?"

"Ah, yeah. Why don't you guys have an apartment like Sam?"

He shrugs. "Dorm's paid for. I'm here on a variety of academic scholarships. Justin's parents won't splurge for an apartment until his GPA comes up." He moves to the door. "There's water and pop in the fridge. Be back in fifteen."

As soon as he's gone, I do fan myself. Shit. I wonder if my face is flushed. I get up and look in the mirror above Romeo's dresser. Relief fills me at the sight of my normal skin tone. I stick my tongue out at my reflection. I spent way too long getting ready this morning and destroyed my room picking out clothes. I didn't want to look like a slob but overdressing was out of the question. After feeling a bit too much like Chloe, I settled on my favorite pair of jeans and a mauve sweater that brightens my light-brown eyes. Then I spent more time getting my makeup right. Not too much but just enough. Ugh. All of that just to study.

Refusing to think of what all that primping says about me or my motivations, I examine the items on his dresser. A brush, Chap-Stick, a stack of papers, and a tube of hair gel look lonely and too neat. Except for the small picture of an older man sitting on a stool and playing a fiddle that's stuck to the corner of the mirror, Romeo's dresser screams boring. The huge mess of papers, hair products, gum wrappers, and pile of clothes on Justin's dresser scream slob.

I move toward the back of the room. Justin's desk is even messier than his dresser. Romeo's is neat and orderly. A closed laptop sits in the center. A nondescript cup holds pencils and pens. Books fill the bottom shelf while three framed photos line the top. Bonus. None are of April. One shows a pretty dark-haired woman holding a toddler. Both are smiling. Another is of the old man from the dresser. In this one he plays an accordion in front of a microphone. And the last is another of the old man holding up a boy who lifts up a red-white-and-blue-striped belt between his boxing gloves. I pick up the last picture for a closer look. The dark-haired boy is obviously Romeo.

"Thought I ruled the world at age eleven with my first title," Romeo says from behind me.

I didn't even hear him come in. Startled, I almost drop the picture. "Was the man your coach?"

"And my grandfather."

I turn. He's too close but luckily looking at the picture in my hand. "The musical one?"

He nods. "Boxing and music were his life."

His voice is almost wistful. I clear my throat. "Marcus said something about you boxing here at the university before."

His jaw tightens.

Does it bother him that Marcus and I talked about him? I lean a hip on the desk. "It was when you were in the cafeteria with all those boys."

He sets the basket filled with folded clothes on the chair in front of the desk. His expression eases as he crosses his arms and sits halfway on top of the desk. "Any sport at this level is a huge commitment, even out of season. I trained and studied, and that was about it. I missed life. I missed music. I was poorer than shit without a job. I decided to quit and start a band. It just made sense at the time."

I can't help a smile. "Well, music makes more sense to me than boxing."

"Me too," he says while his gaze goes back to the picture. "But it was a hard decision. My grandfather boxed for half his life. He never made it big, but he was good enough to make a living at it. He wanted me to go further than him, but I just didn't have the same drive for the sport as he did. But I do have that drive for music."

I lower the picture to my side. "So you want to take the band past college?" I joined to keep playing drums. The idea of anything bigger scares me.

He shakes his head. "I'm majoring in music. Minoring in business. I'm thinking of getting a master's degree in music technology and production next or something in a related field."

"You want to produce music?"

He shrugs. "I'm not sure, but a degree in performance seems useless to me."

I frown at him. I've considered a performance degree.

His lips twist into a slight smirk. "I'm not saying people shouldn't get a music degree, but I'm getting the experience I want through the band."

"Managing experience too?"

He nods.

I blink. "Um . . . wow, you have everything perfectly planned out."

"You must have some plans."

A miserable laugh escapes me. "My plan was to get to an out-of-state college and play the drums. Education was part of the package deal."

He raises a questioning brow.

"This is going to sound stupid, but back in freshman year of high school they drilled college down our throats. Probably hoping we'd become serious students. Well, it worked with me. I became obsessed with the idea of moving away and going to school. My parents had a modest college fund going for me. I was a good, not awesome, student. However, I did play the drums awesomely, and our school went to several competitions throughout the year." I shrug. "I became obsessed with getting a percussion scholarship."

His head tilts. "You did get one."

"I did, but things didn't work out."

"Your mom?"

I nod. "And my sister."

His eyes turn into melting dark chocolate as his warm gaze studies me. "That's pretty amazing for you to give up your dream for them."

"Ah yeah, it doesn't always feel amazing," I say as my cheeks heat. Feeling warmer by the second under his gaze, I set the picture on the shelf. "Between the scholarships and the band, I'm sure your grandfather's still proud of you even though you don't box."

"He would be."

"Oh . . ." My eyes round with the knowledge that his grandfather must have passed away. "I'm sorry."

He shakes his head. "Don't worry. It's been over five years."

I don't entirely believe his causal tone. Obviously, his grandfather was someone important in his life. "Well, you're still involved with boxing right? You were pretty impressive keeping that group of boys controlled."

"I'm shocked," he says with a grin.

"Why?" I say slowly, confused by his announcement.

He leans closer. "You, drummer extraordinaire, just complimented me."

Ah, so that was the reason for his astonishment. I lean over the desk too. "Was that a return compliment?"

His full mouth curls into a wide smile. "I believe it was."

My eyes lock on that mouth for two seconds too long. When I look up, Romeo is watching me. My whole body warms. "We should get back to studying."

His lashes lower. His full lips part. "We should," he says but sways just the tiniest bit closer.

I sway in too.

Anticipation and want sizzles in the air between us for several seconds, until the sound of someone turning the doorknob has us jumping apart.

Justin walks in. I'm in the corner next to the little fridge, and Romeo sits on the desk with his arms crossed. Justin looks back and forth at the two of us. "What's going on?"

Hell, my face burns at his words.

Romeo points to our calculus books on the floor. "We're just taking a break from studying."

I bend down and grab the first thing my fingers come into contact with in the fridge. Unscrewing the cap on the bottle of water, I let out a little laugh. "It's more like tutoring. I'm not doing too hot in the class," I say, hoping Justin will buy my embarrassment as academic.

Justin finally pulls his eyes from us, then moves to the mess on his dresser. "Well, you came to the right place. Nobody's as smart as Romeo," he says sarcastically.

Romeo gives him a level look.

I let out another little laugh. "Yeah, I just might pass tomorrow's test."

Justin plucks a beanie from the tumbling mound of stuff on his dresser before yanking out a jacket from the closet. "Sam's having a poker party at his apartment if you get done early." He opens the door. "Twenty will get you in."

"Um . . . maybe," I say, still feeling like an idiot.

Justin nods. "Later, losers," he says, shutting the door.

Running his hands violently through his hair, Romeo stands. "Fuck," he snarls, then turns and punches the wall.

The bottle almost slips from my grip as I step back and bump into the fridge.

"I told myself this wouldn't happen." He holds his fist. "Between the band and your boyfriend, I'm acting like a fucking idiot."

His actions and his words shock me, but two words have me completely confused. "My boyfriend?"

He gives me a cold look. "Goes by the name Marcus."

What the hell? "Marcus isn't my boyfriend."

His expression becomes shocked. "You broke up?"

I shake my head. "We've been friends since second grade. Nothing more."

He holds up one finger. "You guys practically cuddled at band tryouts." He holds up another finger. "Him getting busy with another girl had you shit crazy." He holds up a third finger. "I referred to you as his girlfriend and he never denied it."

I wince. Though I'm still upset about how he treated Chloe, I'd been feeling sorry for Marcus. Romeo's revelation has me pissed again.

"Marcus was never my boyfriend." I set the water on the desk. My hands fist on my hips. "You read the first two wrong. The third is a lie by omission. But how can you even spout this crap at me when it's obvious you're at least dating April?"

He crosses his arms, leans against the desk, and gives me a flat look. "I dated April last year, but we're just good friends now."

Everything inside of me pauses at that news.

Romeo sighs and folds his arms behind his neck. "None of this shit matters because if Sam or Justin ever knew we messed around . . ."

He doesn't finish the sentence and I don't tell him I know about his asinine pact from Justin. "I should go."

I start throwing stuff in my bag. The fact that he'd kick me out of the band if someone else hit on me pisses me off. That he's the one—manwhore Justin doesn't really count—who hit on me pisses me off more. Or maybe it was me who hit on him first. Whatever. "Let's just forget about this again." I stand slowly and meet Romeo's gaze even more slowly before lifting my chin. "And other than band practice and calculus, I think we should stay away from each other."

His eyes nearly burn me to the spot. His full lips are drawn into a thin line, but he only nods.

"Thanks for the help," I say over my shoulder before shutting the door.

I walk out of the building in a strange daze while replaying the last hour over in my head and trying to figure out where things went wrong. Of course, the almost kiss was the beginning of the end of our truce.

"Riley?"

About to open my car door, I look up to see Marcus getting out of his car. He rushes over to me. "What are you doing here?" His hopeful tone—he must be thinking I came to see him—helps defuse my anger at him.

"I was studying with Romeo. We have Calc Three together."

His face falls but he asks, "You're tutoring him?"

My laugh is miserable. "Ah no. I'm actually having trouble in that class."

He twirls his key ring around his finger and tries to look nonchalant. "Look, Riley, I'm sorry if I put you on the spot last night, but I'm not going to take it back. I'm bat-shit crazy about you. However, I won't pressure you or anything. Things can stay like they are. Or maybe you'll come to your senses," he adds with a grin.

His lame attempt at flirting has me gritting my teeth because no matter what he says, I'm 99 percent sure he doesn't like me that way. For some strange reason, he has talked himself into thinking I'm the one. "Tell me something, Marcus. Is there anyone other than Romeo who you let believe I was your girlfriend?"

His eyes round as his feet shuffle over the curb. "No . . . it's just that after we saw the band the first time he seemed to be fishing for information about you, which I thought was odd. So I let it slide when he referred to you as my girlfriend."

How many times can I want to junk punch him in twenty-four hours? "You were protecting me?"

"Yeah," Marcus agrees with a slow smile.

I unlock the car door and throw my book bag across to the passenger side. A multitude of bitchy wants to erupt out of my mouth. I check it. My relationship with Marcus is already heading into disaster. "Regardless of your feelings, please don't ever lie about me again."

Marcus's smile fades.

I shut the door, turn on the ignition, and back up without looking at my male best friend. My irritation turns to frustration as I drive home. Marcus thinks he's in love with me, but I'm pretty sure he's majorly interested in Chloe. He just can't seem to admit it to himself. Then there's Romeo. He may be a player, but I'm becoming aware the intense attraction between us isn't one-sided. And the fact he was asking about me after the first concert is beyond weird. We didn't even talk to each other that night. He just caught me staring and couldn't have been attracted to me. I looked like crap after skateboarding then crying. And that was before Chloe's makeover that everyone seems to find so sexy.

So why was he asking about me?

Chapter 20

Sam, Justin, and I sit in the tiny hotel lobby and wait for Romeo to check us in. I'm feeling guilty about not being with my sister on Halloween. My mom took the night off so she's taking Jamie trick-or-treating, but my sister had looked crushed when she found out I wasn't coming. However, not only is this our best paying gig so far, it's our biggest one. The venue is in a Detroit suburb, and it took us forever to get here, with Sam sleeping on my shoulder and drooling on me most of the way. Romeo drove the van. Justin sat in the passenger seat. They talked about set variations for the entire two hours. Every time Justin would turn around and try to relieve me of boredom, Romeo had another suggestion. He can talk band shit forever.

My phone beeps with a text.

Chloe: Sorry, I couldn't make it. You'd better wear my outfit. Beat the shit out of those drums for me. Love ya and happy Fright Night!

Since I'm getting my own room, I begged Chloe to come. Unfortunately, her full-time cosmetology course runs every other Saturday until four o'clock, and we had to leave by two. I'm about to text her back but Romeo returns.

"We've got a problem," he says to us all but his eyes are on me. "They're booked. We can only get two rooms."

"Well, then I'll stay with Riley," Justin immediately says.

"I don't think so," Romeo says tightly.

Sam winks at me. "I can then."

Romeo reaches for his bag. "Not going to happen."

"So you're staying with her? That's bullshit. Why do you get to decide?" Justin turns to me. "Who do you want to room with?"

"I . . ." The thought of sleeping in the same room with Romeo has my heart pounding in hormonal dread. But to pick Justin or Sam instead would be band-harmony suicide. "I'm not answering that. It's similar to a girl asking a guy if her butt looks big."

Justin and Sam laugh.

"She's staying in my room, so drop it," Romeo says in the same tone of authority he uses at practice. He hands Justin the standard envelope with keys tucked inside and the room number scrawled across the hotel logo. "You're on the third floor. We're on the fifth. Be back down here in an hour and we'll go over the set plan one more time."

With that Romeo turns toward the elevator. I grab my bag and run after him. "What's your problem?" I ask as the elevator doors close.

"I don't like this."

"So why didn't you put me in Sam's room?" I say because he probably is the least of my worries. Though he constantly flirts, he has never truly hit on me. Can't say that about the other two.

"You're not staying with either of them."

"Why?"

"Because I don't trust them," he says, stepping out of the elevator.

"Oh, and you trust yourself?" I say sarcastically, following him. His narrowed look over his shoulder has me adding, "Don't worry about me. Last weekend killed all Romeo-attracted hormones."

He slides a key card into the door. "Is that so?" he asks evenly.

"That wasn't a gauntlet. It's the truth," I say, lying and then sweeping into the room. I stop abruptly and he runs into me. "Why is there a whirlpool tub in our room?" My eyes round, taking in the king-size bed. "And why is there only one bed?" The question comes out in a screech.

Romeo throws his bag on the dresser. "This is all they had left." He gestures to the small couch. "And that folds out and into a bed."

"Okay . . . but why didn't you let them have this room?"

He cocks an eyebrow. "Justin and that tub together spell party. He'd invite as many girls as possible back to the room. There are not enough funds in a bona fide band account to pay for that mess."

I tilt my head in thought. My imagination agrees with Romeo. "All right, I'll take the couch."

He shakes his head. "You can have the bed."

"No, really. You're a lot bigger. The couch will be fine."

He glances at the clock next to the huge bed. "We don't have time to argue. It's almost six and we go onstage at nine. For once we're the opening band. I need fifteen minutes to get ready. That leaves you with about thirty. So get going."

Rolling my eyes at Mr. Business, I head to the bathroom.

He's sitting on the couch when I come out. His eyes flick from the TV to me and grow huge. I'm wearing black hot pants over black tights, black combat boots, enough black eyeliner for three people, a tight silver-sequined tank top, and a headband with silver bunny ears. As his eyes roam, a smirk threatens to escape me, but I somehow keep a blank face. "Bathroom's all yours," I say lightly.

He gets up and stalks over to me. My heart thuds. He stops inches from me and my chest goes into overdrive. He leans forward. I'm hyperventilating at the thought of his lips on mine, but all he does is peek over my shoulder. "Oh, hell no. I'm going to be beating guys off you all night with your drum sticks."

Though I highly doubt that, I ignore the continued thudding in my chest from his proximity. "Because of a silver fluffy tail?" I ask, referring to Chloe's sewing job.

He looks at me hard. "You should change."

"Chloe is the only one I allow to tell me how to dress. And that's usually a fight. Besides, it's not even that revealing, and it *is* Halloween." His eyes turn harder. I adjust my ears. "Your fifteen minutes is inching closer to ten."

He stalks past me and the bathroom door slams.

I have a feeling it's going to be a long, long night.

The venue is huge. An endless bar runs the entire back wall. The crowd is wild and drunk and dancing. I'm sweaty and exhilarated. Silver sequins stick to my skin. The set has been one long burst of energy, bouncing back and forth from the band to the mob of people dressed up in every costume imaginable. My drumming bubble combined with the crowd has been therapeutic after a long, tension-filled week.

Wearing an open white shirt, black eyeliner, and a long scarf on his head, pirate Justin goes on about what a great crowd they've been and how we'd love to play all night. Blah. Blah. Blah. I suck down water. Dressed in their normal black attire, Romeo and Sam stand with their instruments hanging from their necks and wait for our singer to shut up.

Justin finally raises his arms.

The lights dim and a spotlight hits Romeo as he breaks into a charging riff. Justin starts singing, and as he says the word *slide,* I begin pounding. The lights hit Justin, then me. He sings louder. Romeo's guitar chords grow in volume. Sam joins in. My beating increases in a crescendo and soon we're thrashing out "Helter Skelter" by the Beatles as the crowd goes wild.

Energy pulses through me, from both the playing and the crowd. I love this. Romeo was right. This is the perfect ending song for a Halloween set. He has a talent for song choices. He doesn't pick trendy. He picks what he knows we'll do well.

Unfortunately, the song ends. We do our bow thing while the energy from playing and the crowd have me buzzing. The mass of people in front of us shout and clap like never-ending thunder and then chant for more, but the next band is scheduled to come on in half an hour.

Behind the massive stage, the second band congratulates us on our performance as the stagehands remove our gear. Sam opens a bottle of vodka and we pass it around before going to help pack up Romeo's van. Once the van is crammed full of our gear, a stagehand leads us to a VIP section at one side of the stage. A waitress dressed in a cat costume hands us bottled beers—I'm guessing the masses get plastic cups instead of glass—as the twenty-odd people already in the section swarm around us. Well, mostly the girls. Statements of our awesomeness reverberate around me. Along with echoes of where to find our stuff online to download. I move toward the back and lean on a speaker. The excitement and adoration is skeeving me out. But Romeo, Sam, and especially Justin seem to bask in it. Or maybe they're basking in the female attention.

The second band starts and the attention turns from our little corner toward the stage. I sip on my beer and watch the other band. They're not as good as we are, but they're loud, energetic, and local. After the surge of energy from playing, I'm looking forward to being a spectator.

Girls bop to the hard music and cling to my bandmates while a guy slides over to me and yells in my ear, "I liked watching you drum better!"

I give him a smile and sip my beer.

By the next song, there's another guy at my side. Both randomly yell in my ear about the band playing or asking questions about my band. One appears college aged. The other closer to thirty. Between their lips close to my ears and their bodies brushing mine, I'm becoming uncomfortable. And the sight five feet in front of me—two girls dressed in skimpy witch outfits hanging on Romeo—isn't helping.

Another round of beer comes. Still sipping my first, I decline.

Three songs in, Mr. Over Thirty starts wrapping his arm around my waist whenever he bends toward me to ask a question. He's bending in and wrapping while I watch Romeo stoop down to hear what the girl next to him is saying. She holds her hat and tilts her head. Romeo's wayward lock of hair hangs forward, obscuring his eyes until he looks over his shoulder. His upper lip curls as he stares at the old man and me together. I have no idea what the idiot next to me just said, but I give him a smile.

The night continues with this stupidity. Between the girls on Romeo and the guys next to me, I can't even enjoy the music. I escape to the bathroom when right-side witch tucks her hand under the edge of Romeo's belt and into his jeans right above his ass.

Lucky for me, the room is empty. I pace in front of the stalls and silently pep talk myself into ignoring Romeo. I should not be paying attention to him. I should not be jealous. Heck, I haven't even noticed what Sam and Justin are doing. My infatuation—there, I admitted it—with Romeo needs to stop for more than one reason. The band being the first. Him being a player the second. And last, since I'm sleeping in the same room with him tonight.

I step out of the bathroom and I'm only partially surprised to see Mr. Over Thirty leaning against the wall of the hallway. "There you are," he says with a lazy smile. "Thought you might have gotten lost."

"Just taking a break," I say, and spin toward the stage.

"Damn," he says catching up to me. "That is hot." His hand slides from the back of my thigh over the curve of my butt to grab my tail.

My head snaps and my eyes widen on the guy's smirk. Before I can smack him or push him or whatever my shocked mind had in store, a blur of black and muscle slams him into the wall. "Fucking pig," Romeo snarls into the man's face.

The man wheezes against Romeo's forearm pressed against his throat.

"You like copping feels? Huh?" Romeo shoves harder.

The man gasps for air.

Shocked out of stunned by the violence in front of me, I tug on Romeo's arm. "Okay, let him go. He can't breathe."

Romeo eyes narrow on the man gasping for breath.

My grip tightens. "Romeo!"

Finally, he lets go and steps back. "Get the fuck out of here."

Holding his throat, the man rushes toward the stage.

Romeo continues staring at the wall.

"Um . . . I guess I should say thanks but that was a bit intense." My fingers are still on his arm. I drop my hand. "You okay?"

He nods but doesn't look at me.

"I guess we should head back." I pivot toward the club.

He grabs my elbow. "I came back here to tell you I was leaving." He gestures with his chin toward the stage. "Those two are getting a taxi later."

"Oh," I say, realizing he means for me to decide if I want to stay. Go back and deal with being in a room alone with him or go back to where Mr. Over Thirty is. I yank my bunny ears off. "Guess I'm ready to go."

Chapter 21

Everything was an awkward argument. We both offered the other the king bed. We both offered the other the shower first. Finally—we could have been sleeping by the time we reached an agreement—we compromised. I got the bed. He got the shower first. After blow-drying my hair to damp, I brush my teeth and groan at my reflection. Thinking I'd be alone, I grabbed the first set of pajamas in my drawer without a thought. I'm wearing a red tank top and matching sleep shorts dotted with hearts. A clearance deal my mother bought after Valentine's Day last year. I keep telling myself a bathing suit is more revealing, but the damn shorts are super short. And I have to cross the entire *fucking* room to get to that huge bed.

I shove my brush in my bag, take a deep breath, open the door, set off in a sprint, and run right into Romeo standing in front of the TV.

"Whoa," he says, grabbing me by the shoulders so I don't fall. My hands are on his naked, hard chest. Apparently, just flannels constitute sleepwear for him. "Why are you moving so fast?" His eyes sweep down. Way. Too. Slow. "Ah . . . nice pajamas."

My hands push at his warm chest. "Shut up," I say, probably turning as red as my top.

"No, really, I like them." His mouth curves into a smirk, but when his eyes meet mine, there is no laughter in them. Instead there's a heat shining in their dark depths that sizzles through me.

My hands quit pushing at his chest, spreading over his skin instead. The lines of his face tense. The feel of warm skin over heavy muscles under my palms has sweaty images running wild in my head. His breath catches as he watches me and the evident thoughts flashing through my eyes.

I tell myself to step away. Now. My feet don't move. His hands slide from my shoulders to my upper arms. I could be imagining it, but the movement feels like a caress. I lean closer.

His eyes flare with want and he yanks me forward.

Oh shit! I think before our mouths connect—more like slam together—and teeth clink. Our tongues tangle and slide against each other while our hands yank and grasp. I'm hyperaware of every eager touch. His fingers gripping and pressing into my hipbones. The hard chest pushing against mine. The tight line of his muscles as I dig my fingers into the back of his neck. Our bodies pressed closely together as our mouths move in a heated tune. The long kiss is wild and messy and desperate and wonderful. And perhaps inevitable. Maybe wrong but inevitable.

Tearing his mouth from mine, he catches my waist, and before I can even figure out direction, he lifts me and sets my stunned body on the low dresser. His chest expands in a deep breath as he holds me there with his hands trapping mine against the dresser top next to my thighs.

My heart beats erratically in the silence. Anticipation hangs in the air between our heavy breathing. His dark hair hides his eyes until he lowers his head and I catch the intensity in his gaze before his teeth nibble on my bottom lip and then his tongue traces the curve of it. My shock dissolves as I melt into him. He lets go of my hands to reach up and gently cup my face as his mouth again devours mine.

We kiss deeply while our fingers explore skin. His under my tank on the curve of my waist. Mine find the ridges of his abdomen. His trace the angles of my ribs. Mine discover the hard mass of his pectorals on either side of the ever-present necklace that hangs from his neck. With each touch we inch closer until I wrap my legs around his waist and lock my ankles behind him. Our kiss goes back to the frenzy of the first. He pushes into the V of my legs and his hands cup my breasts.

My gasp breaks the kiss. I gasp again at the hard, rubbing pressure of him between my legs mixed with the sensation of his calloused palms on my skin. "The bed. Move to the bed," I say within a rush of air.

He buries his head into the spot where my shoulder meets my neck. His hands grip my waist tightly as he draws in a deep breath. The release of air warms my skin while the shake of his head has his dark hair tickling my collarbone. "I don't have a condom," he says harshly.

His words slowly break into my haze of lust. Is that what I was thinking? Me, who made Aaron wait seven months? Yes it was. "How could *you* not have a condom?"

"I don't carry them."

"What?" I say in a long screech, and the bubble of desire I'd been in bursts. My legs drop to the dresser.

His hands slip out of my tank top and he steps away.

My fingers dig into my thighs. "Um . . . are you looking for a disease or a baby's momma?"

He slowly sits on the edge of the ceramic tile around the whirlpool tub. Bending over, he lowers his elbows to his knees and steeples his hands over his face. The muscles of his back ripple with his deep inhalations.

It slowly dawns on my dumb ass that he's unworking what we worked up. I lean back against the wall and rub my temples.

"It's not like that," he finally says, sitting up, lifting a knee, and draping an arm around his leg. His long musician's fingers wrap around a flannel-clad shin.

"Um . . . non-condom use will probably result in one or the other. Maybe both."

He rests his chin on his knee. "Contrary to popular belief I'm not like Justin or even Sam. I don't sleep around. Thus the need for carrying condoms is unneeded."

He watches as confusion filters across my face. He has no reason to lie. It's not like he's trying to get in my pants. Rather the exact opposite. I recall him coming back alone to the dorm the first night we kissed. I remember him leaving the bar alone. But then I recall all of the girls hanging on him, including the two tonight. "Then why do you let girls hang all over you?"

He shrugs. "It's expected. I'm in a band."

My brows lower. "So you play the part?"

He nods.

I think of Kendra's confusion at his flirting. "Ugh. Just when I'm starting to think you're not an asshole."

His full lips flatten as he gives me a questioning look.

"You're leading them on."

"I let them hang on me and flirt a little. I'm not promising them anything. And I'm sure as shit not Justin, fucking them and then moving on to the next one."

"Still," I say stubbornly.

"What if they came on to me and I ignored them? How do you think *that* would go over?"

"As long as the band remains popular, girls and their feelings are a means to an end?"

He runs a hand through his hair and the sexy flop that usually threatens to cover one eye stands at an angle. "I work my ass off to keep the band going. Justin sings. Sam plays. You play. I set everything up. I spend hours on the phone with contacts. I listen to music mostly for research instead of pleasure. I'm constantly at meetings for possible gigs. I'm not going to let pissed-off fan girls screw with what I've built. It's not exactly easy telling a girl who has some ridiculous notion about you after seeing you onstage that you're not interested."

Unrequited love—more like lust here—isn't easy to deal with. Heck, my Marcus letdown wasn't too suave. But Romeo's band mentality is overboard as usual. I love playing in the band, but the band seems to rule his life. And because of that, I'm guessing that tonight is a onetime thing. It should be a onetime thing. Or I guess it's a second-time thing. "Well, maybe you could tone it down. You must have when you dated April."

He nods. "It's easier when you have a girlfriend. I do try to keep the flirting to a minimum. I don't like fucking with people, but since the girls who hit on me have this preconceived notion about guys in a band, they tend to be a bit forward. So I just go with the flow and try to keep it light." After giving me a look that conveys the conversation is over, he drops his knee, turns, and flips on the water.

As the sound of rushing water fills the room, I'm about to ask him why he's filling the tub—because he is *not* filling that tub or getting into it in a condomless environment—but spotting the ink across his ribs, I blurt, "You do have a tattoo."

He reaches down and sets the plug while looking over his shoulder but doesn't reply.

Engrossed by the sight of the elegant lines that start and end with a Celtic symbol covering one side of his ribs, I stand. Instinctively I'm aware his hidden tattoo, unlike Justin's noticeable body art, means something. "What does it say?"

He turns back to the tub and runs a hand under the water, checking the temperature. "It's from a song."

"What song?"

"'Raglan Road.'"

"I've never heard of it."

"It's an Irish folk tune."

"What are the lyrics on your skin?" I ask persistently.

He sighs, then says: "That I had loved, not as I should/A creature made of clay,/When the angel woos the clay, he'll lose/His wings at the dawn of day."

My palms flatten behind me on the dresser at the realization that someone broke his heart. More important, I'm wondering if she still holds it. "Why those words?"

He faces the water, yet I can see his pensive expression in the mirror on the wall behind the tub. "It was my grandfather's favorite song. I played it at his funeral. My mother sang."

"Oh . . . that's both lovely and sad." Though I'm beginning to understand how much Romeo's grandfather means to him, I'm not sold those haunting words don't represent something else.

The blast of water fills the silence until Romeo turns it off, stands, and flips on the jets.

I cross my arms and give him a level look. "Don't tell me you're getting in there."

He shrugs. "I'm feeling a bit tense. Might as well use the facilities." He gives me a half smirk. "Want to join me?"

I lower my chin.

Copying me, he lowers his chin and meets my stare. "I'm not the one who suggested we move to the bed."

Humiliation hums under my stern expression but he does have a point.

"I'll wear my boxers. You must have something that represents a swimsuit," he says, obviously referring to underwear. His eyes glint with a look of challenge. "And maybe we should talk about this." He rocks his index finger and thumb between us.

That glint of challenge is what does me in.

Steam rolls off the whirling water. Romeo and I sit across from each other. Though we both sit diagonally, our limbs brush every now and then. I can see the blur of his blue boxers through the bubbling water, but by the time I'd found enough bravado to exit the bathroom in a black sports bra and black panties I'd worn under my costume, he'd already entered the tub. Cute Riley would have jumped in that tub before four beats of a drum. But the Riley who believed Romeo when he said she was beautiful took her time. His eyes roamed, burned into my body, as I dipped a foot in the tub, then slowly stepped over the edge and even more slowly lowered myself into the water. However, he lay back and closed his eyes with a content sigh as soon as the water covered me.

The swirl of the water is the only sound in the room except for the splash when I reach up and tighten my messy bun. I might as well be alone except for the infrequent brush of his thigh. Supposedly, we were going to talk. After almost ten minutes of silence, I decide *I'm* going to talk.

"So you've never, ever had a one-night stand while in the band?" I ask incredulously.

"None," he says, slowly opening his eyes.

I can't stop the huff of disbelief that escapes me. Two years of girls throwing themselves at him and not even once?

At the look of skepticism on my face, he moves toward me and water sloshes. He pulls me by the waist until my legs overlap his and we're sitting in the center of the tub. My eyes grow huge at the contact of our skin and the intensity of his gaze.

He leans closer. A flaring hunger scorches in the depths of his dark eyes. "Sex can be lust, but it can be so much more when trust and respect and affection are layered into it." His lashes lower and his wet finger traces my lips. "I once had enough lust to last a lifetime." His calloused palm presses against my cheek. Dark eyes burn into mine. Burn into me and sear me with their heat. "I want the more," he says huskily before his lips cover mine in a searching kiss.

My head spins from both his words and his lips. If I was confused, I'm brainless now. Who gave him all that sex? April? And who does he want the *more* from? Me? He sucks on my upper lip. Yeah, a good guess would be me. I push at his shoulders and break the kiss with a gasp. "What about the band?"

His hands cup my shoulders as his lips curve into a frown. "I wanted you since that first time I saw you play. The other reasons I told you about not wanting you in the band were true, but that was the strongest one. I knew you were going to drive all three of us nuts, but especially me. The deal was no girl drummer unless we all agreed to keep our hands off."

Since I already knew this, I just nod. It's really all I can do after his admission of wanting me since seeing me play.

He leans his forehead against mine. "Please don't take this the wrong way, but could we just see how things go before we let them know about us?"

The gurgle of the tub whirls around us along with a hazy steam, and like our passion earlier it feels like we're separated from the world.

"You want me to be your dirty little secret?"

He rears back and his expression turns contrite. "Ah, Riley, I'm sorry about that. It's just . . ."

A laugh escapes me—I can't hold it in any longer. One, because of his regretful look. And two, because I'm relieved that this isn't a onetime thing. I'm relieved and ecstatic there is an us.

His brows lower in confusion.

I rein in my laughter. "What's between us isn't really any of their business."

His full lips curl into a smirk. "Did you just play me?"

"Yes. I am a bit dirty," I say, pulling at his necklace until he bends. I smile against his mouth and his wide eyes close at the touch of my lips.

Chapter 22

I wake to bliss—I'm lying in Romeo's arms—and to torment —someone is pounding the shit out of the door to our room. We both sit up at the same time, but Romeo jumps out of bed first.

"Fuck. That has to be one of them." His shocked eyes travel around the room. "Take care of the bathroom. I'll get the couch."

He wrestles with the couch while I pick up towels on my way to the bathroom. I yank my damp bra and panties and then his boxers off the shower rod. After a tame—compared to earlier in the night—make-out session until the water got cold, we both changed then fell into an exhausted snuggle. The thought of Sam or Justin showing up in the morning didn't cross our minds. Now it's on our minds. Big time.

The addition of shouting reveals Sam is the one pounding on the door.

After shoving damp underwear into my bag, I ask Romeo, "You ready?"

He dives onto the open couch. "You'd better not let him see you in those pj's for more than two seconds."

I roll my eyes and go to the door. My fingers fumble with the chain longer than necessary. "What the hell? Is the Mafia after you?" I mumble, opening the door.

"Whoa," Sam says with a whistle. "I like the little nightie thing."

"Shut up," I say, stepping into the bathroom. "It's shorts."

While I brush my teeth and get dressed, I can hear Sam exclaiming something about a hot tub, something about a hot drummer, and something about Romeo being gay. My vote is a definite no on that one.

They're watching TV when I return from the bathroom. Romeo's still lying on the fold-out bed and Sam is sitting on the edge of the king bed. He frowns at my sweatshirt and jeans. "I liked the nightie better or maybe that outfit from last night."

Ignoring his clothing choices for me, I ask, "Where's Justin?"

"MIA. Went home with some girl last night." He throws a pillow at Romeo. "Get in the shower so we can go to breakfast. They have a diner attached to the hotel on the first floor."

Romeo gives him the finger but gets up.

During most of breakfast, Romeo ignores me as usual. Sam flirts. Romeo looks like he wants to stab him. The diner is busy. The food greasy. I start hungry but as Romeo keeps ignoring me, I push scrambled eggs and hash browns around my plate.

Romeo sends Sam to pay the bill, then leans over his plate. "I'm sorry. This is harder than I thought it would be."

I wave my fork. "Don't worry. I get it. But I'm going to be honest. I can only deal with the pretending crap for so long."

Nodding, he tears open a sugar packet. "You're not the only one." He stirs the sugar into his coffee while studying me with darkening eyes. "Want to study together tonight?"

Studying with him in the dorm room he shares with Justin could be dangerous.

As if reading my thoughts, he says, "I could come to your house."

Sam slides into the booth. He looks at Romeo suspiciously. "Why are you going to Riley's?"

I shove my plate away. "Because I'm close to failing calculus."

Sam rolls his eyes. "Ah, as usual boy genius to the rescue."

Romeo's only response is an eyebrow arch. Probably at the *boy* reference.

After breakfast we go back to the hotel and wait in the lobby for Justin to show up. We wait awhile. Romeo sends him several texts warning that if he isn't back within a certain amount of time, he'll need to find a different ride home. Justin shows up later than all the times threatened. Looking rough, with bloodshot eyes, he grins at Romeo's scowl.

The ride back isn't much different from the ride to the gig. Sam sleeps on me. Romeo and Justin talk band business in the front.

Romeo drops me off first. The house is empty. My mother left a note on the counter about her and Jamie going to the library and then to dinner. Sunday is the one day each week my mother still acts like a mother. Well, sort of. Cooking seems to be beyond her skill set of late.

Later when I'm in the laundry room off the kitchen trying to make a dent in the mountain of dirty clothes that grew overnight, I get a text from Romeo about him coming over in an hour.

I stare at the text like it's an alien life form. Though we all have each other's numbers since we're in a band together, I've never called or texted any of them. Especially not Romeo. The sight of his name over the text brings reality to me more than last night, more than this morning. I'm seeing Romeo. As in dating. As in possible boy-friend. As in holy hell what am I doing?

I sink to the bench below hooks covered with raincoats and scarfs. Deep, deep down I want Romeo with an intensity that borders on insanity. But then there's the band. The multitude of girls who hang on him. And last, my sorry little heart that Aaron stomped on. He may not have crushed the organ, but he sure as hell bruised it. Those bruises have *almost* faded away.

My fingers tap out a beat on the edge of the bench.

I'm an adult. Lately, I run a household. I'm going to be nineteen soon. I should be able to date a hot, slightly moody guitar player without falling in over my head.

Yet strangely, the fact that he doesn't sleep around and doesn't really date has me worried. Because of all the girls he could have, why me? What draws him to me? That I drum? That I don't appear—even though I am—in awe of him? I'm afraid that whatever's attracting him will soon fade away.

My fingers stop their rhythm.

I need to keep this light, fun, and carefree.

I can't fall too hard. I can't let it feel as deep as it already does.

"Ah-ha!" I say, snapping the back of the book closed. "I'm right. You're wrong." I flick Romeo's paper with a finger and it falls off the counter.

He quickly shuffles to the answers in the back of the book. "Damn. That's a first." He snatches my paper and picks his up from the floor.

While he compares the two, I go to the fridge and fill two glasses with ice and water. Setting them down in front of our mess on the counter, I smirk at his wrinkled brow. "Figure out where you screwed up yet?"

"Yeah, I forgot to take the derivative the third time."

I feign a look of surprise and move around the kitchen island. "Genius boy forgot?"

Perched on a stool, he swivels and pulls me between his legs by the belt loops of my jeans. "Did you just call me a boy?"

A grin explodes across my mouth. "I believe I did."

He removes the grin off my lips with a hard, deep kiss. "Did that feel like a boy?"

I brace my hands on his thighs. "That felt very manly. And pretty damn hot," I add, inching closer to him.

He groans and drops his forehead to mine. "What am I going to do with you?"

"Should I answer that?"

He shakes his head. "Not when we're in a house alone."

I drown in the lustful thoughts that flip-flop between our gazes, but my mother and sister could come home at any second. "Should I call you Justin now? When we're alone at least?"

"Ah no. After living with Justin for over two years, I like Romeo better." His hands tighten at my waist. "We should tell the guys. Hiding like this . . . I feel disrespectful to you and to them."

The mood suddenly changes with those words. I step back and sit on the stool next to him while he watches me. "Today sucked, but usually the only time I'm around is at practice." I slide my textbook closer to the edge of the counter. "I think you were right last night. Let's wait it out and see how things go. There's no reason to get everyone riled up before anything's . . . real."

His dark eyes pin me to my stool. "This feels real."

Under the intensity of his stare, I'm wondering how to respond to that when the door to the garage opens. "Romeo's here!" Jamie squeals.

I introduce him to my mother while Jamie bounces around him. My mother is polite but seems disinterested, which is totally different from the way she acted when I brought Aaron home the first time. With Aaron, she hovered and questioned. She's almost dismissive with Romeo. I'm not sure if her indifference is because

I'm technically an adult or if she can't care about anything outside of her bubble of depression, but her reaction bothers me.

Jamie brings her DS to the kitchen. My mother, seeing we're studying, takes her upstairs for a movie. Fortunately, the seriousness that hovered between Romeo and me is absent as we finish going over the sections for tomorrow's quiz.

At almost ten o'clock, I walk him to his van, which is parked in the street. After he tosses his books inside, he reaches for my wrist, but I step back. "I wouldn't do that here."

He cocks his head in question and that angled fringe of hair falls over his eye.

"Marcus lives across the street, two houses down. And though he's at the dorm, someone in his family might see and say something."

He lifts his chin and his jaw tightens. "So we're going with the dirty little secret thing?"

"Though I don't like this pretending crap, I'm just not ready to deal with Justin and Sam yet."

His expression is conflicted, but he says, "All right, I'll see you tomorrow."

I go to the sidewalk and wave to him as he drives away. I actually don't want to deal with Sam or Justin, but the truth is I'm not ready to make Romeo and me official yet.

Chapter 23

I finish the last problem on the calculus quiz with confidence. Professor Hill likes to save the fun for the end of the class. However, as I pack up my bag and slip on a jacket, my nervousness about my grade sets in. The professor will hand back last week's test when I hand in the quiz. Tests are worth 50 percent of the grade. If I didn't do well, my college career will start out in a slump. Taking in a deep breath of courage, I march past the last two people still quizzing and plop my quiz on the pile with the others.

Professor Hill looks at me through thick glasses. "Riley Middleton, right?" he asks quietly. After I nod, he shuffles through the papers and hands me the test.

"Thanks," I mutter, turning away and lifting up the stapled mass of paper. The score on the top has me rushing into the hall to find Romeo.

He waits near the door to the outside entrance. No surprise, two girls are talking to him. But as I get closer, I am surprised when one of them turns her head in a giggle. Kendra obviously is still hoping for a fuck fest. Ah yeah, over my dead body.

I shake my head at Romeo as he tries to break away from his stalkers.

He seems to get my point, because he stays put. Yet when I pass, he yells out, "Hey, Riley, you said you'd give me a ride to . . . the mall!"

To the mall? That was lame. I stop and force a confused look. "Oh yeah, I almost forgot." That was even lamer. In fact, this whole secret thing is lame every time it comes up.

Kendra turns toward me. "Hey, Riley." She gestures toward Romeo with an eye roll. "We should meet you at the mall."

My hand tightens on the strap of my bag. "Ah . . ."

Romeo steps between the two girls. "We should, but we'll have to do it another time. We have a . . . quick band errand to run."

Kendra visibly deflates. Her tall, pretty friend, whom I've never met, stares at Romeo as he slides up to me.

We step away and Kendra yells, "Call me later, Riley!"

I quickly slip out the doors to cut off a possible answer.

A few steps into the brisk wind of the day, I'm glancing at Romeo's profile as we walk along the sidewalk that leads to the parking lot. "She asked you about a girlfriend didn't she? And you told her you didn't have one."

His head snaps up. "I thought we were hush-hush."

"She was asking about April." That he thinks I'm referring to me is a bit scary.

"You told her I was dating April?" he asks as his winged brows meet.

"I thought you were when she didn't understand your flirting then quick departure."

He nods slowly. "Guess I do need to tone it down."

I give him a look. There is no way in hell I'm going to watch girls hang all over him now.

"Like to an almost nonexistent level."

"Ah, I knew you were smart." Stopping at the curb, I lift my test up. "Look at this."

"A ninety," he says with a lopsided grin that threatens to steal my breath. "I think I deserve a kiss for that."

I grin back. "I think you do too. But *not* here."

His eyes roam over me slowly. Slow enough that I can feel the heat of his gaze in the brisk wind. "We should celebrate."

"Thought you had work."

"I have two training sessions tonight but not until seven."

The temptation wanes as I think of the time. "I have to pick up my sister." My mother usually picks Jamie up on Mondays since it's her other day off, but today she has a counseling appointment at the Child and Family Services Center. I had to nag and beg, but she finally made the appointment.

"We could pick her up and take her with us. You'd just have to bring me back by six thirty."

Temptation becomes sweet reality. "Okay, but we're not going to the mall."

"How about pizza at your house?"

I grin at him. "Pizza at my house would be perfect."

On the way to pick up my sister, about two miles from the university, Romeo reaches across me at a four-way stop and puts the car into park. Confused, I turn to him.

He grins. "Time for my tutoring reward."

I'm grinning too. At least for a quick second.

He wraps a hand around the back of my neck. His strong fingers press me closer. His lips first suck on mine, then he sweeps his tongue in for a thorough kiss.

A horn sounds behind us but his kiss has me prisoner.

He lets me go.

The horn blares again.

My eyes flutter open and stare into those nearly ebony eyes. "That was nice." I touch my lips. "As in sizzling."

He sits back, a smug expression on his face. "Maybe you should drive."

I shift the car out of park.

The person behind us holds the horn down.

"Yeah, yeah, I'm driving," I say, and wave behind me.

On the rest of the way to my sister's school, he looks through my iPod and randomly makes comments about drummers and their limited song choices. All loud banging and fast beats. And here I thought my music selection was eclectic.

We wait for Jamie until the long line in front of the sprawling elementary school is reduced to a handful of cars. Since she usually comes out with the first wave of students, her absence has me worried.

Romeo waits in the driver's side while I go into the school. The halls are nearly empty and she's not at her locker. Her classroom's empty of students too, but when her teacher sees me she smiles. "I figured you'd show up, Riley." Every time I come to this school I like Mrs. Hess more. She wowed me with her politeness at the open house—my mother couldn't attend—but right now she's confusing me.

She reaches for a stack of papers and books on her desk. "Here's the work. Depending on how she's feeling, she may not be able to get all of it done. Math and reading are the most important."

I meet her halfway across the room and take the pile. "Jamie didn't come to school today?"

She shakes her head. "Your mother must have called. The computer had her marked as an illness."

"Oh," I say, perplexed because Jamie was watching TV and bouncing around the living room when I left this morning. I tighten my grip on the stack of books. "Okay, I'll make sure she gets most of it done."

In the hallway, I'm on the phone with my mother in seconds. Her sigh is loud and irritating as I demand to know why Jamie didn't go to school.

"I overslept, all right?"

"Why didn't you bring her in late at least?" I ask, exiting the building.

"I only get one day off with her, Riley."

There's a long pause between us. I never missed school unless I was extremely sick—like deathbed sick. My mother drilled the importance of attendance into me for thirteen years, six of which I received an award for perfect attendance. But my mother's new-found irresponsibility isn't the biggest issue. "So you missed your counseling appointment."

She sighs again. "I can reschedule."

I wander to the lawn at the edge of the sidewalk and kick leaves. "So you haven't yet. What exactly did *you* do all day?"

"I think you're forgetting who the parent is."

"Well, it's kind of easy when you don't act like one," I snap.

She hangs up on me.

I get in the passenger seat, then toss Jamie's books *and* my phone in the backseat.

One look at my furious expression has Romeo saying, "I'm guessing the celebration has been canceled."

I yank at the seat belt.

He turns the key in the ignition. "And I'm guessing I'll be driving back to the dorms."

The seat-belt buckle snaps loudly into place. "I don't know who my mother is anymore."

He glances at me with a sad look but stays silent and drives.

I sink down in my seat and push my feet up against the glove box. "I used to wake up to bacon and pancakes. Now she doesn't get up. Holidays used to inspire a decorating frenzy. For Halloween she put one plastic pumpkin on the coffee table this year. Until I was in high school, she went over my homework with a fine-tooth comb. Now she's letting Jamie stay home on a whim."

Romeo keeps his gaze on the road but his mouth turns down. "Things like divorce or the death of a loved one are stressful and can change people, Riley. Is your mom going to counseling yet?"

My fingers rub my temples as I shake my head. "She was supposed to go today, but the not big *effing* surprise is that she didn't. I knew she'd find a way to weasel out of it."

"Sounds like she's afraid to go."

"No shit."

"You need to be patient with her."

"I am but for how long? How long does Jamie have to live with half or less of a mother?"

He gives me a pained glance before turning onto the highway.

"And I'm not her. I'm not Jamie's mother. I try to do what I can for both of them. But it's obviously not working! Everything is just getting worse!"

Suddenly, Romeo pulls off to the side of the road. He reaches for me and I fall into the warmth of his body with a shudder. Even with the console between us and the sound of cars whizzing by, I'm encased in tranquility. I breathe in his clean scent, press my face farther into his chest, and tighten my hold on his back. The world stops spinning as I let his embrace strengthen me. The highway disappears and there's nothing but Romeo and me.

Sometime later the earth rotates again when Romeo pulls a few inches away and tilts my chin up with a finger. "Better?"

I nod and fall back against the seat. He finds a song with a somewhat slower drumbeat before merging back onto the highway.

My fingers play the song on the dashboard as he drives to the dorm. He rolls his eyes at my playing but it calms me.

Romeo doesn't turn off the car when we pull in front of his building. He watches a few students coming and going before turning. "Will you call me if you need to talk?"

I nod slowly.

With his grip on the door handle, he asks, "You're coming to practice tomorrow?"

I reach for the passenger handle. "Of course, playing keeps me sane."

He smiles weakly and shakes his head. "And people say I'm obsessed. Can we do something after?"

At the thought of being alone with him, I can't help a wide smile. "Yes. I'd like that."

Chapter 24

Over the past week and a half, Romeo and I have seen two late-night movies and gone to a twenty-four-hour diner for coffee three times. After each outing—two after band practice—we fog up the windows of my car or his van. Then there are the late-night calls. Sometimes they're deep and thoughtful and revealing. I could listen to Romeo talk about his musical, boxing grandfather for hours. The only person he respects more is his hardworking single mother. He understands my conflicted feelings about my father—the man he is as opposed to the man he was.

Other times we stray into insignificant and silly. I text him pictures of my drumstick collection. He raps old Celtic songs to me over the phone. We argue over music. He likes the new wave of folksy stuff like Mumford & Sons and the Black Keys. I'm into classics like the Beastie Boys and Nirvana. Strangely, our taste in music rarely connects. Yet when we're together, we exist on an island for two where sincerity and benevolence are intertwined in the warm breeze. And while I try to tell myself our secrecy is keeping things slow, my heart feels like it's falling way too fast.

Especially when he touches me.

And as usual, he's trying to touch me as we walk through the theater parking lot.

He reaches for my hand. I smack his shoulder. "Stop it before someone sees," I hiss, then add, "You already held it for the entire movie." And did sexy things with his fingers the whole time. Who knew the brush of a thumb on a wrist could be hot? I never imagined such a thing before. Now I'll be imagining it all the time.

He shrugs. "We're already here together. So what if someone sees us?"

"Well, hand holding is not as easy to explain as two friends going to a movie."

He gives me a level look but doesn't reply until we get to his van in the last row of cars. Then his reply comes in the form of pressing me against the cold side of his vehicle and kissing me hard and long until I'm gasping for breath. He steps back, panting into the cool night air. "Did that feel like a *friend?*"

Under the dim parking lights, the hard lines of his face twisted in anger make him look sexier than usual. And his usual is pretty damn sexy. I yank a lapel of his black wool coat and he's close again. "That felt like the guy I can't stop imagining about."

His dark eyes flare. "Tuesday you should come to the dorm after practice."

"What about Justin?"

He shrugs. "He always stays until the bar closes."

I give him a skeptical look.

He places a hand on the side of the van next to my head and leans near my ear. "I'll play the fiddle for you."

Now that is more temptation than I can handle. "All right, you win," I say, thinking I'll have to park in a different dorm lot because of Marcus.

His lips brush the skin of my neck. "Early night, right?"

I nod as a shiver runs through me. I'm not sure getting home after midnight constitutes an early night. "Eight o'clock class tomorrow morning."

He straightens his arm and looks down at me. "I'm booked tomorrow so except for calculus . . ." He sighs. "It's going to be a long wait for Tuesday night."

This is why I'm falling so fast. His wistful eyes and impatience to be with me. The almost tangible pull between us. The dark scruff of his jaw. His thumb caressing my wrist. The tone of his voice when he talks about his family. Okay, every single thing about him has me falling too fast.

"Riley?" Someone shouts across the row of cars.

I push away from the van and Romeo to see Marcus staring at me from over the roof of his car. His roommate, Dan or something, stares too.

Shit. "Hey, Marcus." I step toward my car parked next to Romeo's van. "What's up? What movie did you guys see?"

He says some title but all I'm aware of is the burn of Romeo's scornful gaze on me. I'm hardly aware of Marcus's question about what movie I watched, but as his words come closer, I break my stare with Romeo.

"So what movie did you guys see?" Marcus asks again mere feet from me.

"Later, Riley," Romeo brusquely says from behind.

I wave a hand but don't turn around. "Um, some crazy action thing. I can't even remember the name of it." Admitting Romeo and I went to some chick flick spells *d-a-t-e* more clearly than us standing close in the parking lot.

Romeo's van starts and his lights shine over us as he backs out. A long honk sounds before he drives off.

Marcus's eyes turn to slits. "Hey, Don, could you give me a minute here." He holds out his keys.

"It's late. I need to get home," I say, desperately not wanting to have the coming conversation.

Marcus shakes the keys. "I just want to talk to you for a few minutes."

He steps closer after Don takes the keys and walks off. "How long has this been going on? Is he the reason your shirt was backward that morning? Did you make up that shit about him wanting you to quit?" He swallows tightly. "Is this why you've been ignoring me?"

I want to snap that whom I date is none of his business, but the hurt etched into his usually amiable features stops me. "You know why I haven't called you. It has nothing to do with Romeo. Have you even thought about what I told you about Chloe?"

"Chloe was a mistake," he says firmly.

"Really?" I cross my arms and give him a sardonic look. "Because half of our high school could have slept with the other half, but the only person you seemed to ever notice messing around was Chloe."

His head rears back as if I slapped him.

"It's true. You've been obsessed with Chloe's sex life or at least the rumors of it since sophomore year. Why is that, Marcus?"

"B-because I was worried about you."

I shake my head but let it go. I'm hoping my words will get him to face his feelings about Chloe, but I decide to be honest with him about Romeo. Hiding a relationship is one thing. Lying about it feels very wrong. Like the dirty little secret thing is true.

"Listen. Marcus, Romeo and I just started dating. It's kind of complicated with the whole band thing, so I'd appreciate it if you wouldn't say anything to anyone."

"You're the last person I would expect to fall for some band asswipe," he sneers.

"There's a lot more to him than who he is onstage," I retort. "I have to go." I hit unlock and whip open the car door.

Marcus's fingers wrapping over the window stop me from closing the door. "We're still friends, right?"

I sigh. "Marcus, we'll always be friends. I just think . . . we should take a break from each other for a while." I pull on the door and he lets go. His face is a mournful picture through the glass.

As I drive home, my thoughts jump from Romeo to Marcus then back to Romeo. I'm trying not to hurt Marcus, but I don't know how to deal with his misplaced crush. But I may have hurt Romeo by jumping away from him and acting like there was nothing between us. I'm not sure if Marcus will keep his mouth shut, and I'm starting not to care.

I pull into the garage but instead of going inside right away, I text Romeo. Sorry, I didn't mean for it to go down like that. I did tell him the truth.

I'm two steps into the house when he texts back. It's all right. Total ambush. I hate to admit it, but thinking that he was your boyfriend for the last three months had me jealous more than anything else.

It's stupid how his jealousy has butterflies swarming in my stomach. I'm thinking of what to text back when the light flicks on and Jamie wanders into the kitchen. I almost drop my phone. "What are you doing up?"

Still wearing jeans and a sweater, she opens the fridge. "Watching TV." At least she's wearing bright pink princess slippers with crowns over the toes.

"Do you know what time it is?"

She shrugs and reaches for a can of pop.

"Put that back. It's after one in the morning. Where is Mom?"

"Sleeping," she says snottily, dropping the can with a thud. She's hardly ever snotty, but then she rarely stays up past eleven.

"Mom went to bed while you were watching TV?"

Jamie shrugs. "She was tired."

Unfucking believable. I'm so mad it takes every bit of control for me to calmly say, "Go brush your teeth and get dressed for bed. I'll be up in a second to tuck you in."

She frowns but scampers out of the kitchen, which is a mess. Dirty dishes cover the entire back counter, and food boxes and papers cover the island. Crap. I'm going to have to clean that up tonight or it will be there until tomorrow afternoon.

I unclench my fists and stuff my phone in my pocket. I don't really have time to text. On my way upstairs, I pass piles of stuff loaded on the stairs waiting for someone—me—to take up. I grab a stack of towels, rush up the stairs, and then pause at the bathroom door. The mess inside halts me in the doorway. Dirty towels are piled in the corner because the hamper is overflowing. Toothpaste smears the sink and spots the mirror. The trash basket in one corner is bursting to the brim with tissues and empty toilet paper rolls.

I didn't grow up like this. I grew up in a clean, organized house. Jamie should too.

This disaster of a house didn't happen overnight. Five dates in nine days and I get a sister up in the wee hours and a house in a shambles. I stuff towels into the bathroom closet as the realization I need to slow things down with Romeo hits me full force. I love being with him, but my mother and sister need me more than I need a budding romance.

I already agreed to Tuesday, then Saturday the entire band is going out for my birthday, but after this week Romeo and I are going to have to slow things down for real. But there's always the phone and the computer and school.

Calculus III never sounded so good.

Chapter 25

I n the soft light from a study lamp on his desk, Romeo sits on the edge of his bed and plays his antique fiddle. I sit on the desk chair. Just like last time I'm mesmerized by the picture of him wrapped in the delicate, haunting melody. The smooth movement of his deft fingers. The shadow of his lashes on his skin. The tilt of his defined jaw cradled against the instrument. And the dark angle of his hair, swaying over his forehead as he pushes the bow. He's actually sexier playing the fiddle than the guitar.

He holds the final note before opening his eyes, then grins at my look of awe.

I unwrap my arms from around my knees. "What was that?"

"'Annie Laurie.' I don't remember all the words. I was always more interested in the tune than the text, but it has something in the refrain about how the singer would lay down and die for her." He sets the fiddle and bow back on the shelf.

I drop my knees and stand. "Well, I might want you to lie down, but the dying seems rather wasteful." Sometimes I shock *myself* with the things I say to him. I've never been a bold person. Guess my response to him proves that wrong.

His eyes darken and his jaw tightens. He reaches out, catches my wrist, and yanks me forward until I fall against him. My knees dig into the bed on each side of his thighs while my fingers grip his shoulders.

He reaches up and releases my ponytail. "Seems like my initial opinion was right. You do have a dirty mind."

"Just with you," I say a little breathlessly as he fans out my hair.

"It better be only with me," he says roughly, his fingers wrapping around the back of my neck. He pulls me down toward his lips. "Your dirty little mind is making me crazy," he says in breath that warms my lips. Inside the curtain of my hair, his mouth brushes against mine until he kisses me fully, exploring my mouth with the slow glide of his tongue.

The next kiss is long and bottomless and has me falling onto his lap. Those full lips move to the corner of my mouth and slide around the curve of my chin. His knuckles brush my ribs as his fingers lift the edge of my shirt. "This okay?" he asks against the skin of my neck.

I clench the front of his T-shirt. "Only if you take off yours."

His quick breath echoes in the room then he reaches behind his head and jerks his shirt off in one quick motion. My hands reach for his skin.

"What about yours?" he says in a husky tone.

I lift my arms willingly, then gasp at the contact of skin against skin as a palm to my lower back nearly slams me to his hard chest. He catches my lips in a hot kiss that has me moaning into his mouth. The strong arms holding me tremble deliciously before his shaky fingers unclasp my bra.

We stare at each other as I help pull the garment away. His eyes lower and darken to a definite black as he stares at my breasts. One hand slowly slides to the center of my back. The other splays across my stomach and pushes until I'm bent back over the floor. I'm suspended in air between his warm palms.

My eyes round and my breath catches as his mouth descends on a breast. The shine of the lamp spotlights his movement. Holy hell.

Romeo's mouth on me is hot as hell. The muscles of his shoulders ripple under my palms. The tug of his mouth has my breath coming out in pants. I'm shocked, but too turned on to be embarrassed at my heavy inhalation. When he moves to the other breast, my lower body instinctively scoots forward until I'm pressing against his erection. He shudders at the contact and groans against my skin. I feel that groan to the tips of my toes.

At the rock of his hips in tune with the suction of his mouth, a delicious friction grows between us causing me to gasp, "You've got a condom here, right?"

His mouth lets go of my skin and presses to the center of my chest. He breathes heavily against my skin, causing tingles to ripple through my body. "I have this one-month-rule thing."

"One month rule?" I repeat dumbly.

"I'll explain later," he says in a ragged voice. The palm on my back presses me up until we face each other. His thumb circles around the button of my jeans. "Right now I want to touch you. Can I touch you?" The question comes out in a harsh breath.

The intensity of his dark eyes and the slow circle of his thumb leave no question of where. Just the thought of him touching me has me melting. His eyes hold the question until I slowly nod.

He lets the button loose and together we tug my jeans off. He lifts me into a straddle over the spread of his legs as soon as my jeans hit the floor. My feet tuck behind his calves and I reach for his shoulders to steady myself. Our eyes lock while his hand moves past the band of my underwear. Then as his fingers glide against me, his eyes close. The lines of his face are strained. He draws in a deep breath and I tremble from both the slide of his hand and the look of wonder and ecstasy on his face. He leans forward, resting his forehead on my shoulder. My own eyes close as my hips move to the rhythm his touch creates.

Pants fill the room like the growing beat of a drum. His know-ing fingers apply pressure, move deeper, and circle my skin. It's evi-dent he knows exactly how to play my body. His fingers move over me as dexterously as they did the fiddle. His palm adds pressure above, and a strangled moan bursts from my throat. My back bows and my fingers grip his shoulders so my melting body doesn't melt into liquid lust on the floor.

I'm startled and slightly embarrassed to find him watching me when I open my eyes. Nearly naked and sprawled across his lap with his hand still cupping me, I recall my strangled frog-like moan.

"Fuck, Riley," he says in a hiss, and slowly removes his hand. "I never thought I'd see anything as beautiful as you playing the drums, but that was fucking gorgeous."

My growing blush instantly dies as his words warm me a dif-ferent way. I'm not beautiful like April or Kendra, but I do believe Romeo sees me as beautiful. I glance at his obvious need under the denim of his jeans. "What about you?"

He smirks painfully. "Cold shower?"

Bolstered by his words, especially *gorgeous,* I trace my fingers along the dark trail of hair above his belt buckle. His entire body jerks from my touch. I unclasp his belt and unbutton his jeans in seconds.

Just as my fingers dip under the band of his boxers, his hand covers mine. "Ah, Riley—"

"Let me. I want to," I say, and cover his mouth in a kiss. I'm not entirely a novice. I've done this once for Aaron, but then I did it out of girlfriend obligation. Now my hands reach for Romeo with a surge of eagerness.

With his head on my chest, his eyes closed, and his fingers making patterns on my hipbone, Romeo appears relaxed. Twenty minutes ago, he'd looked tense, almost in pain, and just like he said about me, fucking gorgeous with his neck muscles straining and a fine sheen of sweat covering his chest as he came in my hands.

I'd never been a prude with Aaron, but I'd never been so sexually blatant either. Something about Romeo weakens my inhibitions. Well, most of them. Though my bra and jeans still lie on the floor, I tugged my shirt on before he laid me across the bed and curled against me. Languid and close, contentment flows between us.

I give his Celtic-knot necklace a tug. "So what is this about a one-month rule?"

The fingers stroking my hip pause. "The accumulation of my past."

"I'm listening."

He sighs. "It's a long story and it isn't pretty."

His response has me begging. "Tell me. I want to know. Tell me everything."

Leaning on his elbow, he props his face up with a palm. "I've never told it before. Let me think of where to begin, how to begin." His fingers draw an invisible pattern on my stomach while he looks across the room. His face tightens in thought. The scruff on his jaw is harsh in the dim light. And the glitter of memory in his dark eyes is far away as his past pushes into our cocoon of contentment.

"Since I can remember, my mother and I lived with my grandfather. My dad took off before I even turned one. My grandfather was old even for a grandfather. My mother was from his third marriage." He chuckles lowly. "He liked the ladies, used to take old biddies on dates to the bingo hall. And he always had one or two at the local bar when he played. After she completed night school, my mom worked as a secretary in an insurance office. My grandfather owned and ran a rundown gym. We didn't have a lot of money.

But I had boxing and music and both of them. Then the summer between sophomore and junior year, everything fell to shit."

He drops his head to my chest and his fingers halt their tracing on my stomach. "My grandfather had cancer. It was in stage four by the time they found it or maybe by the time he decided to go to the doctor. It was like one day he was there and the next dying in the hospital."

His words reverberate against my chest as a lump forms in my throat at the obvious pain of his grandfather's death. Hoping to offer comfort, I trail my fingers through the silk of his hair. But I don't interrupt. The tightness of his tone reveals how difficult this story is for him. I'm thinking it's easier for him to tell it with the top of his head tucked against my chin and his face hidden from me.

"I always worked at the gym more during the summer, but that summer I worked all the time. Nights were spent at the hospital. A girl came in one warm June day. Though I didn't know her name, I recognized her from school. Some popular cheerleader a grade ahead of me. She just worked out and flirted that first day. The next day she cornered me in the office, and before I knew what was happening we were having sex on the desk."

My fingers pause before I grip his hair too hard. Instinctively, I understand this girl is the lifetime of lust he was talking about that night in the hotel.

"She came to the gym every day. Sometimes we'd go to the office. Other times I'd take a long break and we'd slip next door to the house for an entire afternoon. I'm not sure how, we didn't talk much, but there was nothing she didn't know or want to do. And I was eager to try everything. I fucked my way through the summer while my grandfather lay dying. There were even nights that my mother went to the hospital alone while I bent my new obsession over the kitchen table."

My mind is screaming, *Too much information!* But I have a feeling that he's keeping the reality of their relationship mild for me.

"Like I said, we never talked much, but I took the things she did with her hands and lips and body to mean something beyond lust. What kid at fifteen wouldn't?"

My fingers grip the short strands of hair at the back of his neck. I try to imagine him at the age of fifteen. He'd be shorter and his face not as defined, but still handsome, still intense. "Wasn't that a bit young?"

I feel his shrug against my shoulder. "I turned sixteen midsummer." His fingers trail on my skin again. "Late summer my grandfather died. Between the funeral and the first day of school, I didn't see her. Yet over the summer she had become my world. That summer with her kept the grief of my grandfather dying from being real to me, which at the time meant everything to me." His thumb circles my belly button.

"What happened at school?" I ask when he pauses, even though I have an idea.

"She ignored me." He lets out a sad laugh that pains my heart. "I must have looked like an idiot standing by her lunch table waiting for her to acknowledge me. I was never in the circle of popularity, but I did have a reputation and respect from boxing. Blew it to hell in one lunch hour. Later that day she did corner me and made it clear the summer had only been a fling."

I want to beat the nymphomaniac to a bloody pulp even now.

"My world stopped. The pain she kept at bay throughout the summer overcame me. And every day I saw her with her quarterback boyfriend, I died a little more inside. I quit going to the gym—even working there. I ignored my friends. I missed my grandfather. My grades dropped to awful. Then I began to hate her and her popular goody act. But I started hating myself more because as the days went on, I realized what an idiot I'd been to think there was anything between us. And yet I still wanted her. It was like all that sex had me addicted to her. Or maybe I thought if she took me back, the pain would end."

He never says her name. As if saying it gives her memory power.

He pushes up, lies on his side, and rests his face against his palm. His troubled eyes meet mine. His expression is a long, sad melody. "The more I isolated myself, the more I sunk into depression. The pain of losing my grandfather pulled me into a black hole and her rejection anchored me there." He takes a deep breath and exhales with the words, "Until one fall evening, my mother found me in the basement with a gun pressed to my head."

I let out a startled gasp. The slow beat of his story built to this revelation. Now the climax of it is tearing through me with a thousand erratic thumps that can't catch a rhythm. I can't make sense of the image his words bring. I could never envision the man lying next to me doing such a thing, but the image of him as a young boy with a barrel pressed against his head in a dark basement fills me with a deep sorrow that has me staring at him in frozen shock. That he'd been so alone and despondent, to the point of contemplating taking his own life, pierces my heart. The sporadic, sickening beat tearing through me breaks free with a whimper and a dripping tear that rolls onto the pillow below me.

"Oh, Riley." He wipes at another dripping tear, then strokes my hair. "It's okay. I'm stronger now. It's years later. I'm here with you right now. I'm a survivor. I haven't been near that dark hole ever again. Not even at the edge."

I exhale slowly. Breathe in and exhale again. There's dignity in his voice, a hardness in his tone as if he's proud of what he's overcome. "How did you get over . . . everything?"

He smiles sadly. "A year of counseling, several months of antidepressants, and my mother's indomitable will. She'd been grieving too, but after that she pulled herself together, and refused to let me wither in my black hole. She made me play music. Came and watched me train at the gym. And when I went back to school at the new semester, she was a drill sergeant about homework. I gradually began to live again and in time found myself."

I wipe at another tear. "Do you still hate *her*?"

He shakes his head. "She was young too. We lived in a small town. Her father was on the town council or something. After I got better, I felt sorry for her. Inside she was something completely different than what she could show the world. But I took something away from the experience with her. I learned that sex is meaningless unless the people involved care about each other."

His acceptance of her has me believing he's over the painful memory more than his earlier words. My fingers brush his ribs and tattoo. "You lost your wings. This isn't just about your grandfather is it?"

He nods. "It's a reminder for me too. To wait and love wisely."

"The one-month rule," I say, understanding its meaning. And though I believed him before about not having one-night stands, now I understand why.

"I don't really keep track of time. But I need to feel committed before I go to that level."

"So we're not there yet," I say tightly, even though I feel like we are. At least I am.

"It's only been a little more than two weeks." He glances at my half-naked body. "And we're already moving faster than we should while we're hiding from everyone."

I wince, suddenly ashamed at my behavior. "I'm sorry about that. It's just that with everything else in my life right now more drama seems unbearable." I feel compelled to add the entire truth after he's shared so much with me. "And you scare me."

His eyes round while they search mine. "I scare you?"

I wipe the corner of a wet eye, scoot over a bit, and roll into a pose mirroring his. "You're Romeo, the perfect guitar player and basically manager of Luminescent Juliet. Girls throw themselves at you. You're beyond smart. You're hotter than hell. And if I can't hold on to some band geek from high school, how am I going to hold on to you?"

His jaw becomes hard. "Are you sure you're over that boy?"

Boy is right. "Oh yeah, I was over him before our first kiss."

His face relaxes and his finger follows the curve of my nose. "You love your family enough to turn down a percussion scholarship. You play the drums like a demon. You're this wild mix of cute and sexy and beautiful. You're snippy and stubborn and funny, and you say the hottest shit that always turns me on instantly." He leans forward and kisses me lightly. "It's not too hard to hold someone who's already caught."

Oh damn, how am I supposed to slow this down now?

"Band geeks are obviously not too smart." His fingers are back on my hip tracing invisible patterns. I realize he can't stop himself from touching me. The whole time he shared his past, he had to touch me. As if he needed the contact. My heart does a little jump, then swells at the knowledge.

"I don't want to hide us anymore," I suddenly blurt, and his expression turns pleased. "Especially from the band. But how do we tell them?"

His fingers pause. "Why not when we go out for your birthday on Saturday? We can show up together and ease them into reality."

"All right," I say, slowly sitting up. It would be more than awkward and drama filled during practice, but all of us out together, it may go over better. "It's getting late. I should go. I don't want Justin to find out this way."

Nodding, Romeo sits up too and reaches for his shirt.

I'm tugging on my pants when I spot a pair of flip-flops under the edge of the bed. Romeo's past filters through my brain along with an image of those ratty flip-flops.

With my pants still hanging open, I point at him. "It was you!"

Chapter 26

Romeo tilts his head quizzically.

I zip my pants then gesture wildly at him with my hands. "That night outside the theater in the smoking area."

He scoots to the edge of the bed and nods. "I always wondered why you never said anything about that night. Never considered you didn't recognize me. I thought the badass drummer was embarrassed."

I ignore the badass comment. "But you don't smoke." And he was dressed differently, but sometimes he does change right before going onstage.

"Once in a while I bum one from Sam, especially if I'm feeling nervous."

I frown. "When are you nervous?"

"I am human, Riley. Playing in front of huge crowds gets to me sometimes."

Yeah, right, and I'm Wonder Woman. "Why did you give me that card?"

"You seemed distraught, lonely, depressed. The card never hurts."

Another revelation hits me. "That's why you were asking Marcus about me."

"Mostly."

I pause buttoning my pants. "Mostly?"

He runs a hand through his hair and sighs. "I was interested in you from the start."

My mouth falls open, thinking of our meeting in that dark, smoky alley. "Why?"

He draws in a deep breath. "Your sadness drew me to you first." His expression turns pensive as he rubs the scruff along his jaw. "Then the fact you were mature enough to respect someone's wishes without hate. And even then you didn't seem like other girls . . . You've never wanted me for something I'm not."

My mouth falls open even more. "Then why were you such an ass at tryouts?"

"You were with Marcus, actually wrapped in his arms." His eyes turn hard at the memory. "I figured he was the guy you were crying about that night. And you didn't look like a lost and lonely girl anymore. You looked sexy and full of confidence. Suddenly unbelievably fucking jealous, I couldn't seem to help myself. Then you played like a drummer goddess and I imagined long practices watching Justin and Sam flirting with you. Of course, I was right. The whole thing drove me insane, especially while I thought you had a boyfriend."

I'm a bit overwhelmed with his perception but I manage to ask, "Do you always carry those cards?"

"I do." He reaches into his back pocket and pulls out his wallet. Under the front flap he shows me a stack of cards. "I also volunteer twice a week for the Child and Family Services suicide hotline. It's where I met April. Her cousin committed suicide when they were in high school."

My fingers pause reaching for my bra before I scoop it up. Poor April. I almost wish things had worked out for her and Romeo. "So she knows about that girl and . . . well, you know."

"A little. Not much. I've never told my past in its entirety to anyone before."

I can't help frowning. "I shouldn't have pried."

He reaches for my hand and squeezes it. "I wanted to tell you. You . . . we . . ." He shakes his head. "This just feels real. And keeping secrets doesn't feel real."

"It does feel real." I reach out to touch his face and my bra rubs against his cheek. I yank my hand down and we both laugh. I quickly stuff my bra in my pocket. "Do you know I didn't want to try out for the band?"

His expression becomes confused and he shakes his head.

"Marcus and Chloe thought it was the greatest idea ever. I thought it was the stupidest." I reach for my jacket hanging on the bedpost. "Even after I watched you guys and thought you were awesome, I had no intention of trying out. But while we waited for you to come out, I looked at the card. I hadn't until then because I thought it was your number."

A winged brow arches.

"I was floored when I read the card. Though I'd never thought of . . ."—I can't bring myself to say that word after his story—"hurting myself, I realized something was wrong with my life and that I needed something. I decided it was playing in the band."

Those dark eyes that reveal so little watch me for a long moment. "So you're telling me I helped you decide to try out?"

"In a weird twisted way."

His lips curve into a close-lipped smile.

"But what I really want to tell you is that you're amazing." He puts out a hand for me to stop. I grab it and hold it in both of mine. "The past you've overcome, that you volunteer, and that you care enough about strangers to offer them bandanas and cards and encouraging words . . . Well, you're just amazing."

He stares at our entangled hands for several seconds, then says in a hoarse voice, "Thank you."

"You're welcome, but don't get too big of a head," I say with a smirk. "There's a bit of asshole in you too."

Though I expected a laugh, he yanks me into his arms and hugs me tight. "I know you wanted to go to Virginia," he says, warming my ear. "I know that was your dream, but I'm so fucking glad you're here."

I hug him back and honestly say, "I'm glad I'm here too."

Chapter 27

Grocery shopping is one of the lamest things I have to do. But in my current domestic goddess status, I've become a pro at it. I clip coupons. I shop for sales. I plan meals. I rock at keeping the bill down. But taking Jaime never helps.

"Why can't we get two kinds of cookies?" she whines, holding two cartons while the pink plastic crown on her head wobbles.

"Because one is enough."

"But I like chocolate chips *and* these marshmallow things."

"Pick one. We'll get the other next week."

She rolls her eyes and tosses the chocolate-chip cookies into the cart. The next stop is the cereal aisle, which always takes the longest. I point out which brands are on sale and which ones I have coupons for, then Jamie contemplates.

My phone vibrates in my pocket while she holds two boxes next to each other and compares. I dig my phone out and smile at Romeo's name across the screen before reading the text: I'm sitting here looking at the white roses you sent me. Their beauty, their scent, their soft petals remind me of you. Yet they're not even close to the real thing. You sure you can't go out after practice? I'd like to thank you personally and make your heart smile like mine is right now.

"You okay?" Jamie asks, dropping her cereal choice in the cart.

I'm standing in the middle of the aisle clutching my phone to my chest. I must look like a lovesick junior high school girl. But I don't care. Romeo is so freaking perfectly awesome. So opposite of what I originally thought of him. I should send him flowers every day. Forty-five bucks is so worth this text. "Yeah, I'm good," I say wistfully.

Jamie gives me an odd look, then pulls the cart forward while I stand in dream mode. I slowly follow. Somewhere between the chips and the produce, I text him back: My heart's been smiling since last night. And don't tempt me.

I stay on a Romeo cloud through the checkout line and then while I toss groceries into the trunk. I'm not even sure what I bought the second half of shopping and I don't particularly care. I float all the way home until I hit the garage door opener and see my mother's car inside the garage. Then I plummet down to earth.

"Mom's home!" Jamie squeals from the backseat.

Needless to say, I'm not as excited. My mom should be at work. Something's very wrong if she's home.

Inside the garage, Jamie grabs two grocery bags from the trunk and rushes inside. I drag the last six into the kitchen. Jamie's two bags along with her backpack lie on the floor. While I put away groceries, I can hear the murmur of my mother's and sister's voices from the living room. The TV blares over their conversation as I load the Crock-Pot with rice, vegetables, chicken stock, and chicken, then wander into the living room.

My mother sits on the couch with a blanket across her knees. She's dressed for work in black pants and a red blouse with her name tag still attached. Curled next to her, Jamie watches TV. My mother stares out the large window of our living room.

"Jamie," I say, reaching for the remote and sitting in the nearest chair. "Go do your homework, then you can watch TV." Hoping to muffle the coming conversation so she won't be able to hear it, I change the channel instead of turning off the TV.

Jamie gives me a sour look.

"Come on, you know the rules." Six months ago my bossing Jamie around while my mother sits quietly would have been weird. Now it's normal.

Jamie rolls her eyes but stomps off to the kitchen. Eight-year-old eye rolls are quite annoying.

I turn up the volume and then turn to my mother. Her eyes look puffy and slightly red. "What happened? Are you sick?"

She shakes her head and picks fuzz off the blanket on her lap.

"Why are you home?"

She lets out a sigh. "I found out something today."

I hold in my sigh. "What?"

"Don't say anything to your sister," she says, lowering her voice. "But your father is getting married in spring."

Oh shit. I just stare at her.

Her eyes narrow on me. "You knew?"

I nod slowly.

She clutches the blanket. "You didn't tell me?"

"I didn't know how. I didn't want to hurt you."

"Well, it would have been better from you than some customer who knows your father," she snaps.

I imagine her behind the counter ringing in items while some faceless bitch talks about her soon-to-be ex-husband getting married. "I'm sorry."

"When did he tell you?"

I swallow. "In August I think."

Her hands drop and her lip quivers. "August? Riley, it's November."

"Mom, he doesn't matter anymore."

She shakes her head sadly. "He may be able to sweep over twenty years of his life away, but I can't." She draws in a ragged breath.

"I still love him. I'm afraid I'll always love him. I'm going to die alone, pining after him while he belongs to someone else. Someone younger."

I lean forward. "Stop it. You'll find someone too. Someone better."

She shakes her head.

I'm not sure if it's my father or her life with him that my mother can't let go. But she needs to let both go. "Did you reschedule that counseling appointment?"

"I find out my husband is getting married and you're worried about counseling?"

"You need to talk to someone."

"I'm talking with you," she says stubbornly.

"Someone who isn't emotionally involved."

"A stranger. You want me to open up to a stranger."

"No, a person whose job is to listen and help."

She looks out the window as if the fallen leaves outside are the most important thing in the world. Then she asks, "Does Jamie know about the engagement?"

Ah, topic switch. Of course. "I don't think so." I should probably tell her Dad has been bringing Sara to dinner most Tuesday nights, but her red-rimmed eyes keep me from speaking.

Rubbing her temples, she continues to stare out the window.

I scoot to the edge of the chair. "I could stay home tonight."

"And watch me mope?" She waves a hand. "Go to practice, Riley. I'll be all right. I just couldn't work. Concentration and cordialness eluded me."

"Okay, if you're sure. I'll be home after nine anyway." I stand. "Dinner's in the Crock-Pot. It should be done by seven thirty."

She gives me a weak smile. "Thank you."

"No problem," I say, watching her stare out the window again. She's right. I don't want to stay here and witness her depression. But her forlorn look almost has me sinking back into the chair. I remind myself I'll only be gone for a little more than two hours. Plus I'll get to see Romeo, even if we're still pretending until Saturday, I'll get to be with him. And being with him is becoming the most important thing in my world.

Romeo and I rarely argue during practice anymore. He's still a slave driver, but he is a perfectionist when it comes to music. Being one too, I usually listen to my slave driver. Sometimes we don't agree. Even though I've come to realize he's a musical genius, I am the authority when it comes to the drums. And he usually accepts my decisions. After I give him an explanation, of course. If Sam or Justin has noticed the change in our behavior, neither of them has commented.

But today he is on my ass. And well, I can't say much. Still worried about my mother, I am off a bit. We're trying to do a cover of "Sweet Sour" by Band of Skulls. Everyone has it but me. And the song is kind of simple, especially for me.

"Fuck," Justin says. "How many times do we have to redo this?"

Romeo glares at him. "Until we get it right."

"We've got it right. It's just Riley, who keeps screwing up. So she's off today. I'm sure by the next practice she'll have her shit back together." He turns to me. "Right?"

"Yeah, right. Sorry," I say with a frown. I should have just canceled practice.

Sam sets his bass against the wall and fishes out cigarettes from his pocket. "I'm taking a break."

"Good idea before I grow hoarse," Justin says, flopping onto a metal chair.

Lifting his strap and guitar over his head, Romeo gives me a questioning look. I shrug, then push my sticks in my back pocket and pull out my phone.

There are several texts. All from my mother. My fingers quickly press buttons and scroll. Skimming them I realize Jamie actually sent them. I go back to the first one and read through them.

Mom is crying.

Mom is acting weird.

Something is wrong with mom.

Mom won't get off the couch.

Come home.

Please.

I'm off my stool, punching in my mother's number, and across the room in seconds.

"Riley?" Jamie answers in an expectant tone.

"What's going on?"

"Mom's . . . drinking," she says in a hushed whisper.

"Drinking?"

"Yeah, like beer but its red. And she keeps crying, but she won't get off the couch."

What the hell? "I'm coming. Send me a picture of what she's drinking, okay?"

"Okay."

"I'll be there in fifteen minutes."

"Hurry," Jamie says.

I change my phone to vibrate, turn around, and nearly run into Romeo.

He catches me by the shoulders. "What's going on?"

"My mom . . . I have to go."

He doesn't release me. "Is she okay?"

"No, she's losing it," I say, and rest my forehead against his chest.

His arms wrap around me. "Do you need me to come with you?"

At the idea of him seeing my mother drunk, I shake my head vigorously and repeat, "I have to go." But my hands clench at the muscles of his back. My face digs into his chest. He feels solid and indestructible and safe. "I have to go," I mumble into his shirt.

Somehow understanding my dilemma, he gently unwraps my arms from around him and steps back.

Justin comes up from behind Romeo. "What's going on with you two?"

"Nothing," I say. My phone vibrates in my hand.

"It sure as shit doesn't look like nothing," Justin says.

Romeo crosses his arms as Justin glares at him.

I stare at the picture of an empty wine bottle on my phone. My mother rarely drinks—usually just at parties and during the holidays—but she drank a whole bottle of wine in a little over an hour? Alone with my sister?

"Are you two seeing each other?" Justin demands.

"No," I say as Romeo says, "Yes."

"What the fuck!" Justin roars, pointing at Romeo. "You said none of us could hit on her! You're the one who made a big deal about the whole thing!"

Romeo glares at Justin but softly says, "It's not like that."

My phone vibrates again. This time the picture is of my mother with her mouth hanging open and she's almost falling off the couch.

"I don't give a fuck what it's like! Your rules always stand, which means she's out." Justin flicks his thumb toward the door.

Romeo growls, "Justin—"

"This is such bullshit!"

My world slowly disintegrates as I look at the picture in my hand again. Maybe I've been blinded by hope, but the picture tears all hope away. My mother is broken. And I'm at band practice trying to play some stupid song.

"We're not getting rid of the best drummer we'll ever have because of your ego," Romeo snaps.

"My ego? Listen motherfucker, you're the one with the ego. You're the one who makes all the rules. You're the one who didn't even want her. And you're the one who's going to stand by your shitass rules!"

I glance up from the horrible picture to see Romeo and Justin standing inches from each other. Both have their fists clenched. Romeo's jaw is tight. Justin's teeth are gritted in an opened mouthed sneer. Someone is going to swing soon.

"This doesn't matter," I say softly.

Leering, Justin leans closer to Romeo. "How long you been taping that ass?"

Romeo lunges and they crash against the wall. "Shut. Your. Filthy. Mouth." He enunciates each word with a shove and dust flies around them.

I rush next to them and pull at Romeo's grip. "Stop it!"

Breathing hard under Romeo's weight, Justin sneers again. "Does she fuck like she plays?"

Romeo takes a small bounce back, and though I have a hold of one arm, quick as lightning he punches Justin in the jaw with the other. Justin slides down the wall. Romeo leans over his falling body. "I warned you."

With a slight shake of his head and rage flying out of his eyes, Justin starts pushing himself up. "You wanna go, asshole?"

"Stop it!" I yell again, stepping between them. With an arm on each of their chests I say, "This doesn't matter." They ignore me and stare daggers at each other. "Because I quit."

Both of them turn to me as confusion changes their furious expressions. I step from between them and race down the stairs. Romeo calls my name as I push out the door, but I'm in my car and gone before he can catch up.

Chapter 28

It's my birthday. Nineteen long years on this earth. So far today I've shut my phone off when it wouldn't stop beeping, got Jamie ready for school, and dropped her off. Next I'm going to confront my mother. She's still lying on the couch, where she passed out last night, and staring out the window. But instead of puffy her eyes are bloodshot.

Over the past year, my mother has deteriorated into a stranger. Yet somehow between stuffing the washing machine and filling the Crock-Pot I missed the complete transformation. Or maybe in its daily gradualness, I became blind to her full change.

I collapse in the chair next to the couch.

Her eyes don't leave the window, but she says in a gravelly voice, "I don't need to hear it right now."

Happy fucking birthday, Riley.

I shoot out of the chair. "You don't need to hear it?" My fists clench at my sides. "Well, you're going to hear it."

"Riley," she says weakly.

"No, you need to listen. I cook. I clean. I babysit. I do the damn yard work. Why? Because I know how hard this divorce is for you. And because I'm hoping if you have less to do, you'll have more time to heal. But you're not healing! You're getting worse!" My arms flap out in frustration. "I'm not even sure why you have custody. I take care of Jamie most of the time. You just sit on your ass and stare into space. And now you've added drinking to the mix."

She sits up slowly. Her brown eyes filled with hurt stare at me. "You don't think I should have custody of Jamie?"

I tell myself to shut up, but the words come out anyway. "I'm not sure. I don't know what to think anymore." I walk past her hurt expression. Her sobs come at me in the kitchen. Ignoring them, I open the door to the garage. At the moment, she can cry all she wants. I don't care.

I end up at the skate park. Lucky for me, when Marcus and I skateboarded in August, I was too lazy to take my board up to my room and instead threw it in my trunk. I've spent two hours trying to do nearly every trick I used to do. I sucked at most of them. Since it's a cold though sunny November school day, I've had the ramps and grid rails to myself. No one has witnessed my many wipeouts. Not that I really care. I was going for mindless, but somewhere in between the multitude of face plants, the truth began to sink in.

I should have never left my mother alone last night. Deep down I knew that, but I wanted to see Romeo. So I went.

Guilt bubbled up in me until it exploded like a geyser and I went to a bench to get my head together.

Now I sit and face reality while absently rolling the skateboard under my feet.

My mother's afloat in depression. My sister's losing her childhood. My father's getting remarried. And I'm holding the tatters of my family together. But instead of putting my family first, I've been selfishly busy lately. With Romeo.

Like a growing drumbeat, guilt pounds in my head. *Boom. Boom. Boom.* The guilty echo has me whipping my phone out. I stare at it for several long moments, then force myself to text Romeo: We can't see each other anymore.

I slide my phone back into my pocket. The booming guilt abates but a different guilt mixed with sorrow pounds through me. I pull my hoodie tighter around me, lower my chin on my lifted knees, and let the tears fall.

My mother's broken and now I feel like I'm breaking.

The wind blows. Sorrow flows from me. The sun shines. The ends of my sleeves become drenched. Dried leaves pelt me. My heart dries up and threatens to stop beating, but the world keeps turning.

Minutes? Hours? Sometime later I wipe my eyes one last time, then lay my head on my knees.

"Hello, Riley."

My eyes fly open and find Romeo standing in front of me. The tight lines of his face are grooved with weariness. Dressed in a long-sleeved thermal shirt and a dark green beanie, he looks cold. Remembering the rough feel of it against my cheek, I wonder where his black wool coat is. Then I wonder how he found me here.

Somehow he reads my thoughts. "Marcus guessed you'd be here." As his eyes take in my red-rimmed ones, he gestures to the bench. "All right if I sit?"

I nod slowly, drowning in the image of him. He sits close enough for me to reach out and touch him. His harsh profile is beautiful in the bright sunlight. An intensity flows through me and threatens to sweep me into his arms. I want to crawl into his pocket and be a part of his everything. I want him to play me music while my heart melts and drips for him. I imagine lying in his bed and breathing in the smell of him until it fills my lungs and becomes part of me. I want to lose myself within him and never get set free.

Suddenly he scares me in an entirely different way than before, as I finally understand my father's excuse of being in love. The entire world melts away when I'm with Romeo. There's just him and me and the overwhelming connection between us.

But even though I've been acting like him, I'm not my father. Falling in love isn't a free ticket to shit on everyone else and live in a bubble of love.

"I got your text," he slowly says.

Obviously. I silently build my wall of resolve and wait for the coming blowout.

He turns to me, his dark eyes contrite. "I'm sorry about last night. I shouldn't have hit Justin, but I won't let him talk like that about you."

I blink, realizing he thinks I broke up with him because of him and Justin fighting. "You shouldn't have hit Justin, but my text wasn't because of last night."

His skin pales. "Then why?"

"I don't want to . . . I can't . . ."

His entire body stiffens and his eyes pin me to the bench. "Have you been mindfucking me the last two weeks?"

I break our locked gazes. Leaves blow across the sidewalk. The high-pitched crunching scrape is a low whine compared to the roaring in my chest. "No. The last two weeks have been amazing."

"Then what the hell is going on?"

"I . . . my family needs me right now."

"So it's okay to throw me under the bus and break up with me in a text?" he asks in a condescending tone.

"No, the text thing was not okay. I just . . . needed to do it at that moment."

The wind blows and leaves swirl around us. I feel him staring at me and imagine the starkness of his gaze.

"Why are you doing this to us?" he asks hoarsely.

I let out a sigh and finally look at him. The pain etching his face almost breaks my resolve. Almost. "There isn't enough of me to go around for there to be an us. Nothing else matters when I'm with you. You're like a drug to me. I always crave more. I feel alive and euphoric when we're together. I feel free. I feel like the person I always wanted to be."

The breeze ruffles the locks of hair escaping his hat as thoughts tumble across his eyes. "Riley, we *can* take things slower."

A miserable laugh escapes me. "The last two weeks were me taking it slower. Slow and you don't work with me."

His gaze moves past me toward the skateboard ramps. His jaw is tight. His long musician fingers press into his thighs. Even the posture of his body screams anger, but when he looks at me again, the sorrow in his eyes rips through me.

"I'm so sorry," I gasp while more tears threaten to escape from the well that I thought had dried. "I feel like I'm leaving you standing in the cafeteria, but it's not like that. This . . . this is hurting me too. I don't want to choose, but I can't be there for them and with you. I just can't." I swallow tightly. "Don't hate me for this."

He reaches for my hand. "I could never hate you."

"Please don't," I say, tucking my hands in my lap.

"I can wait," he says so lowly I almost miss the words.

For a second the promise of his words deadens the cold wind and warms me, but I shake my head and the chill blows through me until I feel empty. "That's not fair to you or to them. My mother's mental health can't be tied to the possibility of us. I already resent her. If I hold on to the hope of us and can't be with you, I'll end up despising her."

He stands, paces in front of the bench, and pauses at a tree. Under his shirt, his shoulder blades tighten like daggers. He raises a clenched fist at the tree trunk. Fury hangs in the air and reels into the wind until he drops his hand and unclenches it. His entire body rises with a breath as he turns toward me. "So you're determined there's no future for us?"

"I've become determined to do the right thing," I say, my fingers curling together so I won't reach for him. I want his arms around me. The desire to give and receive comfort nearly overwhelms me.

Several windblown seconds tick by.

"I don't think you should quit the band," he says without looking at me.

Strangely, abandoning Luminescent Juliet and drumming doesn't seem too momentous compared to what's between Romeo and me. "I have to. My family needs me too much right now."

He shakes his head. "What about you, Riley? What about the fact that you love to play?"

"I love my family more," I say simply.

His dark eyes are hollow as he stares at me in silence. The wind grows colder and dry autumn leaves circle us. He takes a huge step and kneels in front of me. I'm cautious at his nearness, pressing myself into the back of the bench back as he leans forward. "I understand how much your family means to you. And I respect you for it. I even get why you need to quit the band. Though it's killing me, I'll respect your decision about us, but I need to be honest. So I'm only going to say this once." His gaze holds mine. "I will *wait* for you."

Not wanting to hurt him anymore, I shake my head as he stands. Halfway up he bends, gently grasps my face between his calloused palms, and kisses me hard. The kiss is searing and desperate and bittersweet. Then his hands and lips release me. "Happy birthday, Riley," he says in a hoarse whisper before walking away.

Tears fill my eyes and longing drills into my chest as I watch him walk away until he's just a speck then gone.

I let out a shudder into the wind.

This has to be the worst birthday ever.

Chapter 29

My life has become a plodding beat. There are no exciting cymbal strikes or booms from the bass drum. The even plod is rarely broken except by small bursts like a high-hat thump with my mother's slow changes.

But she *is* changing.

She took the long talk we had after I returned home from the skate park to heart. I firmly and honestly told her that if she didn't start getting herself together, I'd be having a serious conversation with my father, who has been hinting at full custody since her overdose. She has been reading to Jamie at night as soon as she gets home from work. She's had lunch with Jamie twice at school. She even made another appointment—I plan to drive her to that one—with a counselor. And she actually helped me cook on Thanksgiving. But she did lie in bed for most of the day yesterday after seeing my father on Saturday, the night he comes over to watch my sister. I'm trying to be patient. I can't expect her to change overnight, so I've become her persistent shadow.

College is the only time I'm away from home. Chloe has been hanging out with me at home more, but I still feel lost without the band and music and drumming, even more so without Romeo. I try not to dwell on him. If I did, I'd become like my mother. Lost in depression. So eating lunch with motormouth Kendra is actually wonderfully, mindlessly numbing.

Kendra saws her pizza into tiny bites. "So is it true you guys canceled playing at the Creed this weekend?"

"I have no idea." I shrug, but the numbness inside of me is hit with a twinge of guilt.

She gives me an odd look.

"I quit last week." Another twinge of guilt hits me.

"Why would you quit?" Kendra asks, smacking down her plastic knife. "I'd practically give my left tit to be near Romeo. Plus, there's you and the whole drumming thing."

I can't help a smirk. "Your left tit?"

Kendra grins and flips back her blonde curls. "I said *practically.* So what gives?"

"I needed to be home more." I twist my milk carton back and forth between my hands. "My parents are going through a divorce."

"Ah, divorce sucks. At least my stepdad is loaded." She stabs a bite of pizza. "You're a far better woman than me. Not sure I'd be able to give up something like seeing the sex god regularly so I could help out my family. But I guess it was about playing with you."

She'd be shocked if she knew what I'd actually given up. And probably super pissed I didn't tell her about Romeo and me. Not that it is any of her business.

Kendra taps the side of her plate with her fork. "Huh, on second thought, maybe I could give up visions of Romeo for my mother. Mothers are the best, you know?"

I nod slowly as a revelation hits me upside my dense head: I've been immaturely looking at the world in black-and-white. Kendra's a selfish beauty queen. Romeo's a player. I'm a band geek. Justin's a manwhore. Except for the last one—Justin is a manwhore—I've been proved wrong on all counts. People are layers of personality and their pasts, but I've been two-toned blind and judgmental. Damn, I need to grow up.

Kendra is pensive and her pink lips turn down. "So not having a drummer, they must have canceled." The look on my face has her adding, "Hey, you had to do what you had to do, right?"

"Yeah," I say, but that twinge of guilt grows.

Kendra starts talking about some guy from her Spanish class. I listen with one ear as my guilt settles more deeply. By the time I'm walking to calculus, I feel horrible. Romeo puts so much time into getting gigs. It's not like we live in some huge metropolis. Maybe I should have given the band two weeks or something to find a new drummer. I just lost it after my mother's drinking binge. Even though she was in the throes of depression, her behavior was extremely out of character.

Last week I purposely arrived late to calculus. I can almost keep Romeo out of my mind, but seeing him brings on a wistfulness that twists my gut and makes me question my decision. He nodded at me when I came in, then made small talk with me at break. Nothing serious, just generic hello-and-how-are-you stuff. My response was just as generic. After we shared such a deep connection, our impersonal exchange tore at my heart, which was a selfish reaction. I'm the one who demanded the distance between us.

Today I'm early as usual. I wait with my books and calculator in front of me. The guilt eating at me goes into overdrive when Romeo strolls into the room.

He's dressed in a dark brown hoodie that matches his eyes. My gaze devours him. He doesn't glance my way but instead sits and tugs his books from his bag. Flips through his notebook while my pencil taps out a nervous beat. The beat, not me, catches his attention. He stares at my tapping eraser, then his eyes shift to mine in a look that says, Please stop that racket. But other than that his gaze is empty.

"Sorry," I say, cringing and setting down my pencil.

"Doing okay?" he asks, and opens his textbook.

"I'm all right." I resist the urge to tap my fingers. "Um . . . I heard you canceled your gig this weekend."

He keeps turning pages and says only, "Yup."

"I feel really bad about that. I could . . . Well, I'd be willing to play just this weekend if you need me."

He slowly turns to me. His dark eyes look empty. "Thanks, but it can't be uncanceled. Don't worry though. It's like I told you, I'm aware the band doesn't trump people's lives."

"Ah, okay. Have you found a drummer?"

He nods, then turns back to flipping textbook pages.

I can't stop myself from asking. "Who?"

"The guy I wanted from the start."

Pain rips through me. I try to blink away the sting of his words. I'm not sure if he purposely wanted to hurt me. I can't read him when he's hunched over a textbook, but it pretty much sounded like he was saying hiring me was a mistake.

Maybe it was.

But I can read between the lines. The bigger mistake was *us*.

I push my chair back. It clanks against the table behind us when I stand. I ignore it and the students looking at me. Professor Hill walks in as I race out. Inside a bathroom stall, I breathe deeply and fight the well of tears threatening to break loose. I've already done this. I do *not* want to do it here. I will not do it here.

I'm almost calm when I hear the creak of the door.

"Riley?" Romeo's deep voice asks.

Shit.

"Are you all right?"

Fighting a new sob, I resist answering. His worrisome tone hurts almost as much as his words. The pain of our breakup is somehow caught in my throat.

"I know you're in here." His voice echoes in the empty bathroom. "I saw you come in."

I breathe through my nose.

"I'm coming in if you don't answer."

"Just go away, Romeo," I say through clenched teeth.

"I didn't mean what you think."

"Just go away!"

"Riley . . ."

"Please!"

I hear a sigh, then the door shutting. I let out a whoosh of air and bang my head against the metal wall of the stall before sliding the lock on the door open. I'm leaning against the sink, clenching the counter and trying to compose myself, when another girl comes in. Her glance at me is dismissive. She goes to the mirror and adjusts her hair before opening a tube of lip gloss. I wash my hands for something to do then take a deep breath, head for the exit, and yank open the door.

I almost run into Romeo coming out of the men's restroom.

"Whoa," he says, catching me by the shoulders.

"Let me go."

"Just give me a minute." His hands tighten on my shoulders as he stares down at me. His dark eyes are full of remorse. "You were the right choice and I'll always be grateful I had the opportunity to play with someone so talented." He takes a deep breath. "And I wouldn't trade any hurt for the time we had together. I—"

"Don't," I say, shaking my head as I pull out of his grasp. "Don't say anything else."

His arms drop to his sides, and he doesn't reach for me again.

The girl from the bathroom comes out. "Oh good, you're still here," she says to Romeo.

I spin around and head back to calculus. Romeo mutters something. The girl's high-pitched laughter rings down the hallway. I shudder before I open the door. Only three more classes and then I'll be free from this agony.

Chapter 30

Over the past eleven months, I've eaten in almost every casual restaurant in the tri-city area. It's as if my father thinks a change in decor and menu will make everything okay. Tonight it's Mexican. And the usual group—my father, his girlfriend, Jamie, and me—sits around the table, with Chloe in the mix this time. I figure if my dad can bring Sara, I can bring Chloe. I need the support, or maybe she's the buffer.

Jamie and my father leaf through a new book, a Waldo title this time. Sara has gotten into the habit of bringing Jamie a book each Tuesday.

Chloe swirls the straw in her glass of Coke and asks Sara, "So you're a lawyer?"

Sara nods. "I work for an environmental agency."

"So how did you meet Mr. Middleton?"

I tap Chloe's leg with my boot. Like I want to know this stuff. They must have met when my parents were still together. Chloe ignores me.

Sara takes a sip of her wine and glances at my father as if asking his permission to share. The idiot just smiles. Sara turns to Chloe and me. "My firm sometimes hires people in his engineering firm for research. I've known him for several years through work."

I choke on iced tea.

Chloe's eyes round. "You guys have been dating for two years?"

"No." Sara shakes her head and glances at me. "We didn't start dating until January."

When he moved out. But the thought of them working together, giving each other looks, and an attraction growing between them for two years, has my stomach turning.

Chloe keeps talking with Sara while my father and Jamie flip pages and look for Waldo. Our food comes. I pick at nachos. My dad asks me about school. I give him basic answers. He doesn't ask about the band. I never told him I was in one. Sara asks me about my major and future plans. I mumble something about still considering my major. This is usually how these dinners go. Tense and slow. But Chloe is soon talking Sara's ear off again, and I'm left alone, picking at cheese, meat, and beans. I shove my plate away when Sara describes the house she and my father are buying.

Chloe follows me to the bathroom. At the sink she says, "I'm not sure what your problem is. Sara seems pretty nice, especially to Jamie. If anything, I'd think you'd find her attitude with Jamie to be the cat's ass."

I snatch a paper towel from the dispenser. "Oh, I don't know," I say sarcastically. "Maybe because she's *not* my mother."

Chloe opens up a tube of red lipstick. "*Fail*. It's not her fault your parents are getting a divorce."

"He wants to start a family with her."

The tube hovers above her lips. "Okay, that's not the easiest issue to deal with, but what are you going to do? Be a bitch forever? Make this harder on Jamie? Are you going to hate a new brother or sister?"

I whip the paper into the trash. "It just feels like I'm betraying my mother."

Chloe shrugs and closes her lipstick. "I can see that. Yet being persistently rude to Sara doesn't equate to sticking up for your mother. And it sure as hell isn't going to change anything."

"You're right," I concede.

When we return to the table, I try to keep the sullen look from my face and even join in on the conversation a bit. This woman will soon be my stepmother. And though I'm not looking forward to that day, I'm thinking Chloe's right. Acting like a brat isn't going to change anything but will only make the transition harder for everyone—because by that time my father will have partial custody of Jamie, which essentially means Sara will be her part-time mother.

Divorce really does suck.

My father hangs his coat on a hook on the wall near our booth before sliding in across from me. "Your call and invitation to lunch was a nice surprise," he says.

For most of my life, I was equally in awe of both of my parents. Both were slightly stern, but they always had time for me, whether that meant watching me play in the marching band or hanging out with me on movie nights or playing the board games I loved as a kid. But my father didn't just break my mother's heart almost a year ago, he broke mine too by destroying our family.

I glance around the diner. "This isn't going to be a friendly lunch."

He raises a brow at me.

"I want to talk about a few things since you and mom can't seem to communicate."

"Riley—"

"Just let me say what I need to, okay?"

He nods as the waitress comes up.

After we order drinks, I take a deep breath and start. "I've been upset at you since you left, and I'm still upset. I'll probably be pissed for a while that you destroyed our family." He leans back as if shocked, probably because of my language, but I don't care. This has to come out and it is coming out honestly. "But Chloe helped me realize my anger isn't helping Jamie, me, or even Mom. More important, Jamie needs to be with you more than six hours a week."

My father's fingers drum on the table. "Until the divorce is finalized that's all you mother will allow."

"I know but Sara said you're buying a house, and maybe if you explain Jamie will have her own room, Mom will cave. But you need to talk with her. Maybe apologize."

"Apologize?"

"Yeah, apologize. You left her. Did you ever tell her you were sorry things didn't work out after twenty-one years of marriage?"

"All of those things were said before I left."

"Maybe you need to say them again."

The waitress sets our drinks down, coffee for him and water for me. She asks if we're ready to order. We both say no at the same time. My dad stares at me as she leaves.

"Listen, I may be pissed at you but I called," I say. "I'm going to try not to be such a bitch to your girlfriend. It's hard to like her because of Mom, but I'm willing to try. Why? Because in the long run my behavior is just going to hurt people, especially Jamie. I don't want my attitude to rub off on her. If I can swallow my anger and pride, why can't you kiss your soon-to-be ex-wife's ass so you can spend more time with your daughters?"

His expression turns angry. "What is with your disrespectful mouth?"

"Sorry, I'm a little emotional. I'll try to tone it down. Please answer the question."

He runs a hand across his face. "You're right. If I can spend more time with Jamie *and* you, me being contrite and pleading with your mother should be feasible."

"Just try for Friday after school through Sunday morning. And you need to be very, very contrite."

His mouth turns down in confusion.

I nod at the huge window, through which we can see my mother walking toward the entrance from the parking lot. Then I slide out of the booth and grab my coat from a hook nearby. "Here she comes," I say. Walking away from my father's wide-eyed look, I meet my mother just as she enters the diner.

"Did you get a table yet?" she asks.

"Um, yeah." I gesture to the booth at the end of the line. "Dad's here."

She pales as she turns and sees the back of his head.

"He wants to talk," I say in a reassuring tone.

"Riley—"

"You need to talk with him. You're both still our parents."

Shaking her head, she steps back.

I reach for her arm. "Mom, do this for Jamie. For me. For you." She looks at me with petrified eyes. I feel like a manipulative asshole, but I press on. I've become persistent with her. "It's just talking. You can do this. You're strong enough to do this."

She gives me a nasty look but takes a deep breath and moves past me. I watch her slowly hang her coat next to his and then sit. Her face is tight, her eyes hostile. I push out the door and go to my car, but I don't leave and instead watch them while my car warms up. My father is talking. My mother is crying. She tears at the napkin holder near the inside end of the booth.

Feeling like a jerk for pushing my mother into this, I sink down in my seat. This might have been too much for her.

But then my mother is talking and moving her hands. My father's shoulders slump. His head is bowed. Her moving hands grip the edge of the table before she pushes away. My father grabs one of her hands, and though I can't see his expression, his posture is repentant.

My mother slowly sits back across from him, then they talk and nod and drink coffee. The guilt in my stomach slowly uncoils the longer they sit. When she stands and reaches for her coat, she lets him help her into it.

I shift my car into reverse as hope replaces my guilt.

Chapter 31

I'm at the kitchen island three days later vigorously studying for my calculus exam when my mother comes through the door. She's talking on the phone. She's hardly spoken to me since the conversation with my father. Obviously, she's angry at me for setting her up. I've chosen to remain patient and wait until she's ready to express her irritation. Though I can't say I'm looking forward to it.

Cradling her phone to her ear, she steps between the island and cupboards. "That's sounds workable. I'll call you closer to Christmas. Okay. Yes. Good-bye."

Though I'm very interested to know whom she is talking to, I continue to crunch numbers.

"That was your father." She drops her phone on the counter.

"Oh." I pretend nonchalance and punch at my calculator.

"We've come to another tentative agreement until the divorce is finalized in February." Her clipped tone clues me in to how stressful talking about the divorce is for her. I remind myself that stress is better than giving up. I set my calculator down and give her my full attention.

"After New Year's he'll pick up Jamie from school on Fridays and drop her off Sunday mornings. I'm hoping you'll go there too and at least spend Friday night in the beginning."

"You'll be okay alone?" I ask, trying to keep elation from my expression. Too much happiness at her finally giving in might freak her out.

She grips the counter. "I'd like Jamie to transition into this smoothly. He wants both of you to spend the twenty-third and part of Christmas Eve at his house. I agreed."

I nod and continue to keep a straight face, but inside I'm ecstatic. They are working things out. Well, maybe as much as things can be worked out at this point.

Her expression tightens as she leans over the counter. "Riley, I get why you did it, but don't ever do something like that to me again."

"All right," I say. We could argue but there's no point. She's doing the right thing and that was my purpose. Plus, she's facing her predicament. That more than anything has me thrilled.

She lets out a sigh and looks at my mess sprawled across the island. "You have exams tomorrow?"

"Two," I say, reaching for my calculator. Philosophy should be an easy A, but I need to get at least an 80 percent to maintain a B in calculus.

"Then I'll cook dinner later."

As she moves toward the laundry room, I can't help a grin. Not because I don't want to cook dinner but because every day I see a little more of my mother coming back. It's been about a month since the wine episode. She's not her old self—she may never be—but she's doing more and getting better. Like Romeo did years ago, little by little she's starting to live again.

For the past two classes, Romeo and I have restricted our communication to simple hellos and nods. We proved a couple of weeks ago that generic conversation was beyond us. I refrain from looking at him as much as possible and try to keep him from my thoughts. When he enters them, the almost healed scab of us on my heart rips open anew, leaving me on the bench in the skate park again. I'm looking forward to running into him only randomly on campus after today. I expect our paths will rarely cross. And sadly, I'm relieved by that future of us.

The exam keeps my mind from wandering, for the most part. Romeo moving or clearing his throat or tapping his pencil in thought pulls me back to him. I can finally, thankfully concentrate when he hands in his test. Finishing and reviewing the test takes me about another forty-five minutes. Confident of at least an 80 percent, I hand it in and leave the class for the last time. The thought makes me gleeful. Various reasons have me despising Calculus III.

I decide to head back to the main building instead of the parking lot. My philosophy professor said he'd probably have grades posted outside his office by this afternoon. I might as well check since I'm still here.

Though it hasn't snowed—much to Jamie's dismay—the air outside is frigid as I cross the commons. The cold temperature and wind has students crossing my path and moving quickly through the open space. I rush into the towered building that's mostly professors' offices but then freeze in my tracks.

Romeo sits in a small, seclude area in front of me. My world stops as he rubs his face with both hands. In between swipes, the scruff along his jawline is visible. His hair looks messy. His clothes wrinkled. Except for showing up onstage, Romeo was never a slave to fashion, but he always looked well groomed and hot and a bit cocky. All of that is gone. The slouch of his shoulders and his disarray paint another picture. A picture that hurts more than the girl who sits next to him, with her hand on his slumped shoulder.

I've kept my gaze from him for weeks, but now the sight of him so despondent has the broken pieces of my heart threatening to shatter.

Just as I'm turning around—the idea of seeing his eyes filled with pain has me desperate to flee—April looks up and her eyes narrow on me. I'm out in the frigid commons in seconds.

Unfortunately, as I reach the sidewalk leading to the parking lot I hear, "Wait, Riley!"

I stop but don't turn around. I'm surprised she's remembered my name.

April steps in front of me. "Why are you doing this to him?"

Minutes ago I'd hoped desperately at the awful sight of him that his despondency wasn't because of me. Now April's demanding question has me feeling ill. "He told you about us?" I ask.

"Somewhat," she says with a slight nod. "I guessed and he needed to open up, but he never said it was you. I just figured that out." My staring at him like a deer in headlights must have given the *who* away. "What I can't figure out is why someone wouldn't want to be with him." She rubs her arms, which are covered only in a thin sweater. She must have taken off after me without grabbing her coat.

"I'm not going to explain myself to you, April. I don't even know you. But I will say I do want to be with Romeo. I just can't."

She watches me, probably trying to gauge the pain that must be evident in my expression. The cold wind blows her long hair across her face as she leans closer to me and says quietly and lowly, "I don't believe you."

I rear back.

She flicks the long curtain of her hair back. "You know why?"

I don't particularly care and I'm about to tell her off with a string of four-letter words.

"If you truly wanted to be with him, you would make it happen."

"Listen, April—"

"No, you listen, Riley. Half the girls on this campus are chasing after him, but he's in love with you, and you're throwing it away."

I hold in a gasp. I'm assuming she's assuming. I will not ask if he told her that, even if I want to, even if her words have my heart thudding like a drum. "Why are *you* telling me this shit?"

"Because I want to see him happy. And you're obviously the one who can make him happy."

My eyes bug out. Just lovely. This girl obviously deserves him. Not me. Why can't Romeo love her? Why can't Marcus love Chloe? Why can't I love Marcus? Why is love such a clusterfuck?

She takes a step past me and says, "Just think about why you can't real closely, Riley. You owe him that much."

Refusing to cry, I stomp toward the parking lot. Every day is miserable without him. My heart is breaking too. Yet there's not enough of it left to owe myself, much less Romeo.

Chapter 32

My father's new house is not as big as our house. But it was constructed decades ago and has a different charm, with its built-in cabinets and window seats in almost every room. There are only three bedrooms. Jamie and I share one. Not a big deal, since I probably won't be here much. The other one is empty and I'm assuming it will be a nursery, which is still surreal.

We opened presents about an hour ago. Christmas music from a local radio station plays in the background. Jamie and my father are in the living room, working on some ridiculous LEGO Café thing. My father always did like toys that made it easy for him to participate. I'm helping Sara in the tiny kitchen. The scent of cinnamon and vanilla hangs in the air. I'm cutting celery and onions. She's cooking French toast for breakfast. Jamie wouldn't let us eat—or shower—before opening gifts. We're all still in pajamas.

I've kept my attitude in check. Both my father and Sara still irritate me, but I'm going to make this work for Jamie. And for my mom.

"The turkey will be done by three. You can stay for dinner, right?" Sara asks.

I keep chopping. "Sure. We'll just have to leave right after dinner. I . . . I don't like my mother home by herself on holidays." I'm not going to tiptoe around my mother as if speaking about my father's wife would be hurtful to his fiancée.

"Of course, your mother needs you right now." Sara's lips press together.

If we're ever going to get along, I don't want her to tiptoe around me either. "Just say what you need to, Sara."

She flips the bread on the griddle, then rests her robed hip on the edge of the stove and faces me. "I'm very much in love with your father. My life has never felt so complete. Yet I'm aware your mother is hurting. I'm aware my joy is her pain. And . . . and that just makes me feel awful, which may sound patronizing in my position, but it's the truth."

I set the knife down slowly and rest against the counter so we face each other. I believe Sara doesn't like hurting my mother. I also believe people make choices. Usually with only themselves in mind. "Please don't take this the wrong way, but do you believe love conquers all? Overrides everything else?"

Offense flashes in her eyes. Maybe there's only one way to take my question in her situation. She fiddles with a knob on the stove, and the diamond on her engagement ring catches the light from the window above the sink. "Every situation is different, Riley. Love doesn't always make sense. To the those in it or to the people around them. The falling can be an emotional, chaotic whirlwind. The landing, jarring and eye-opening. But if two people are really in love, there's nothing in this world that can overcome it. Even if they can't be together, love doesn't cease."

I'm suddenly very angry—interpreting her stupid love words to mean that she and my father were in love before he left us—and I force myself to murmur, "Um, okay." Though I tried to avoid sarcasm, I know it laced my tone. Frustrated, I pick up the knife and start chopping again.

Sara doesn't move. "Your father never asked me out until after he left your mother."

He'd obviously been planning on hooking up with Sara, but I just nod and chop. Sara goes back to the griddle.

There's no way around it. I'm always going to resent my father for leaving my mother. Maybe if he had gone to marriage counseling or tried to rekindle their love and then left, I wouldn't be so resentful. Maybe not. It doesn't really matter, because I'll never know.

I scrape up onions and celery with the knife, then violently toss them into a bowl for the dressing. Sara raises an eyebrow at the smack of the knife against the bowl but doesn't say anything.

The stupidest thing about this whole scenario is that I'm the one sacrificing for my family while my father plays house with Sara. They're all happy and in love while *my* heart is breaking.

My father comes in from the living room. He wraps his arms around Sara from behind and kisses the top of her head.

The embrace makes me want to vomit.

"Breakfast almost ready?" he asks.

Sara puts down the spatula and reaches up, wrapping her hands around my father's neck.

I set the knife down with a clank. "Think I'll go take a shower."

Neither of them responds. My father just nuzzles Sara's neck.

Barf. Barf. Barf.

Rushing up the stairs, I sadly realize my mother and father never acted like that.

Two days after Christmas, Chloe shows up to check out my Christmas haul, as she's called it for the past four years. I usually get a ton of clothes for Christmas since my mother works at a department store. Though Chloe is far more curvy than I am, she can fit into about half of my outfits. Most of them are not her style, but she still likes to look.

She pops her head out of my small walk-in closet. "There's hardly anything new in here."

I pull a poster from a box. My walls have been empty since May, when I had packed for college—thinking I was headed for Virginia. "I told my mom not to worry about me and to spend her money on Jamie."

Chloe curls her bright red lips. "Why do you have to be such a lame-ass martyr?"

I roll my eyes and push a two-step ladder against the wall. "There's stuff in there with tags on it from last Christmas."

"So?" she says, turning back into the overstuffed closet. "A girl can never have too many options, at least when it comes to clothes."

I unroll a Led Zeppelin poster while the sound of Chloe pushing hangers around echoes from the closet. Zeppelin's drummer, John Bonham, has been my number one idol since my father introduced me to the band in seventh grade. I'm tacking the psychedelic print back on my wall when Chloe comes out of the closet holding a shimmery black dress that still has the tag on it. I think the designer label priced at less than ten dollars lured my mother into that purchase. Not the idea that her daughter would actually wear it.

She presses the black silk against her body. "Lame?"

"No. You'd look great in it." I turn back to the poster and push a tack in. "I'd just never expect you to pick it."

"I'm thinking New Year's Eve."

I pause from pushing the tack in. She broke it off with the way much older man more than three weeks ago. "Where are you going? And who are you planning on getting all worked up with in that dress?"

"Marcus."

I glance over my shoulder. "How?"

She clutches the dress tightly to her chest. "He called me last night."

"Get out!" Swinging around, I about fall off the ladder.

She shakes her head. "It's official. We're going on a date."

"Now that is the cat's ass." I'm off the ladder—safely—in two seconds, then hugging her. We pull apart and bounce across from each other in circles like idiots. "You're going out with Marcus! On New Year's Eve!"

"I know! I know! I know!"

"This is fan-fucking-tastic." I suddenly stop. "Why didn't you tell me right away?"

She draws in a deep breath while her eyes find the floor. "I don't know. I just . . . You and Romeo . . . and, well, I didn't want to make you feel bad."

"Oh, Chloe, I already feel like shit twenty-four/seven, but why would you going on a date with Marcus upset me?"

Lipstick smears her front teeth as she gnaws her lip.

Suddenly it makes sense. "You're going to see Luminescent Juliet."

Her eyes are sad as she nods.

She's right. The news has me feeling like shit. Drumming and Romeo are two of the things I like best in this world. "Well, that should be fun," I force myself to say nonchalantly while reaching for another poster. "Where are they playing?"

"The Razor."

"Huh? The club's doing an eighteen-and-older for New Year's?"

Biting her lip again, she shakes her head.

Sighing, I unroll a Blink-182 poster. Their drummer, Travis Barker, is another of my idols. "Justin's getting you in."

She nods slowly. "I'm sorry, Riley. If it had been anyone but Marcus, I would have said no."

I push the ladder over. "It's all right. I'm happy for you. And if you and Marcus work out, it won't be weird with him anymore." I push a tack in. "There's that right?"

I haven't talked to Marcus since I asked him to pick up his kit for me. Realizing Romeo and I were done, he started in on his stupid crush shit again. Feeling like a skipping record, I once again pushed him to examine his feelings for Chloe. He's been so resistant about Chloe, I never thought he'd take me seriously.

Chloe looks up at me. "Why don't you come with us?"

I imagine hanging out with the band and almost shudder at the thought of being around Romeo for an entire evening. "I don't think so."

She leans against the wall and stares up at me. "Why are you doing this to yourself? You're crazy about him. He's crazy about you. Why do you both have to be miserable?"

"I already explained why," I snap. "Besides, how do *you* know he's miserable?"

"Marcus said it's pretty obvious."

My heart lurches. If it's obvious to clueless Marcus, then it's bad. My chest tightens. I'm hoping he's not as bad off as what I witnessed the day of exams.

"I get why you don't think you can date him, but then I don't," she says.

"Just drop it, Chloe," I say in a warning tone. I'm reminded of Romeo all the time lately, while I'm *supposed* to be getting over him.

She lets out a huff. "Okay, I just wish you were as happy as me right now, but then who knows how things will turn out. Marcus and I plan on taking this slow, you know?"

"Ha!" I say, jumping off the ladder. "Marcus has let his guard down. One date with his eyes wide open and he's going to be in so deep he won't know what hit him."

Her heavily lashed eyes grow round. "You think?"

"What man can resist Chloe the Testosterone Conqueror? Especially in that dress," I say, gesturing to the black silk she's still holding.

Chloe looks down at the dress, then grins at me. "You're right."

I grin back but inside I'm breaking.

Chapter 33

I decided to go to the New Year's Eve show. By myself. I didn't want anyone to know, but I wanted to see Luminescent Juliet, and of course, Romeo. The show had already started by the time I entered the club. The walk in was freezing since I dressed in one of my band outfits. Shorts, a tank top, combat boots, and a velvet hoodie. I lied to the bouncer at the door and told him I was playing a set tonight with the band. I was lucky he remembered me from the last time we played and he didn't even bat an eye.

Keeping my emotions in a tightly packed coil, I pull my hoodie up over my ponytail and move to the far corner of the club while Justin sings a cover song. People jumping to the beat of Green Day's "Holiday" pack the dance floor wall to wall. The tables near the floor are packed too. Near the back, tables are sporadically filled because most people push toward the stage. I pull a chair away from a table, lean it against a wall, and sit on the back with my feet on the seat.

Shrouded in the shadows, I take in the entire scene. The lights. The stage. The crowd. The pulsing music. Then I zone in on the drummer. He's good. Not as good as me, but I can admit he's talented. Justin belts out lyrics. I wouldn't have thought it, but he does justice to Green Day. Wish I had a chance to play this band. Their music has a certain energy I admire as a drummer. Sam plays his bass, bounces to the beat, and yells out the *hey*s exuberantly into the microphone.

Finally, unable to stop myself any longer, I look at Romeo. He steps toward the edge of the stage and starts the guitar solo. His back bows. The muscles of his arms clench when he lifts the guitar. His fingers fly over the stem. Dressed in designer shredded black jeans, a chrome belt, black boots, and a black collared shirt, he looks like a rock god. And sitting out here on the other side, I can see why girls fall for him. Not that I didn't fall for him on the inside.

Want rolls through me. I'm fascinated with him all over again. But now I'm just one of the unknown faces in the endless sea of the crowd.

The song ends and Justin starts spouting his blah-blah-blah. Here's one thing I don't miss. Romeo goes to the back of the stage and chugs down water. Justin continues his lame rhetoric while some guy I've never seen before comes out with a keyboard.

I sit up straighter, wondering what's going on. Romeo comes back to his microphone. He gives Justin a look and the ass finally quits talking. The lights dim. I'm on the edge of my seat. Romeo breaks into a loud, powerful riff. Lights flash.

The crowd goes wild and I stand on the chair.

Oh hell no. This was my idea. I wanted to do this damn song. Really, really bad.

Sam steps up to the center microphone and lets out a scream that morphs into the Beastie Boys' "Sabotage," which sounds as energetic as I knew it would. Sam belts it out in a perfect nasal twang like the original. I'm pissed it sounds so awesome. I'm also ecstatic.

But even with my love of the song, I'm soon watching Romeo playing instead of concentrating on the music. I drink in the sight of his carved profile. The harsh line of his jaw. The flop of his hair. From this distance, I imagine the flash of his dark eyes. Then I remember the low, deep rumble of his voice near my ear paired with his fingers making patterns on my skin.

I collapse against the wall.

More songs come but I pay little attention. I'm lost watching the one thing I want most in this world but cannot have. My stupid, stupid heart is twisting and fracturing, but I can't look away. I'm wilting, morphing into a wallflower with torn petals and a broken stem. I'm suffocating yet alive. Finally, they take a break and I can breathe fully without Romeo in my vision.

I slide down onto the chair.

A buzz of conversation breaks out that's louder than the music coming from the speakers overhead. The people wandering around me don't seem to notice the girl sitting with her heart bleeding in her hands. Bright and bubbly in their fancy party clothes, they laugh and cheer and drink. They wait for the New Year.

I wait for nothing.

They're excited.

I'm empty.

A low light flicks over the stage, with two vacant stools in the middle. A hush goes through the crowd, and the entire mass presses forward again.

Great. Acoustic music with Romeo singing. Just what I need to hear and see. I'm guessing the new drummer hasn't had enough time—though I learned enough in a month and a half—to play three sets. So why not crush me some more?

Sam and Romeo come out carrying acoustic guitars. Of course, Romeo doesn't say anything. They just sit, he taps a foot, and they break into music. I don't pay attention to the particular song. Feeling miserable, I just stare at Romeo again. Though he glances at Sam and the audience every now and then, his gaze is mostly downward. His expression is a shield. After several songs—I can't say how many—someone hands Romeo a banjo and takes his guitar.

Sam taps his foot on the floor and they break into a fast, folksy rhythm. The song sounds familiar, but this folk stuff is more Romeo's thing than anyone else. Suddenly the music slows, Romeo's face tightens, and he sings the first line.

The words jog a musical memory—Romeo talking Mumford & Sons I think—but I'm too entrapped in the vision of him looking grieved and broken as he sings and plays. His eyes close as he sings the refrain with Sam. The refrain that contains the same words he said to me on the bench in the skate park.

My hands clench in my lap. Frozen, I'm back on that bench in the skate park with him kneeling in front of me telling me he *will* wait for me. But the world keeps moving while the sad rawness of his voice wraps around me and sinks into my chest. The audience sways to the music but I'm falling a million miles away with each passing note. Romeo's forlorn expression etches itself into my memory as I fall farther. And yet he keeps singing about waiting.

The song ends and I finally land.

Sara's words from Christmas Eve rush into me: *"The falling can be an emotional, chaotic whirlwind. The landing, jarring and eye-opening. But if two people are really in love, there's nothing in this world that can overcome it. Even if they can't be together, love doesn't cease."* And suddenly her words become clear because I am in love with Romeo.

The stage is dark and empty. My mind, shocked glass.

Justin comes out. The crowd goes wild. They're in front of me but they are far from me. The room is a blur. Justin's words incomprehensible. I'm drunk on self-awareness. I teeter on the edge of the chair from the clarity of my feelings. Justin and the crowd screaming a countdown to midnight cracks into my consciousness, but I bring my knees up and curl into a ball.

The truth has been with me for a long time. In my misery, I refused to acknowledge it. Now the feeling roars through me and I can't pretend anymore.

I'm in love with Romeo.

"Three! Two! One!" the crowd and Justin roar. The stage lights up. The crowd turns wild. A guitar wails. Drums pound. The boom of a bass joins in. High-energy music. My favorite kind. But the music doesn't marry into a song for my ears. All I can hear is . . .

I will wait for you.

The last twelve months of giving and giving roll through my mind. I've given up almost everything. A scholarship. Time. Playing the drums. And mostly Romeo.

I'll keep giving and giving. My mother and sister are worth the giving.

But he's waiting.

For me.

My eyes lift to him in all his rock glory while the rest of the room is a blur. There's so much more behind the facade he creates on stage. So much more than his masculine beauty. Peeling back the raw sexiness of him exposes an astounding determination, a deep honesty, boundless compassion, and a startling intellect. Between his past and the man he has become, he's perfection.

How can I just give him up?

The song ends. The stage empties. People mingle and drink around me. The scene before me continues to be a blur. My arms tighten around my knees as I question my resolution. Question how much I can give up until I lose myself. I feel like I'm back in time watching that first performance of Luminescent Juliet and staring at the card Romeo gave me while wondering if my life needed a change.

Until love brings clarity.

My mother and sister are worth sacrifices, but so is Romeo.

And so am I.

With the heartache of the past year, I lost sight that my life is mine, is for me too. Taking care of my family shouldn't eradicate my chance at happiness. I can't be there for my family if I lose myself and melt away. Six months ago, even a week ago, I wouldn't have agreed with that perception, would have thought it selfish. But with each passing day without Romeo, I'm becoming a drained shell while my heart breaks. I'm losing myself from the misery of losing us.

Yanking my hood off, I stand and look around the huge room. Though I planned on slipping out quietly after the performance, I rush and shove through the crowd toward the empty stage. I spot Justin and Sam surrounded by girls at a table off to the right. I can't see Romeo. Enclosed between a rail and a wall, a different bouncer guards their section of tables. They raise shots and cheer inside their secluded area.

The bouncer doesn't recognize me and refuses to let me through.

"Justin!" I yell but the music above is loud.

Yet someone notices me. Chloe, looking sexy in that black dress, comes over to the rail. "Riley! What are you doing here?"

My hands grip the metal between us. "Where's Romeo?"

Her expression brightens but before she can answer, Marcus is behind her. "Out back. He's packing up, then leaving."

Without another word, I whirl toward the back door. A bartender yells but I ignore him and dash through the rooms filled with jars of olives, napkins, and maraschino cherries. Practically in a full run, I push the door open and fly outside, but the sight in the alley has me halting. Or at least trying to. Unfortunately, it's snowing and the ground is slick. I don't stop but rather slide into the side of Romeo's van. My head and body hit the metal with a thud before I hit the ground with a second thud.

Romeo's and April's blurry faces appear above me. My vision of the world is spinning. Not just my mind.

"Damn, Riley, are you okay?" Romeo asks, reaching for my hand.

No, I'm not okay. I just saw him and April in a tight embrace. Never mind the double collision or the fact I'm lying in several inches of snow or that my head is whirling. "I think so," I say, becoming embarrassed at bursting in on their private moment and hurt because they had a private moment.

April grabs my other hand and they pull me up. April lets go of my hand. Romeo doesn't. He bends and slaps snow from my legs and backside with the hand not enclosing mine. "What are you doing here?"

"I . . ." My head is pounding for several reasons.

"I should go," April says, stepping toward the door. Her long hair spins with the movement and catches falling flakes. "Have a safe trip, Romeo."

My eyes search his and the sound of the bar door shutting echoes in the alley. The falling snow muffles the noise of the city, and leaves me feeling like I'm encased in a snow globe that could be shaken or shattered at any moment because I can't read anything in the dark depths of his eyes.

"Where are you going?" I ask.

He breaks our locked gazes, bends, and finishes brushing snow from me. "Home for a few days."

"Oh." My head actually, really freaking hurts but his hand wrapped around mine helps.

"Why are you here?" he asks again.

"I came to watch the band."

"I mean out here."

"Oh. Yeah. Um . . ." Shit, I sound like a goose-headed idiot. I reach up and touch my forehead. I *am* a goose-headed idiot.

Romeo gently pushes my hand away and brushes his fingers across my skin. "You're not okay."

"Are you with April now?" I blurt.

His gaze turns cold as he lets go of my hand and lowers the other from my head. "You think I'd use her that way?"

"No," I say slowly. "Of course you wouldn't." Snowflakes fall between us. "I didn't think. It was just an emotional response."

"Emotional response?" He crosses his arms over the front of his wool coat. "What's going on, Riley?"

I concentrate on the falling snow in the spray of light above the door to the club before my gaze meets his. "I missed the band. I came to watch. Alone. And then . . . and then I watched you. You sang that song about waiting. It seemed like to me." I press my hand against my chest. His eyes watch the movement. "And—and my perception of everything started to shift. By the time you finished the song I realized something."

"What?" he says, his eyes remaining emotionless.

"That I'm in love with you."

He continues to stare at me without even blinking. I'm not sure what I was expecting in reply to my admission—perhaps a little excitement and definitely reciprocation—but he's as cold as the snow-filled air.

"Okay, um, I should go." Tears sting my eyes. They're from the pain in my heart, not my head. I've been breaking, but in seconds I'm going to shatter into a million broken pieces of despair.

His hand clamps down on my arm. "Will admitting you love me change anything?"

My gaze whips to his. "I want to be with you."

"What about your family?"

My head pounds in confusion. Why is he being difficult? Everything seems perfectly clear to me, even with a goose egg starting to throb on my forehead. "I want to be there for them and with you."

"Can you do that?" he asks while his dark eyes drill into mine.

Slowly moving beyond the pound rattling in my head, I realize he's scared I'm going to leave him again. "Yes, I can," I say in a tone laced with conviction. Because I will. Because I want to. Because I need to. "It isn't always going to be easy, but I want this misery we've been in to end. I want to be with you."

Relief flashes in his dark eyes and his posture changes from stiff to fluid as he steps forward and cups my jaw tenderly. "Though only months, it feels like I've been in love with you forever," he says. His thumbs stroke my skin while snowflakes fall on my upturned face. His eyes burn into mine with the intensity that is Romeo. "I want to be with you forever," he adds in a broken whisper, then his lips brush against mine. I sway from the power of his words and the feel of his lips. He pulls back. "I don't think you're okay."

"Oh, I'm good." I lean closer until I'm only centimeters from his lips. "Actually, other than my head, I've never felt better." My lips cover his and the pounding in my head dissipates from the heat of our kiss.

I refused to go to the hospital even though Romeo was afraid I might have a concussion. He wouldn't let me drive home. So in the van I went. Because of the falling snow and the concentration it took for him to drive, the ride home was quiet. Except for the ding of my phone.

Chloe keeps texting me, asking what's going on. Lying on the couch at home, I finally answer her.

Me: Slid through the snow. Bumped my head. At home. Romeo's with me.

Chloe: Ouch, you clumsy beeyatch. Romeo's with you? Does that mean what I want it to?

Me: Yes.

Chloe: Hot damn! Finally.

Romeo comes into the living room with a bag of ice and a dish-towel. "I think it's gotten bigger," he says, staring at the lump on my forehead. He sets my phone on the table, gently lifts my shoulders, and slides under me. With my head in his lap, he lays the towel-wrapped ice on my forehead and uses his other arm to hold me by the waist.

I close my eyes. The ice helps. Being held by him helps more.

"You sure you're okay?"

With my eyes closed I smile at him. "I'm good, actually great."

He reaches under my head and loosens my ponytail. "Your mom, she's better?"

"She is. She's getting there."

"Is that why you came tonight?" he asks as his fingers travel through my hair.

My eyes pop open and meet his. "No."

He looks away as the line of his jaw tightens. "Riley, it's okay if you put your family first."

Struggling between the pain in my head, the ice on my skin, and his hold, I sit up until I can face him. His expression is cautious and weary as my hand rests on his cheek. "It was never like that. You weren't second. Ever. It was about who needed me."

His expression doesn't change. "And now?"

I draw in a deep breath. "I need you."

The tight lines of his face smooth into reverence. "I need you too," he says softly, wrapping his hand around mine before pressing his mouth to the center of my palm. Then he gently pushes me back down onto his lap. He again sets the ice on my forehead. "And the band? Even after Justin's temper tantrum and me punching him, they'd take you back."

Music will always be part of my life, and one day I'll play again—I'll be drumming until I'm an old lady—but now is not the right time. "I'd love to be in the band, but there isn't enough time between school and family and you. I'd rather be with you."

He chuckles lightly. "Did I hear that right? Riley Middleton, drummer extraordinaire, would rather spend time with me than playing drums. I think the world just stopped spinning."

"No, it's still spinning." I cover his arm across my waist with my own. "Someone recently told me that if two people are truly in love, nothing can overcome it. Guess that includes an obsession with drums. I've become obsessed with you instead. You'll always be first in my heart." The pleasure in his gaze has me smiling. "But do you think I could step in once in a while? I was thinking I could do "Sabotage" every now and then."

His arm tightens around my waist. "Riley, I'll let you have whatever you want."

"I just want you."

His smile is sweet and sexy. "You've had me for a long time."

I return the smile, close my eyes, and burrow deeper into his lap.

Sometimes life is hard and painful and just plain sucks. And other times life is beautiful and brilliant and amazing. Right now, in Romeo's arms, the brilliance of life shines on me with a ferocious glare.

A Month and a Half Later

My mother signed the papers a week ago. The divorce is finally official. And though she has been getting better, it's Valentine's Day, which has me worried. Memories of special events bring her down. Since it's a Friday and Jamie is at my father's, I put my trust in Romeo and let him plan the evening, with my mother included. Yet I have no idea what we're doing. He wants to surprise me.

When he pulls up in front of the antique store—the band practices above it—I'm in total surprise.

I give him an odd look. "What's going on?"

His dark eyes shine with mischief. "Part one of the night. You get to play."

Though I was hoping for some alone time, excitement rolls through my gut at the thought of playing. "What about my mom?"

"She's meeting us here after she gets out of work. We have two hours." Reaching behind the seat of the van, he pulls out a small bag, then leans toward me and gives me a quick kiss. "Let's go."

Upstairs, Justin and Sam already wait. After some hugs and fist bumps, I'm behind the set. Unbelievably, within minutes, Romeo's barking off instructions and handing out music sheets. It's like I've stepped into a time machine as my fingers itch to give his skull a whack with one of my sticks. And the strangest thing? He's decided Valentine's Day is somehow connected to the eighties. He has us playing "Livin' on a Prayer" by Bon Jovi and "Should I Stay or Should I Go" by The Clash.

But hey, I'll play anything with a lively beat. Once we start rolling, I'm just into the rhythm and loving every second. Except for in between playing when my boyfriend's barking orders and back to being the dick I met in this room. But behind the drums, I can handle him being a jerk.

After almost two hours of playing, Romeo announces a break. Sam slips downstairs for a smoke. Justin's immediately on the phone with some girl. Romeo gives me a grin. Except for that grin, it's like nothing has changed.

"Come here," I say.

He sets his guitar on a stand.

When he gets close enough, I give him a light thump on the top of his head. Though it couldn't have hurt, he scowls at me.

Now I grin. "I've wanted to do that forever."

He rolls his eyes while reaching into his back pocket. He pulls out a silver-wrapped present. "I get whacked and you get a gift. How does that work?"

I snatch the gift from his hand and ignore the question because I'm wearing his present underneath my clothes. Wanting to surprise him, I finally let Chloe take me to Victoria's-Slut-Secret.

I tear off the silver paper in two seconds flat. A custom set of drumsticks lies in my palm. Tiny skateboards over flames curl around each one. I let out a laugh. "How cute! They're perfect."

Romeo gives me an eyebrow arch. "Just don't use them to tap on my head."

Before I can respond, Sam returns with my mother and another woman. Romeo goes over and gives the woman a long hug, then introduces his mother to mine. I slowly get up from the stool. Romeo and I have been trying to plan a weekend to visit his mother, but the divorce becoming final has kept me from leaving mine. So I'm stunned that I'm meeting his mother tonight.

Tall and dark haired like he is, she's attractive, with strong features. After Romeo introduces us, she wraps me in a warm hug and I'm still shocked. My mother laughs at my expression, then gives me a long hug and a warm kiss on my cheek. Once the introductions are finished, Romeo sends both mothers to chairs against the wall and me to my spot behind the drums.

Suddenly his eighties revival makes sense, considering our audience.

We play the two songs for our mothers and they tap their feet, clap to the beat, and laugh. Playing, I remember thinking I'd never see my mother happy again, but even beneath her laughter, the tight expression she has worn for the last year is gone. Between her entry back into the real world and her weekly counseling sessions, she's almost the mother I once knew.

After our impromptu concert, Sam and Justin take off to a bar. I'm thankful they're not coming to the late-night dinner with the mothers and us. I wouldn't be surprised if, from mere habit, Justin hit on one of them.

My mom offers to drive Romeo's mother to the restaurant and I'm all smiles. Once they exit down the stairs and the door shuts behind them, I tackle my boyfriend. We fall against the wall as my legs wrap around his waist and my lips devour his.

He breaks the kiss and rests his forehead against mine. "You're not going to get me out of here if you keep this up," he says raggedly, rubbing his knuckles across my cheek.

I cover his hand with mine. "You're so awesome. I love you."

His lids lower as his full lips curve into a grin. "I know."

My own lids lowering, I reach behind me for a stick.

He laughs and grabs my arm. "Drummers and their damn tempers. You don't have to beat it out of me." He presses my hands against the wall. "You know I love you. How could I not?" He places our tangled hands against his ribs. Over the tattoo under his shirt. "You've given me back my wings."

Acknowledgments

T hank you, Lisa, for always reading. I'd also like to thank the three musicians who helped with the drumming scenes. You know who you are. Last, I'm hugely grateful to my husband and son for putting up with my writing addiction and helping out so much. I'm the luckiest gal in the world to have you both.

About the Author

J ean Haus is the author of the Luminescent Juliet Series, which revolves around a sexy, talented indie band in a small college town. She lives in Michigan with her husband and son, where she spends almost as much time teaching, cooking, and golfing as she does thinking about the tough but vulnerable rockers featured in her books. Visit Jean online at www.jeanhaus.com.

Turn the page for a sneak peek at the second book in the series, *Ink My Heart.*

Ink My Heart

Chapter 1

I need a beer, a shot, and a woman. Or several of each. And not necessarily in that order. After five hours of singing, my voice is hoarse, my throat is sore, and I want to get away from the three other twits in my band. I've been playing *and* arguing with them all day. The van has been tranquil since we left the recording studio. The echoing bump of the highway is the only sound other than snores as we travel north from Detroit to mid-Michigan, where we go to the local university as juniors—well, except for Gabe. The loser goes to community college.

We'd still be in the recording session if Gabe, Sam, and I hadn't forced Romeo to call it quits. Romeo the perfectionist, our lead guitar player and my annoying roommate. His fingers should be bleeding after playing the guitar so long, but no, the bastard is one big callus. He could have put in another five hours, but instead, he's had a pissy look on his face the entire drive home while I've been in the passenger seat ignoring him and trying to doze. Snores are coming from behind us. Sam is sleeping on the first-row bench seat. Gabe is passed out next to his drum set on the floor in the back.

It was Romeo's asinine idea to make an album of his originals. He hopes it will make us a few bucks on the indie scene. He may be right, but after the hell of a day we had at the studio, we'd better make more than a few bucks.

A beep from my phone wakes me up fully. I dig it out of my pocket. A picture of Mara, one of my regular girls, appears on my screen, and the text: *You coming out tonight?* I don't text back but keep Mara as a reserve while hoping for the possibility of meeting someone else. A sexy new adventure.

Romeo takes the exit ramp into town, and I drop my feet from the dashboard. "Just take me to Rats."

He gives me an irritated glance. "I'm going over to Riley's. Not coming back into town to pick you up later."

I shrug. Though the main strip of bars downtown isn't as busy in the winter, I can usually find a girl to take me home. If no one else, there's always Mara. "I'll find a ride."

Waking up, Sam stretches and yawns. He runs a hand over the fuzz of his buzz cut, then punches the back of my chair. "Shit, Justin, you're a machine. How can you go to a bar after partying last night and working all day?"

"It's Saturday," I say with a tone of obviousness. Sam likes the attention we get from women too. He just likes partying a lot more and, as usual, went overboard last night. His bright blue eyes, which the girls gush over, are bloodshot today.

"Thought you would have got enough ass last night," Gabe says from the back.

"Never," I say.

"Well, that was one seriously *big* ass you went home with."

I recall Emily—or was it Emma?—with a slow smile. Gabe's girlfriend is stick skinny, with huge tits. Nothing wrong with *that,* but I like all women. I like the way they smell. I like the soft sighs they make. I like how they ease my loneliness, if just for a night. I like them in all shapes and sizes. Toned and angular or round and soft. Lingering on that last thought, I say, "Oh, she was big in all the right places."

"Dude, there's nothing you won't sleep with," Gabe says sarcastically.

"I have standards." I raise one finger. "They have to be hot." I raise another finger. "They can't be wasted." I don't take advantage of the incoherent. "And they can't be a bitch," I say with the flick of a third finger. Because Gabe is always such a prick about everything, I add, "Which is why I turned down your cousin."

"Stay away from Rachel," he snaps. "But what is that supposed to mean?"

"Well, the girl is hot and she didn't drink too much last night. So figure it out."

"Mother fucker!" Gabe yells, and dives toward the front of the van as instrument cases clank and roll around the back.

While I laugh, Romeo throws up his arm in a clothesline move and Gabe's lanky body bounces backward.

He crashes into Sam, who immediately sits up on the first-row bench seat and says, "Shit, Gabe! I was sleeping!"

"I'm kicking his ass," Gabe shouts, his longish brown hair falling into his face. "In this van. Now."

Sam hauls Gabe back by the sweatshirt, but he kicks at my seat. I keep laughing. I have several inches on Gabe and almost twenty more pounds of muscle. "More like get your little bitch ass kicked."

"Fuck, Justin. When are you going to grow up?" Romeo says, clutching the steering wheel. My laughter instantly dies. I'm sick of

Romeo telling me I need to grow up. I'm busy staring him down when a fist connects with and then slides from my jaw. "Asshole," I gasp, letting my seat belt loose and turning.

"Stop it, Gabe!" Sam yells. "And Justin, shut the hell up!"

I'm ready to pounce when the sight of Gabe struggling like a hyperactive kid in Sam's grip makes me pause. I want to punch Gabe back, but I'm not like him. I don't throw blows when a guy is being held down or not looking.

Gabe starts repeating, "I'm going to kill him."

Sam is becoming red in the face from holding Gabe. Though Sam is the most muscular of us all, Gabe is wiry, pissed-off strength.

Trying to control my urge to sucker punch him, I glance out the window. I want to relieve Sam. "We're almost downtown. Just let me out."

"Good idea," Romeo says under his breath, hitting the brakes. I brace myself on the dashboard with a spread hand.

Sam and Gabe bounce off the back of my seat, then thud to the floor as I jump out of the van.

Before slamming the door, I say, "Tell Riley I said hi."

Ignoring me Romeo takes off with tires squealing. He's in a rush to drop Gabe off at his hovel across town and dump Sam at his apartment so he can race to his girlfriend's house. Romeo's pussy whipped in addition to being a band dictator.

The brisk air stings my arms. The cement under my feet is crusted with dirty bits of remaining winter snow. Shit. I forgot my coat in the van. Cars whiz by as I take in my surroundings while rubbing my sore jaw. I'm in a part of town I don't know well, but I can't be too far from Rats. Fucktard Gabe. Ever since he joined the band more than three months ago, he's been a prick because I didn't pick him to be our drummer when he'd first auditioned. Instead, I'd picked Riley—a girl—and the dude was never going to get over it.

The little bitch wasn't pissed at Sam, who also wanted Riley, just me. Now I'm walking because of his stupid ass, and freezing.

After trudging through the cold, I get my bearings and realize it should be less than ten blocks to my favorite bar. Two blocks later, a bright neon sign across the street catches my eye—DRAGONFLY INK. I stop rubbing my jaw and stare. Either the tattoo parlor is new or I've just never noticed it. In seconds, after waiting for a car to pass, I'm crossing the street.

My motivation isn't just to get out of the cold—I'm addicted to ink and body piercings. My body art started as a silent *fuck you* to my parents, but even though it didn't get their attention, I continued doing it because I liked it. The sting of the needle and the bold statement of the ink on my skin has become addicting. Adding a bit of tarnish to my pretty boy looks is a bonus.

I warm up in seconds inside the shop, but it takes my eyes a minute to adjust after leaving behind the cold dusk outside. Track lighting illuminates the framed art on the walls, and the space is filled with glass display cases of jewelry.

A girl comes out from behind a counter in the back. She's smoking hot in her slinky half shirt, which shows off the circular tattoo around her pierced belly button.

"Can I help you?" she asks. Her gaze slides over the tattoos on my arms and pauses at the ring in my eyebrow while she flips her long brown hair behind a shoulder.

"Maybe." I give her a slow smile. "I want to check out some of your art."

Her hips sway and her heels click on the floor as she steps closer, pointing to framed pictures on the walls. "Those are our most popular basics." She then points to a rack of laminated images. "These are more intricate." She taps her nails on the cover of a binder on the counter. "And in here we have the works of art." She leans with both hands behind her on the counter and sticks her chest out. "Have anything in mind?"

With her tits beneath my nose, there's not much in my mind besides what's right in front of me. "Not sure. Just checking things out."

Her frosted lips curve into a knowing smile, and I grin back.

"Mandy," a male voice says from the far end of the shop. "You need to schedule Jack's next appointment."

"Give me a sec," she tells him, still staring at me. She pulls her hands from behind her on the counter. "Take your time—I'll check on you in a bit."

Mandy can check on me anytime. Smirking, I nod and watch her saunter away toward the guys waiting near the counter. I reach for a binder of designs, but really, I'm waiting on Mandy. Appears I may have found my "sexy new adventure."

After glancing at the barbells, earrings, and gauges in the glass case, I page through pictures of skulls, stars, crosses, and tribal art designs. Nothing's really grabbing me, so I open a binder labeled *Custom Designs*. Inside are a bunch of photos with people showing off their awesome tats. There's a sexy '50s pinup girl, a flaming sun setting into its reflection on rippling water, a rose that looks like it's growing out of a woman's hip, an arm sleeve of Japanese art . . . The intricate ink is blowing me away, but I'm brought back to the shop when someone says, "Show me your other side, Paul. Let me see how Todd did on the last one."

Though the words are commonplace for a tattoo parlor, the feminine voice grabs my attention—it's dripping with sex. Low and husky, the voice wraps around me like a lush naked body might, taking me to dark, sweet places.

Pretending to examine another book, I glance at the owner of the voice.

She is bending over and staring at the guy's ribs. Dark auburn curls spill across her profile. I can't see her clearly, other than her lowered thick black lashes and the pout of her red lips.

"Very, very nice, Todd," the voice purrs to the other guy, who I'm assuming is the artist—but fuck, I wish she were talking to me.

Hell. My hands grip the edge of the glass countertop. If she keeps that purring up, I'm going to get hard just listening to her.

The guy drops his shirt over his tattooed ribs. "You should design my next one."

Nodding, she turns toward the counter and away from me. "Anytime, Paul, just set up an appointment with Mandy."

The guy beams at her as I flip through the book of photos absently. I'm guessing the owner of that voice designed the ink in the pictures—and all I can think about is how to get an introduction to her. I haven't been this fascinated by a girl since . . . Damn. I don't remember when. And I haven't even seen her face yet.

I'm staring at art that I'm not really seeing when a finger drumming on the counter pulls my attention from the binder. Expecting Mandy, my mouth falls open at the sound of that voice.

"Finding anything interesting? Anything giving your skin an itch?"

Her sensual tone shoots lust down my spine and right to my dick. I gradually flip a page, getting control of myself, then at last look up and take in the face that owns that voice.

Holy shit. She's better looking than I could have imagined. Two tiny silver stars dangle from the barbells at the end of one eyebrow. A lip ring I instantly want to suck pierces the corner of her lower lip. Her gray eyes fringed in black stare back at me. Those eyes are as erotic as her voice. She's all contrasts. Pretty, yet edgy with her piercings. Her pale skin and light eyes paired with rich auburn hair and dark, slashing winged brows make another contrast. She's sexy as all hell. *Get a grip, Justin. Do not drool,* I think. I tap on the book. "These are really good," I say.

She stares at me wide eyed for a moment before coolly saying, "Thanks. I take pride in my work."

Standing up straight, I feign stupidity. "These are yours?"

Her black lashes lower as she glances at the book. "Every one."

My eyes wander over her, taking in the loose sweatshirt with the store's logo and the leaf tattoo that wraps around her wrist. She's not like Mandy, who is in-your-face hot. Instead, she radiates a half-buried sensuality that has me wanting to peel back her cool demeanor and get a glimpse inside. I want to find out what's beyond those slate-gray eyes watching me warily. They remind me of mournful lyrics, the way they hint at deeper emotions and pull at your soul.

"Well, judging from these photos you have to be the most talented tattoo artist I've ever met. And I've met a lot," I say smugly.

Her smoky eyes narrow a bit before her gaze travels the length of my arm. "Looks like you're ready for some real ink."

As long as you keep looking and talking, you can do anything you want to me, baby. "Yeah, I'm ready for something a little more . . . in depth."

"Any ideas rolling through your head?"

About tattoos? Not fucking one. Considering what a tattoo artist might suggest, I blurt, "Something more personal?"

She lets out a low chuckle and leans forward. "So you have no clue?"

I glance at her short silver nails while I rack my lust-ridden brain. "I'm thinking something relating to music?"

She cocks one eyebrow, and a silver star jingles. "You're a musician?"

"Kind of," I say, reluctant to admit I'm in a band. I instinctively know that bragging won't get me anywhere with this girl. I look her over slowly, so there's no confusion that I'm checking her out. I slide my hand across the counter and flick a finger toward her wrist, nearly brushing the skin. "That your only tattoo?"

She stands and folds her arms across her chest. "Oh, I have others."

"Really?" I gaze at her intently.

She leans against the wall behind the glass case. My body wants to get closer to hers, and I fight the urge to jump the counter. "They're not available for stranger perusal," she says.

I run my eyes over her body and imagine where the ink might be. When I look again into her gray eyes, they have a sparkling defiance—but I hold out my hand anyway. "Nice to meet you," I say. "Name's Justin."

Her lips twist into a smirk, but still leaning against the wall, she shakes my hand. Her palm is soft and warm, but I can feel the rough, callused skin along her index and middle fingers, right where a pencil would lie. She must sketch a lot. The contrast makes her even more interesting.

"Al," she says in that smoky voice, then she releases my hand. "And the tattoos are still under wraps."

"Al?" I say, forgetting about the tattoos for a moment. "That can't be your real name."

"Short for Allie."

"Allie," I say softly, lowering my chin, "is far prettier than Al. But I'm still interested in those tattoos . . . or maybe in the idea of what inspires you."

She lowers her eyelashes. "Since *you're* not inking me, let's stick with what inspires *you*."

Her tone has me changing tactics. Obviously, the traditional smolder that I pull out to make most girls melt isn't going to work on this one. "Do you only design?" I ask.

She shakes her head slightly. "No. I ink too."

"How . . . fascinating," I say. And hot. Propping my elbows on the counter, I lean toward her. "We should go out for a drink and talk about what inspires both of us."

She blinks at me with those eyes the color of gunmetal. "Ah, I don't date potential inkees."

Shit. Still trying to move too fast here. "I'm not a customer . . . yet, but a drink doesn't mean a date. People do go out to converse—don't they?"

"Maybe I don't drink."

"Coffee then?"

Her chin drops. "Caffeine is the world's most addicting drug."

I'm getting desperate here. "Milk shakes?"

A deep, sexy laugh escapes her. "If you're really interested in me designing for you, Mandy"—she nods toward the back counter—"can set up an appointment. But I have to get back to work."

Damn. She's leaving me high and dry, and all I want is to hear more of that voice. "Oh, I'm *interested*." Those eyes. That lip ring. I force a smile. I can't keep my tone from conveying that I'm interested in more than her talent.

Her chin lifts slightly. "Okay then, I'll see you soon, Justin."

"Very soon, Allie."

She gives me a slow nod, then walks away.

I watch her—a figure dressed in a shapeless sweatshirt and tight jeans—until she disappears into a hallway beyond the counter.

After taking in a deep breath and snatching a hooded sweatshirt from the shelf at the end of the glass case, I move toward the counter.

"What did you decide on?" Mandy asks, giving me hot eyes.

She hasn't gotten any less sexy since I walked in the door, but—with Allie now in the mix—my lust-o-meter isn't registering even a one for her. "This," I say, dropping the hooded sweatshirt on the counter. "And I'd like to set up a design appointment with Allie for Monday, if possible." I'm already haunted by her smoky voice and those stormy gray eyes.

Fuck. I've fallen in lust. Big time.